Bohin Manor

BOHIN MANOR
Tadeusz Konwicki

Translated by Richard Lourie

faber and faber
LONDON · BOSTON

First published in the USA by
Farrar, Straus and Giroux, Inc, New York
and simultaneously in Canada by Harper and Collins, Toronto
First published in Great Britain in 1992
by Faber and Faber Ltd
3 Queen Square London WCIN 3AU
Originally published in Polish under the title *Bohiń*

Printed in England by Clays Ltd, St Ives plc

Portions of this book have appeared, in a slightly different form, in *Translation*

A CIP record for this book is available from the British Library

ISBN O 571 14437 3

2 4 6 8 10 9 7 5 3

Translator's Introduction

This book can be enjoyed for what it seems to be: a loving re-creation of the past, a genre painting of life on the manor in old Lithuania, the sky tending to be overcast, the pine woods running deep and dark. But though the depiction of mores, sentiment, conveyance, fashion, and utensil is accurate and obeys the conventions of nineteenth-century realism, there are a few details in this work that utterly transform its nature, revealing that what the artist has attempted is the rendering not of a time but of time itself.

The first crack on the surface of illusion is the voice of the author/narrator as he wonders aloud who his grandfather will be. Which of her two suitors will his grandmother choose—the Polish noble of perfect manners and dubious manliness or the young Jew roaming the world like a redheaded Zeitgeist? Only in the realm of fiction can a grandmother still be a virgin; only in fiction can there be tenses like this past future imperfect.

Konwicki's voice, abraded by the smoke of cigarettes and the exhaust of cities, is absolutely essential to this work, and yet as completely out of place in it as would be a rear bumper and taillight of a Polish Fiat protruding from the hay barn at Bohin Manor some twelve years after the failed Polish uprising against Russian rule in 1863. His voice seldom intrudes, and never for long, and it is the measure of Konwicki's deftness that he knew how many such beats would be the absolute correct number. Here the voice of the author showing through the narrative is not the literary equivalent of a painter leaving some of his initial pencil marks on the canvas. Here it is the very source of narrative. And a coy reminder that this is a genetic reverie, not a historical romance—a conceptual novel in more ways than one.

As if to emphasize that the novel's lens of perception is flawed by its own vantage, images of the twentieth century are perceived in the landscape of the nineteenth. The point is not, however, only to create an aesthetic Heisenberg's principle but to demonstrate that our century issued from the last as much as Konwicki did from his grandmother and grandfather-to-be.

Lenin, Pilsudski, Stalin, and Hitler—the quarternity of political men who would shape Poland's destiny in the twentieth century—appear in various guises. Post-uprising Poland was under Russian police rule; and by his name, Vissarion Dzhugashvili, we recognize the local magistrate as the father-to-be of Joseph Vissarionovich Dzhugashvili, alias Joseph Stalin. But the name is misleading, for it is Stalin himself who dashes about the Lithuanian countryside like a hound out of hell. That land of small, swift rivers, meadows, and forests is haunted, moreover, by a legendary monster who burns and devours people alive. Sighted by many, this monster is known only by its demonic name of Schicklgruber, which in the next century would be the given name of Adolf Hitler. The little boy who hitches a ride with Konwicki's grandmother is Jozef Pilsudski, the gruff, mustachioed military man who would lead Poland to independence after World War I and who, when parliamentarianism failed, would step in to stage a coup and save the country. Pilsudski was the Father of the Fatherland, for whom, Konwicki sometimes fears, every Pole longs in his heart. And to readers in Central and Eastern Europe, the young child born to a school inspector in Simbirsk is unmistakably Lenin, who is, of course, a nice boy liked by all.

But the nineteenth century was not only the progenitor of the twentieth. Blind to the distant future and to the future right at hand, it existed in and of itself, and transpired, as all centuries do, as a succession of days and nights. Still, it would not be Konwicki's Polish-Russian-Lithuanian nineteenth century if it bore no trace of the two great bards who appeared with almost mystical synchronicity: Adam Mickiewicz in Poland in 1798, Alexander Pushkin in Russia in 1799.

In *Bohin Manor*, Mickiewicz is embodied in a prose poem counterfeited by Konwicki; Pushkin, in the pained memory of a real poem. Adam Mickiewicz, whose verse epic *Pan Tadeusz* is even more central to Polish literature than Pushkin's *Evgeny Onegin* is to Russian, was as a young man known for his ability to improvise. And it is the youthful Mickiewicz, not the grand poet in exile in Paris or dying in Turkey while forming a battalion to fight Russia, who has left his trace at Bohin Manor: an improvised prophecy of Poland's greatness and diaspora, as recorded by one of the locals with literary hankerings.

Pushkin is also represented by his son, who seeks to settle among the Poles and atone for the sin of the father—since the father was a poet, the sin was a poem. In 1831, after the Poles had risen against the Russians for the first time, Pushkin had dashed off a response to outraged European public opinion. "To the Slanderers of Russia" reminds Europeans that Russia did not bend to Napoleon's will and that Russia has plenty of room to bury anyone foolish enough to take up arms against it. Europeans should mind their own business. Those lines, imperialistic in the very framing of the question, still echo in the Polish memory, if only because they still apply:

. . . *What has outraged you? Disturbances in Lithuania?*
Stay out of this quarrel among Slavs,

an old family quarrel, one already
on the scales of fate, and past your influence.

In this unequal contest, who will prevail:
the haughty Poles or the true-hearted Russians?
Will Slavic streams merge with the Russian sea?
Or will that sea go dry? That is the question . . .

Konwicki is not alone among Poles in believing that, in Lithuania, history is a local crop, like barley. One proof, if proof is needed, is that the truest and greatest Poles come from Lithuanian Poland—Mickiewicz, Pilsudski, Czeslaw Milosz. Konwicki, therefore, should have been delighted but not overly surprised when it was Lithuania which, in late 1989, was the first republic to assert its independence from the Soviet Union. But the Polish myth of Lithuania omits one rather vital element—the Lithuanians themselves: not Slavs, speaking the most ancient of living Indo-European languages, the last nation in Europe to remain pagan, accepting Christianity only in 1348 as part of the political alliance that bound Poland and Lithuania into a state that stretched from the Baltic to the Black Sea and that regularly defeated the Russians, who were just back on their feet after two and a half centuries of Mongol domination. It is no wonder that today's drive for self-determination in Lithuania has been not only anti-Soviet and anti-Russian but anti-Polish as well.

Local legends and conditions aside, what matters most of all in a novel is the myth, the magic of fabula becoming fable. In this post-Holocaust nineteenth-century novel, Konwicki is attempting something quite rare in Polish literature—the depiction of a Jew, not just as a minor character, local fauna, but as vital to the inception, progression, and resolution of the ritual enacted by the plot. As soon as it is over, the story suddenly attains the mysterious clarity of a dream in which everything is both itself and its own significance. And like such dreams, it bears and demands multiple interpretation. Seemingly the most accessible of Konwicki's novels, *Bohin Manor* is in fact his most deeply Polish work.

Richard Lourie

Bohin Manor

1

Miss Helena Konwicka rose that day right after dawn, as she usually did during the week. The whole house was still asleep. The white-washed walls were still sleeping, as were the mahogany wardrobes, the muslin curtains on the windows, and the floorboards, which had creaked and groaned for a long time the night before, crackling dryly every so often. The servants were asleep and so was Helena's father, who had locked himself in his study.

A large drop of dew clung to a vine leaf, sparkling like a fortune-teller's crystal ball. Helena suddenly began peering at that drop gleaming with points of colored light, peering until pain came to her eyes, until tears came to her eyes and that night-born drop of moisture dissolved into a pale-green blur.

"Just a minute," said Helena to herself, "why have I been shaking inside my skin since yesterday, why did I keep waking up during the night, why am I afraid, more afraid than I've ever been? That's right, I had a dream about a tooth, my tooth. It was jagged and covered with blood as it fell from my mouth to my cupped hand."

She started dressing slowly in finery that had been laid out the afternoon before. With deliberation she drew her corset laces until the ends were the length of her ring finger. Yes, I've put on weight again, even though I worked so hard the past year. Without knowing why, she whispered aloud to herself, "But I always mark the Jewish New Year."

The house was still asleep. Sparrows were already chirping in the trees and swallows flew from their clay nests under the manor's eaves but kept cutting back, at an angle, to the gray grain sacks that hung from the edge of the roof. Out past the park and what was left of its old, neglected trees, a cow began bellowing like a steamboat. Miss Helena Konwicka, my grandmother, stopped in front of her window, and once again glanced at a dewdrop containing a likeness of the holiday morning's light. Then she ran her eye over the vegetation, its green faded now, wearied by the long summer, the scorching heat, and its own luxuriance.

The sound of the Wilia must have been audible, approaching, receding. That old river formed shallow semicircles there, right past the fence; then, to make up for lost time, it would quicken its pace. Sometimes people visited that spot from far away to listen to the sound the river made there, its murmur and loquacious hum.

"Let things fall as they must," said Helena with a sigh, though she was well aware that nothing would happen and that this, her thirtieth birthday, would be as lackluster as all the others.

But I am still far away from my grandmother, who is young but already getting along in years, my grandmother who rises with the day, the Feast of the Assumption of the Blessed Virgin, which was her birthday—though no one was certain of that, because back then people baptized their children when they felt like it, health and time permitting. But I am still far away in an ice-cold night under the watchful eye of my cat, who charms my life, though my life is still not charmed.

I am working my way through the back streets of time, through the numbness of the imagination, through my own river of pain, and I must make it to that other shore, to my grandmother Helena Konwicka, a young lady slowly aging in a sad time, a dreary era, a hopeless hour of dispassionate history which floods behind us, beside us, ahead of us.

Now I am above the banks of the Wilia, a dark-green river with blue ripples on its serene waters. Now I am elbowing through a thicket of plants, grasses, and herbs whose names I can't remember because I never had to commit them to memory. I have to strain to recognize the tall wild mint that is now releasing fragrance in the steady sunlight; I pass hemlock and fondly stroke currant bushes whose berries have already begun drying up. But I have no time to linger because I am hurrying to my grandmother, who is celebrating a birthday today on a small family farm, a modest gentry dwelling some ten miles from the recently built railroad.

And so, Miss Helena Konwicka rose that day right after dawn. The whole house was still asleep. She dressed in front of an elegant mirror which had a gilded frame but whose glass was clouded and speckled with tarnish. She viewed herself as if she were an apparition, and every so often that faraway woman in the linen nightshirt seemed to be executing movements a bit at variance with her own, performing an inexact imitation, trailing behind her with a strange and significant delay, and at any moment might suddenly make a mysterious signal or open an invisible door into the unknown, the unknowable, the unfathomable.

"This moment is going to last forever," she said softly, while at the same time inwardly telling herself that no, that was impossible, soon the hour of some fall or winter day would strike.

Her body was still young, beautiful, alluring, yet somehow alien, not a part of her, from some other world. Abruptly she raised her hands to the window filled with the rising sun. Her fingers grew warm-pink, dark streaks of bone and joints were visible. All of a sudden there was a flash of light—as if from summer lightning, for there had been no peal of thunder and the birds were still calmly chirping on the roof of the manor and in the trees in the park.

"I must have imagined it," she said softly, at once thinking that talking to yourself is one sign of spinsterhood.

Again a light flashed, shooting past the front porch, the park, and the outline of the farm buildings. She blinked her eyes, waiting for lightning to strike or for the hollow rumbling surge of thunder. But the morning quiet remained unbroken, filled only with cheerful birdsong.

"Everyone's asleep. I'm the only one who saw it," she said softly, pulling her dress crinkly with starch over her head. "Maybe it was a sign. A sign for me alone. But from whom?"

She suddenly crossed herself and started whispering a Hail Mary. In the next room, the clock's springs twanged as it began striking the hour. But she failed to count how many times it struck. Maybe five, maybe six.

She set off toward the front hall through a series of small, low-ceilinged rooms. Her step was so light that the old floorboards did not creak even once. Though slender and not particularly tall, she had an air of strength about her. Her small head was held proudly. She had a great head of hair the color of dried frangulin, hair with red highlights like that of my father, whom I remember from the infinitely long moment of his death. Helena's face was small and fine, her well-shaped nose was slightly aquiline and sprinkled with dark freckles. Her lips may have been a bit too thin, which was why she would often push her lower lip forward, to make it seem larger. In time, foible became habit. Helena's lower lip began protruding with increasing frequency when she was with people and sometimes when she was alone, even once or twice while saying her prayers. Her eyes were dark blue but sometimes looked gray, and other times tended toward green. Faces like Helena's used to be called sweet, and indeed there was a sweetness to it, a childlike innocence, and that look of reverie found on the angels who once populated heaven and earth but whose current whereabouts are quite unknown.

Out of habit Helena glanced into the kitchen. Emilka had

risen from her bed on the huge slab at the base of the soot-caked oven.

"There's not a breath of air," said Emilka with a yawn. "Soon as the sun's up, it's scorching."

"Are the horses harnessed?"

"Should be," she said, the palm of her hand covering a wide-open mouth full of teeth that were still surprisingly white.

Helena went out onto the porch and stood between two small wooden columns whose limewash was flaking.

"Where am I going?" she asked herself. "And for what?"

Everything suddenly seemed meaningless: the grotesque old park covered with the August dust that rose from the sun-warmed dirt roads, the grayish sky, the vine-entangled porch, and she herself, struggling with a yawn she'd caught from Emilka.

From the direction of the Wilia, from the woods on the other side of the river, came a strange, piercing sound, like the cry of a huge flock of birds or the lamentation of a great throng of people. Helena knew that blood-chilling sound from somewhere, or thought she did.

Just then she noticed that she had neither her prayer book nor her rosary. About to turn on her heel, she decided against going back to her room.

"This must be right, then," she whispered.

She set off down the path that led through high nettles to the farm buildings. On the way she passed a small old orchard, the apples that had thudded to the ground now warm in the morning sun.

In front of the coach house with its collapsing walls, Konstanty the coachman was hitching the horses, an unmatched pair—one dun-colored, the other black. They were both bony, their ribs making shocking washboards of their sunken flanks, and both were poorly groomed and crestfallen. The carriage itself did not look any better. It tilted to one side as if a spring had given out, and its straw-strewn interior had become the domicile of an old hen which, no longer fit for soup, was leisurely awaiting a natural death.

"Praised be Jesus Christ," said Konstanty, pressing his knee against the horse collar while fastening it with a strap.

"World without end."

"I'm all set, miss."

"So let's not be dawdling, then."

"I'll be quick. We'll be there by seven."

2

They drove for a short while through fields of half-harvested grain
and soon plunged into a woods, composed at first of deciduous trees,
then of pine, frequently interspersed with birch. The strong aroma
of juniper and moss damp with dew swept over them. Konstanty
lashed the horses' lean rumps with a lazy whip and the horses broke
into an ungainly trot, farting merrily. It was then that Konstanty
turned in his seat and glanced at Helena, as if taking a hint of
pride in his team of horses, their trot, and that holiday morning.

"How old are you going to turn this year, Konstanty?" she said,
asking the same question she always did to make the ride pass more
quickly.

"Must be a hundred and eighty-two."

"Does that mean you're the oldest man on earth, Konstanty?"
Helena asked laughingly.

"Like as not I am," said the driver with dignity. "Well, but
people do say that in Apan there's one man even older than me."

"And where might Apan be?" asked Helena, her laugh softer
now so as not to offend Konstanty.

"Out that way," he said, pointing with his whip to the heart
of the forest flickering with white fire, the first traces of the sun,
which was rising toward a zenith misted with gray.

As they drove, they would suddenly enter thin clouds of the
night's final chill, then emerge onto sun-warmed hilly ground where

fine sand spilled out through the breaks in the moss as from a cracked hourglass.

"It's a terrible thing to live that long," Helena whispered to herself.

But the old man had turned in her direction, his large, gnarly hand cocked to one hairy ear.

"A terrible thing," he agreed with a sigh. "Sometimes I even think I'm doomed never to die."

He lashed the horse on the right with his ancient whip, then lapsed into reverie. A shot rang out in the depths of those woods vast as a wilderness. Konstanty crossed himself, then cast Helena a cautious glance.

"He turned up for spring again," he whispered with a knowing look.

"And who would that be?"

"You know," he replied reluctantly. "He hasn't shown his face since the uprising, but now he's gone and done it again."

"Have you seen him, Konstanty?"

"Of course I've seen him."

"What's he like?"

"Don't ask," said the old man with a dismissive flick of his whip. "Back under the last king he betrayed people to the damn Russians and the damn Prussians, both."

A roe deer was standing by the edge of the woods, her large moist eyes fixed on the approaching carriage. The deer would chew for a moment, then freeze.

"Is that one of ours?" asked Helena.

"Must be," said Konstanty.

"Come here, Malwinka, come here."

The deer hesitated, pricked up her ears, then took a few steps forward. The horse on the left, the dun-colored one, grew flustered, tossing its rump and snorting.

"Must not be one of ours," said Konstanty, pulling on the reins.

"Here, Malwinka; here, girl," called Helena.

The deer waited until the carriage had passed, then walked onto the road, its deep sand gray as birch ash. Now without fear, she watched them drive away.

I know those woods, that ruined manor, and that river which bears pitch-blackened rafts. A brightly colored butterfly hung suspended over a juniper bush and a split second later it collided painfully with my window, which is covered with transparent frost. I can hear a shrill whine, something like telephone lines whirring before a change in the weather, or the distant rumble of German armor, or just the walls of an old Warsaw apartment groaning in the night. The apartment where I am now. I'm at the threshold. I've come to a stop at the door. I see so poorly. If I cross the threshold, there'll be no turning back. I have a faint headache. I know that pain from somewhere. I can see that forest as if through a morning mist. The carriage wheels creased the ashy sand.

3

Helena emerged from her reverie. "So, tell me, Konstanty, should I get married?"

The driver did not turn around and remained silent for a long while before finally saying slowly, "You'd be the best judge of that."

"And will you drive for me when I live with Mr. Plater?"

Once again the old man was silent for a time. "I would. But it wouldn't feel right. I drove Mr. Konwicki, the squire, my whole life, so how can I change horses in my old age? Wouldn't feel right."

Helena smiled sadly. The coachman's circumspect answer concealed an odd dislike of the Platers. As if to cover his confusion, Konstanty began lashing the horses with the stringy whip. The horses broke into an awkward trot.

"Maybe I should wait a little longer," Helena whispered to herself. "But what's there to wait for now?"

In the far distance, an Ave bell rang, sounding hurried and thin. Helena raised her head. The tops of the pine trees were already filled with sunlight.

"Will we be there on time, Konstanty?"

"Why not, I'll speed it up."

She opened her small white parasol. There was already a delicate tan on her shoulders, though it wasn't clear just where or when she'd gotten it. The carriage rocked every which way, bouncing on tree roots concealed by the sand. Helena sighed. The old man's head turned alertly, but only partway, so that it would seem he was just casting a glance deep into the woods.

"Man's not a free creature," he said softly.

"And what made you say that, Konstanty?"

"Because that's how it is. Everywhere, all over the world, people are ruling over other people. If not one way, then another. It's all God's will."

"Does that mean I'm supposed to get married?"

"You'd be the best judge of that."

A sudden shiver ran through her and she seemed unable to catch her breath. Her lips parted wide, she began gulping the damp, resin-scented air. But that was of no help. She jumped up from her seat and seized the rusty rail that separated the coach box from the carriage. Konstanty failed to notice her fit of gasping, for he was busy retrieving the reins, which had fallen and were dragging along the ground.

Out of the corner of her eye, Helena saw a large brown boletus mushroom at the edge of a rut in the road. What do I care about mushrooms, she thought. At a time like this. I have to calm down. Collect my thoughts. The scattered thoughts of a young lady who's not so young anymore. When did it all go by, where did it all go? The uprising seems only yesterday. It was supposed to have marked a new life. Late-night conversations. Journeys at dawn. The piano out of tune. Distant gunfire in the forest. And sometimes a clatter of hooves just before daybreak. And I was eighteen years old.

A low pine branch grazed Konstanty's cloth cap, but Helena had time to lean out of the way. Now she saw that her fingers had gone white clutching the iron rail around the coach box. Slowly, one by one, she released her fingers, which had adhered to the rusted metal. The carriage lurched over an unseen rock and Helena fell aslant back onto the seat. Tufts of sea grass protruded from the old, crinkled leather upholstery.

"This can't be all there is," she said softly.

"Huh?" said the coachman, who was both coachman and wagon driver. But he was a wagon driver more often; that he did every day.

"It just can't be," she said. "Tell me, Konstanty, how old are you really?"

"I can remember back when we had a Saxon king, miss."

"I felt ill. I almost fainted."

"There's a storm coming. It'll hit around dinnertime."

A column of mosquitoes or some sort of small flies wavered over the road. For quite a while now they had been following the horses, whose ears were adorned with pieces of coarse cloth edged in red to protect them against insect bites.

I feel better now, thought Helena. A momentary attack of fear. But fear of what? A storm's blowing in from the north. Animals are afraid of lightning and people are afraid of the fires of heaven, or perhaps those of hell, she reassured herself.

"Still, it's a shame about Piotrus," said Konstanty pensively, out of the blue.

"What reminded you of him, Konstanty?"

"I always think of him when I'm driving through here."

"It's been so many years. I don't know anymore whether it was all real or not."

"I feel sorry for Piotrus. He was born to do great things."

They could hear the wheels lazily grinding the ash of the road. The woods resounded with the cries of birds awakened by the sun. Helena suddenly lowered her parasol so that it covered her face, and wiped some dampness from her eye with the flat of her hand.

"Why are you talking about that, Konstanty?" she whispered in despair.

"I was driving for them at the time. The snow was heavy. They'd gotten hold of some horses. And the Cossacks were advancing from Oszmiana. A whole horde of them. Piotrus and the others had to flee over this way."

Konstanty fell silent, twirling the old whip in his fingers. "He might even have thought that if he had to die, better it be here, near his own people."

I've already forgotten him, she thought. What he was like, tall or short, blond hair or brown, whether he was jolly or more on the staid side. So many years ago—ages. But that's not so. I remember his eyes, his lips, his smile, the energy radiating from his hands and shoulders, the feel of his curly hair. The strange sound she had heard that morning rose out of the woods again. As if the orbiting earth had rubbed against the walls of heaven or of hell.

"Do you hear that, Konstanty?" she asked.

"You probably think it's that Schicklgruber shedding tears for his sins, isn't that so? But it's just the marshes waking. They stiffen up at night, but now with the sun out they're coming back to life. There now, you see," he groaned in despair at the end. "Whoa, you wolf meat . . ."

He reined in the horses, yielding the way to someone coming from the opposite direction. A fierce white horse flew by hitched to a fanciful runabout. Helena glanced back at the albino horse.

"My respects, your ladyship," said the runabout's driver in Russian. A short man but wide as a safe, the chief of police was in uniform. His small dark eyes laughed with good humor in a huge face adorned with a copious mustache—a gray and horribly pock-marked face.

"Good morning," said Helena with reluctance, shielding herself with her parasol.

The runabout darted by in a cloud of dust. The sound of its little bells hung Russian-style on the horse's collar could still be heard for a good while after.

Gesturing broadly, Konstanty made the sign of the cross. "Begone, you evil spirit. Look at how he flies around in that runabout of his. He's here in the morning and outside Bezdany by evening. He sniffs around like a hound dog."

But now she thought she could hear the Wilia. At that point the road did indeed run closer to the river, along a steep cliff at whose base the water gurgled through the upended trunks of old pine trees. Where do I know that sound from, she wondered. I know it from somewhere, somewhere outside my own life. What's happening to me? It's nothing. Tomorrow we must get started putting up the jam. I've been letting my work slide. I've been waiting for this day. But this day is no different from any other.

Yet once again she could feel that slight, cold, unpleasant shudder run up her spine. Well, I'm thirty years old now. The doorstep to old age. Old age without having had a youth or being an adult. That's what God wanted. What God ordained. What God bid happen.

She made the sign of the cross furtively, glancing both ways to check if anyone could see her.

"Forgive me, Lord God," she whispered, "and grant me the grace of faith."

4

She raised her head abruptly and saw Konstanty's faded eyes before her. He regarded her in silence, paying no attention to the horses, which were walking in step, their heads hung low. Then he turned slowly back around.

"Konstanty, it's simply impossible that you're one hundred and eighty years old," she said with a certain sudden anger.

"One hundred eighty-two," corrected Konstanty, still facing forward.

"No one ever heard of anyone living that long. Why do you say such nonsensical things, Konstanty?"

"But doesn't the Bible tell of people living that long? So many people have died in my lifetime. Polish kings and Napoleon. Many tsars passed away too, and Kosciuszko, may God rest his soul, was born within my memory. He fought here and in America too, but it was in some other country overseas that he gave up the ghost."

"Konstanty, how long will I live?"

He turned slowly, smiling almost imperceptibly under his mustache, which had once been gray but now had become green as river algae.

"You've a long way to go yet, my lady. You're only just at the start."

Again she felt that strange shuddering and suddenly could not get her breath. She closed her parasol as if the small circle of batiste had been blocking the flow of air, which now smelled of the river and sun-warmed blackberry patches. She had gasped for breath like that once before, and a similar chill had run up her spine. God, when was it? In her infancy—and later described to her by her nurse; in her childhood—and mentioned at times thereafter by her father and the others in the household; or in her youth—which even she was now slowly forgetting. Or perhaps in the coffin in which she had been encased for all time.

The horses came to an abrupt halt. Helena raised her eyes and, looking between the horses' heads, saw a youth in the middle of the road, his clothing like that of a student expelled from high school or an itinerant craftsman.

He bowed, perhaps a bit too low. "I beg your indulgence, ma'am. I've injured my leg and can't walk."

"And where are you headed, young man?"

"Just to Bujwidze. Not far from here."

"It's quite close by," said Konstanty in a friendly tone.

Miss Helena suddenly felt faint, yet was still able to say, "Have a seat, then, young man."

He walked over to the carriage and placed a foot on the step, showing a respectable boot. The carriage lurched violently to one side. Seizing the railing, Miss Helena cried imperiously, "Not in here. Up there on the coach box!"

There was something strange about the way he smiled before climbing nimbly up from the hub of the wheel to a spot by Konstanty on the coach box. Only now did she notice that he was hatless. His thick red hair fell onto his high forehead; abrupt movements caused it to hide his lean and restless face, which was crossed by flashes of feeling that seemed at odds with one another. On the verge of smiling, he would grimace in pain or wink a knowing eye. She regretted her impulse a second time.

The horses pulled away, the bone-dry carriage creaking. A heavy bird started up from a berry bush, holding something black in its beak, and flew awkwardly off into the depths of the forest. The passenger had begun speaking softly to Konstanty, who mumbled back approvingly. She noticed that the young man's coat looked too large on him, like a hand-me-down from an older brother.

He turned around and looked at her for a very long moment, just a touch of insolence in his smile. Against her will, she lowered her eyes, and was angry at herself for having done so.

"I beg your pardon, ma'am, but I really did injure my leg. What I mean to say is that my heel's been rubbed raw, I was on the road so long in this heat. People don't like to pick up travelers these days. Everyone's afraid of strangers."

"And have you come from far away?" she asked, to hide the odd confusion she felt. Today's not a good day. It's hard even to draw a breath. And that shuddering. A violent storm was heading their way.

"Oh, pretty far," he said, again with an insolent smile. Or at least so it seemed to Miss Helena. He spoke boldly and was free in his ways, not like the people from those parts. "I walked halfway around the world. And did the rest by ship."

"And where are you going?"

"I'm going home. To my people."

Now she noticed that he was not at all a gangling youth. It was only his being slender that made him look so young. The shadow of mysterious experience lay across his fine face. What was the point of all this? Why had she allowed him onto her carriage? A shudder ran up her spine again.

"Konstanty, speed up the team. We won't be there before noon."

"Giddyap, won't be long now," said Konstanty, clicking at the horses, which paid him no attention.

The road took a downward turn, heading toward the stream. Now blackish alders appeared on both sides of the road and the horses automatically quickened their step.

The redheaded passenger turned around with a smile that changed at once into a grimace of pain.

"I've had a headache all day. Since dawn, actually. I wake up, I look around, the sun's rising through some sort of strange, dark clouds that look like long, dirty towels. If you'll pardon me for saying so, I was sleeping on a pile of grain. It was awfully uncomfortable. Bits of rye kept getting inside my collar."

Only then did she see on his knees a knotted bundle of coarse cloth, like that of a peasant woman bound for market. What do I care, she thought. Still, it's a bad sign. God, what red hair. Judas must have looked like that. I'm turning thirty. My life's more than half over. A lace cap and spinsterhood until the day I die. Is this the freedom that was always so important to me? Once again, in the far distance, as if from the ends of the world, that same strange, unidentifiable sound. It reminds me of a huge cast-iron lid being closed, she thought.

"I hear it too," said the traveler. "It's the Day of Atonement coming."

"What day of atonement do you mean?"

"Just the Jewish Day of Atonement."

"What concern is that of mine?"

"But you were talking about it yourself, ma'am."

"I was?"

"Yes, you were talking to yourself. I talk to myself sometimes too. Talking to yourself is like drifting off to sleep."

When they had passed the stream, full of vegetation undulant as eels, the road climbed to a sandy rise again and the forest receded, revealing at its edge the little town of Bujwidze. They could see, amid the trees on a hill, the church encircled by a wall of fieldstones; the sloping square in front of the church on which there stood carriages, chaises, and ordinary peasant wagons; a few booths selling cracknels and spice cake; and all of this surrounded by the scant few houses that made for the heart of that little town lost in the forest.

The uplifting sound of the church organ coursed through the warm air. There was a smell of horse sweat and the honey aroma of spice cake.

The carriage stopped by the building which housed The Golden Apple, a small store belonging to the Jew Goldapfel. Helena raised her eyes, surprised by the license Konstanty had taken. She was about to admonish Konstanty when the redheaded passenger suddenly appeared by the step to her carriage. He was standing close to her, his elbow almost touching her hand, which rested on the lowered hood. He peered at her with eyes whose color changed from brown to green but was mostly gray as the August sky over the Wilia. He was about to smile, but must have lacked the courage. He had suddenly parted his lips and seemed on the verge of apologizing, but then abandoned the notion. No, that was no high school student—though he wasn't her age yet, either. Helena felt a sudden sadness, a nameless regret. Crows clamored in the tops of the yellowed lindens around the church. The holiday had them in a flutter too.

"I came back here to see you, ma'am," said the young man softly.

"What are you talking about?" Helena snapped out of her reverie, at the same time wishing to defer reaction to this unexpected effrontery.

"You don't remember me, ma'am. But I remember you."

"Where do you know me from?"

"From a long time ago."

"What's all that supposed to mean?"

He stood before her in deep shadow, for the sun was behind his head, the August sun, shapeless, spreading like liquefying butter. A ladybug was confidently climbing over his red hair. What's that supposed to mean, she repeated inwardly. A ladybug means good luck or disaster. What a strange day. The first such birthday ever. Unforgettable.

Suddenly he placed his warm hand on her fingers.

"Don't you dare!" she cried, jerking back. Her parasol fell from her hand and rolled to his high boots, which were like those worn by Russian officers. He bent down and picked up the parasol, but she turned vehemently away, as if from an evil spirit.

"Konstanty, what are we standing here for?" she called out. "Get a move on!"

"The one on the left must have foundered," said Konstanty, flicking his whip at the dun-colored mare.

The carriage rocked, its desiccated frame rattling, and headed off toward the square in front of the church. You mustn't look back, otherwise God only knows what that vagabond will think. But then, to her horror, she cast a quick glance backward, as if only opening her parasol, though she had no need to do so. He was standing in the same place, motionless, his bundle in his lowered hand. He did not bow or make any gesture of farewell. He stood there as if rooted in the sand, still as a sack of buckwheat flour. There was an air of conflict about his stance: regret that he had returned in vain, a sudden despair, and determination to return whence he had come that August night.

5

My grandmother Helena Konwicka, my grandmother whom I never saw in this life—and I do not know when and where she died—my grandmother Helena, along with her father Michal, ran the farm at Bohin at that time; it had been leased to them by an obliging neighbor. Their own small estate, Milowidy, which lay close by, had been confiscated after the failed uprising of 1863. Michal Konwicki had been the civilian leader of the district, a distinction that had been uncovered by a special investigating commission which, for a few months after the rebellion had been put down, had interrogated the local landowners, and not just landowners but peasants, foresters, some townsmen, and even Jews.

That strange uprising which had moved through the center of Europe like a summer storm, erupting suddenly and blowing over quietly, imperceptibly, that strange uprising weighed heavily on the lives of those people for whom it had flashed through the morning like a dawn, dying out before they were even up and on their feet; that unforgettable uprising hung in the air over the Wilia, howled in the marshes by night, and in the winter sucked away the air in the dark recesses of country homes buried up to their chimneys in snow.

My grandmother was an orphan just like me. Her mother, Maria Konwicka, died in childbirth. It was the first time she had given birth and the last. She was buried by the road to Daugiele, in an ordinary grave heaped with earth and marked with a cast-iron cross. I don't know why she was given such a poor burial when she should have lain in Bujwidze, or perhaps even in the Niemen region, and now I'll never know. But I think that must have been her will, and the dying woman's instructions had been honored by her bereaved husband, Michal Konwicki, my great-grandfather.

Helena was now sitting in one of the patrons' pews of the church in Bujwidze. The tall windows were full of sunlight slanting into the church's interior and settling on the walls, the modest-Baroque walls of a country church in a place where the Baroque was finally coming to its end. Those windows were full of birds as well, mostly pigeons warming themselves in the rays of the August sun, and higher up, beneath the nave, sparrows squabbled and chattered so loudly that their innocent voices pierced the music streaming from the old organ on which the self-taught organist pounded away. The church smelled of wax, fading flowers, and of incense, of course; and all those details, so banal, so commonplace, and so obvious nowadays, at that moment put Miss Helena in mind of something terribly far away—or perhaps even close at hand, but blocked by a monstrously thick wall, the wall of nothingness, the wall of non-being.

Once again she was shaken by a strange shudder, neither cold nor hot.

"I know all that," she whispered to herself. "But how do I know it—not from my childhood, and not from daily life either. The heat is horrible. The common people say the end of the world is coming. Judgment Day is coming, but no one knows from where. I caught a chill yesterday in the river. You shouldn't go swimming after sunset. Who used to say that? It might have been my mother. But I never had a mother. It's so airless. I might start screaming."

The lame sexton assisted Father Siemaszko, whose peasant boots shiny with age peeked out from under his alb. Helena had been feeling someone's eyes on her for quite a while, and knew who was looking intently at her, wishing to bow and give a discreet sign of his presence.

Helena waited. With absurd vindictiveness she delayed the moment when she would glance to the right, to where he was sitting by a white column, his rifleman with him as always.

Turning from the altar, Father Siemaszko assessed the interior of the church like a good steward and he was clearly displeased by the attendance; yet when his eyes met Miss Helena's something like a smile appeared on his face, which had not been shaved with excessive care.

Rising, she looked to the right, slowly, deliberately, and with seeming reluctance. Then Mr. Alexander Broel-Plater paid his respects by bowing his head. Already graying slightly at the temples, he was neither a young man nor an old one. He was on the fleshy side now, but one could imagine that in his youth he had attracted attention with his uncommon, almost girlish beauty. His delicate features had coarsened with time, and perhaps from rich dining as well, but he was still a strikingly handsome man—though there was always an air of dissatisfaction about him, of hurt feelings or just plain pride. A dark, lean, good-looking lad with a sullen gaze, Ildefons, his rifleman, was sitting beside him. He bowed too, but somehow perfunctorily, carelessly, even perhaps a little impertinently.

When Mass was over, the priest, cup and paten in hand, and escorted by the sexton, whose left leg was dragging, spoke in Helena's direction, his voice deep and unrestrained, "Don't forget about lunch, my child. Why don't I see your father here?"

Miss Helena only made a gesture of helplessness. But the priest hadn't waited for an answer. He was heading for the sacristy, questioning the sexton on the way: "Was there a lot on the collection tray?"

The sexton mumbled uncertainly.

"You don't remember? I'll give you something to remember, you game-legged devil."

She glanced at the clock on the wall whitewashed with lime. There was still plenty of time before noon and lunch with Father Siemaszko. She walked indecisively out onto the steps in front of the church. Plater was waiting there, and behind him, like a black shadow, stood Ildefons the rifleman.

"A good day to you, Miss Helena," he said, bending with seeming nonchalance to her hand—but she sensed in him a certain tension not attributable to respect alone. "You're not going to turn down the good Father's invitation, are you?"

"How could I dare to, though I'm not feeling my best today."

"It's the change of weather. Even the animals feel it. Just look at the birds."

And indeed, sparrows, or perhaps cuckoos, were flying low over the ground as they cut the scorching air. A flock of crows or rooks circled restlessly above the roof of the church.

Mr. Korsakov, the current owner of Milowidy, appeared out of nowhere. A gray-haired man dressed nattily in black, he had a certain nervous energy about him, a forced heartiness, and an unpleasant familiarity.

"May I wish you a good day?" he asked eagerly.

Without a word, Plater turned his back on Korsakov. Miss Helena nodded silently, keeping her hands behind her, holding her parasol.

"Murderous heat," said Korsakov with a thick Russian accent. "Well then, I don't want to disturb you."

He walked briskly off toward a chaise by which a footman stood waiting.

"He's got some gall, that one," pronounced Plater. "That must be the hundredth time I haven't returned his greeting, but he doesn't care, he's always friendly and cordial."

"He invites us to Milowidy for all the holidays."

"Yes, he grew callous in the service of Moscow. May I walk a little way with you?"

"Oh no, thank you," said Helena in alarm. "I have an errand to run for my father."

"All right then, I'll see you later."

"Yes, till then."

She ran down the steps, and for a time, he watched her go, as if appraising her clothing and the lightness of her movements. Then he looked into the dark eyes of the rifleman, who had been standing motionless behind him.

Helena opened her parasol and began walking across the square, which was overgrown with chicory thick as wool. Out of the corner of one eye she could see Konstanty in the shade of a linden tree, whip in hand as he lazily gossiped with the other drivers. She took the road which led to the estate of Bujwidze, but soon changed her mind and turned onto a path that went through fields to the river. A slight chill drifted from the nearby woods, a timid foretaste of the forest's cold. Now she could see peasant women on their way to a Mass that would be said by a visiting priest. They were carrying bunches of herbs to be blessed. Blessed herbs were better for healing and would last all year until the next Feast of the Assumption.

"Will I really favor his suit?" said Miss Helena softly, then turned around quickly, but there was no one behind her. Everything was caught in a haunting stillness. Everything grew gray, ashen, colorless.

Then in the distance she could see the tall, slender figure of a man standing between blackthorn bushes on a broad strip of rye stubble. He was looking in her direction. And that man with the boyish silhouette seemed to have red hair that was ignited by the sun now lazily cooling itself in a gray mist. She stopped and looked ahead with uncertainty. He shaded his eyes with the palm of his hand, trying to tell who she was at that distance. Then he moved unhurriedly off to the side, toward the forest that stood straight and still. The rare cries of the birds were the only sign of life on that blistering August day.

She went down to the river that flowed soundlessly westward, though at that spot it happened to flow northwest. The river too had gone gray and only near the shore did it take on a deep shade of greenish brown. Upstream, an old moss-and-algae-encrusted ferry barge was moored to the shore. And downstream, by a gentle bend, there were rafts, resin-stained logs stripped of their bark and lashed together.

She sat down on a stone that seemed to have been warmed in bathwater. Suddenly desiring to pray, she made a small sign of the cross over her breast, feeling shame as she did so. But there was no one else there beside the silent river. Small butterflies fluttered over the weeds that grew by the shore, a tern bearing tidings good or ill raced high above the watery depths toward distant islets or channels. And once again she heard that deep and distant sound which seemed to come from under the ground.

6

Helena sat at the table between the priest and Mr. Plater. They ate their cold soup in silence, the sound of the leisurely conversation between the sexton and the rifleman Ildefons reaching them from the kitchen. A friendly sort, the sexton tried to get the rifleman talking, asking him questions good-naturedly and no doubt offering him one tasty tidbit or another; but Ildefons replied charily and his voice did little to conceal his sullenness. The clock in the sitting room struck the hour jarringly, but as usual, no one quite managed to count how many times it had struck. And so the soup continued to be eaten in a troubled silence. To lighten the atmosphere, Father Siemaszko slurped his soup loudly. Alexander Broel-Plater cast a pitying glance at him. Miss Helena did not raise her head.

There was a great clatter of wheels outside the rectory, and despite themselves, they all looked out the open windows curtained with billowing muslin whose cleanliness was not of the first order. Through the branches of the old linden trees they could see past the church wall to the sloping square. His uniform unbuttoned, the police chief cut across the square in his runabout. The peddlers and peasants with their Sunday-best whips in hand turned and silently watched the police official hastening on his way.

"He's sniffing around again," said the priest, stroking his beard. "He dashes from one end of the district to the other like a hound dog. People say that there're revolutionaries in the vicinity, foreigners, students."

"Your Reverence," said Mr. Plater, "the chief of police dislikes all this newfangled dabbling in nationalism. And Petersburg is sour on those Belorussian fashions."

"That's true," sighed the priest. "I know what you mean. But, Count, I come from an old Belorussian family and I'm not ashamed to recall those traditions which go back to the great princes."

"You don't have to convince me, Father. I have nothing against Belorussians or Lithuanians. But, just in general, it's better to be careful."

"That's true." The old priest sighed again, deeply this time, and stroked the thick gray bristles on his large head.

They gazed pensively out the window at the square, where the market had resumed its leisurely pace. Some of the peasants were watering their horses with beer from thick bottles. Barefoot children were running, pulling wooden butterflies on wheels whose brightly colored wings kept opening and closing. Half drunk, some-one was singing mournfully on the other side of the fence. The police chief's horse had left behind a little cloud of transparent dust that settled slowly back onto the square.

The sexton came into the room, dragging his game leg behind him. Using both hands, he was carrying a large wicker basket that was dripping water.

"Mr. Korsakov sent over a whole basketful of peppermint," said the sexton hoarsely, after clearing his throat a few times.

"There, you see," said the priest unhappily. "He's trying to worm his way in with presents again. He has no shame."

"Well, you ought to accept once," said the sexton. "It's not right to keep sending them back all the time."

"If you accept once, you foolish man, he'll show up here with his whole entourage. Take it away and tell him we have no need of it."

"Oh, what a bother," groaned the sexton, and limping even worse than before, he lugged the basket back to the kitchen.

Impetuously, the priest shoved his plate aside. "He's shameless, shameless. How dare he! Especially with Miss Helena here."

Helena smiled sadly. "If he hadn't bought Milowidy, some real Russian would have. But this way it's still ours a little. Aren't the Korsaks from outside Worniany?"

"No, my dear Miss Helena," interjected Mr. Plater. "Those Korsaks are good people. To a man, they all went off to fight in the uprising. They're from the Nalibocka Wilderness and the Ruska Wilderness. But that renegade comes from somewhere near Dukszty, if not even farther away than that."

"They say he used to travel to Istanbul as the Tsar's envoy," said the priest.

"That's right, he distinguished himself in the war with Turkey, then later he served in the Ministry of Foreign Affairs. To advance his career, that traitor even changed his last name to make it sound Russian."

"Lord, Lord, the times we live in. Mikolaj, where are those dumplings?" shouted Father Siemaszko.

"Coming, coming," snapped the sexton from the kitchen.

Three plates of dumplings were served, and to go with them, the priest ordered an herb liqueur from his cellar; he had made it himself from an old recipe that dated back to pagan times. "One drink won't hurt," he said with a sigh, filling their glasses.

Helena was seized by a sudden sense of estrangement. Outside, someone was singing a wistful song in Belorussian, in the next room, the clock was ticking, and patches of sunlight crept across the old walls, whose lime was flaking. What am I doing here, she thought. Any second now my fourth decade will begin. Why is Mr. Plater blushing like that? That color doesn't suit him. There's something womanish about him you can feel a mile away, even though he is so mean and disdainful. Why wasn't I born a man? I might have had an easier life.

"One drink won't hurt," said the priest sweetly, to numb his own conscience. "What's this, aren't you drinking? It's a sin not to drink with dumplings."

Plater raised his glass of greenish liqueur to Helena. "To good fortune. May God grant us all good fortune."

"Good, very good," cried the priest, sweating profusely now. "It's high time for that. We can't let the Muscovites eradicate us. God, back in '48, I . . . Shhh, what am I saying . . . not a word to a soul . . ."

He gulped the liqueur until his Adam's apple, the size of an egg and covered with tufts of gray hair, lurched downward, then returned to its place.

Alexander Broel-Plater hesitated for a moment and then, with a certain air of refinement, moved his heavy oak chair closer to Miss Helena. "Please don't be frightened," he said softly.

"I'm not afraid of anything."

"You're not frightened of me?"

She looked intently at him. Yes, he had been handsome once. The beloved only son of a deranged countess (though they did seem to belong to a branch of a great family, one that was content to rest on the laurels conferred by its coat of arms). Indulged to excess and loved with a hysterical love, he neglected his studies, did not complete his education, and went away, perhaps abroad, only to return somehow dishonored, his name somehow sullied—or that might have been only an aura around him caused by unkind gossip. He's hesitating, his lips are moving, his lids are half closed, he wants to say something but now he's lost the desire. He looks as if he's dying to shed that haughty, mocking pose for a moment, but something won't let him. It's habit that puts a scowl on those lips, a bit too full, soft, and very red. Oh, Mother, how am I supposed to stand it all for the rest of my life, sighed Helena inwardly.

This is how my grandmother spends the day in her Lithuanian village, which is actually more Belorussian than Lithuanian. A holiday in a horrible province that no one in the world has ever heard of. Where minutes drag on like hours, and hours like weeks. Where a woman is born and lives in the same little spot till she dies, married to a neighbor against her will by her parents. But before she dies, she dreams day and night of the great feelings inspired by the magazines that arrive once a month from distant Warsaw or by the books that come once a year from France (which may or may not really exist). Sunday Mass in the parish church, grand name-day parties every so often, a timid flirtation at a distance with a stranger chancing to pass through those parts, a serious illness at the end of the winter, prayers for her native land, and the still living memories of uprisings long dead. The poverty of the commonplace where poverty is commonplace. The fine stitchery of life, a faded holy picture specked by immortal flies.

7

They sat on the rectory porch, which was of course festooned with grapevines that had already gone yellow. That's the way all the rectories in that region looked back then, with vines entangling the small white columns on the porch, clinging to walls whose bluish plaster was usually peeling. Father Siemaszko was smoking a pipe and sipping mead from a misshapen glass. Mr. Plater puffed on a thin foreign cigarette and blew a smoke ring at the little clouds of mosquitoes that had wended their way there from the cooling garden, or perhaps from the cemetery, which faced the village of Bujwidze, where the red sun now made ready to sleep. Her hands clasped around her knees, Helena looked straight ahead at the little town, the small square, and the few Jewish homes around it. The square was almost empty now. There were only a few wagons and carriages left. The Jews had come out and were standing in front of the fence, having a look at the horses, the church, and the rectory. They were discussing the day's modest events, gesturing dramatically and constantly shielding their eyes against the low sun.

The priest closed his eyes, rested his head against the cracked column, his pipe going out slowly on the lap of his cassock. Night was on its way, an early-fall night but a long one, filled with an awful, ringing stillness. Helena sighed. She'd better be going if she was to cover most of the way before nightfall. She could feel his gaze on her. He smiled amicably, crushing out his unfinished cigarette.

"I would so very much like to hear a word of promise from a neighbor I hold in such esteem."

"We have time, Mr. Plater. We have plenty of time. We're in no rush. I'll get there, as Konstanty says."

"All the same, a decision must be made. Neither of us is as young as we used to be."

"Yes, we're not as young as we used to be," repeated Helena, recoiling from an unwelcome chill on her shoulders. "It's getting cold. It's time I left. The storm probably won't come. I can see dew on the flowers."

"You're not playing fair."

"Oh, I don't know anymore. Maybe I shouldn't leave my father all alone."

"What do you mean? We'll all be close by."

The rifleman emerged from the darkening trees. "Sir," he said to Plater, "the coachman is drunk and getting rowdy."

"All right, we'll get on the road right away. But you go back to the carriage now."

"I was just leaving, I had no intention of staying," Ildefons replied sullenly, and walked away through the trees.

The two of them were silent for a time, listening to Father Siemaszko snore.

"Let's wait a little while," said Helena. "Let's wait until after the harvest. It's not a good time for me."

He opened his mouth and was about to speak, but she forestalled him, saying, "Everything will be fine."

"God willing. Well, let's be on our way."

"I'm staying here a little longer. To visit the cemetery."

He rose and, looking off to one side, said after a certain artificial delay, "Oh yes. The cemetery. We have too many cemeteries. But how could it be otherwise. I'll say goodbye, then. Until next Sunday."

He took her hand in his very cold palm and kissed it ceremoniously. When Plater had left, Helena stared blankly at the priest, at his hair cropped close to his large head, his frightfully thick eyebrows, his lump of a nose and jowlish cheeks—a face at once comical and kindly. Then she noticed one of the last flies of the year straying down the priest's nose, en route from his eyebrows to his mouth, and saw the mosquitoes preparing to land on his creased and sweat-dampened forehead, and she said softly, "Praised be Jesus Christ."

Unexpectedly, Father Siemaszko opened his eyes and, in a soft and oddly lucid voice, asked, "And do you believe, my child?"

"Do I believe?" repeated Helena, shaken.

"Yes, do you believe?"

She took a long moment to collect her thoughts. For the first time in her life she was afraid to answer, but without knowing quite why. His heavy lids once again covered his bulging eyes.

"I do the best I can to believe. Though I am a sinner."

"What do you know about sin, my child? Well, get going home now, otherwise Schicklgruber will be coming after you in the night."

"Have you ever seen him yourself, Father?"

"He burned down a temple full of Jews in Mira. He's a cannibal. A Beezlebub that devours human flesh."

Then all of a sudden she asked a question she did not even wish to ask: "And what about your own faith?"

"What are you saying?" he said, switching to Belorussian and keeping his eyes closed. "My respects to your father. Go now, go. I want to nap here a little longer."

She walked past the orchard and into the small cemetery, which was on the far side of the church hill and sloped down toward the village. Smells both cool and warm came at her from every side.

The aromas of cooling flowers and still warm herbs, the breath of the nearby trees and of distant fields with their sheaves of grain.

As always, her heart was wrenched by the sight of the grave and the moss-covered stone with its weathered inscription: PIOTR PIESLAK. She walked over to the grave and knelt beside it with a sigh. How many times had she knelt there? It was a habit, like saying her prayers at night. She used to go there with despair in her heart, wanting to kill herself on that grave. Later, she began kneeling beside it as before a roadside shrine; while now what she felt was fear or sadness. She crossed herself, but, thinking she had skipped a part of that sweeping gesture, repeated the sign of devotion. Lord, let his soul rest in peace—but do I still remember what he looked like, she thought. She tried desperately to recall the young insurgent's form and features, and it was only with great difficulty that she was able to distinguish in the darkness of memory his black, bushy hair; his swarthy face, with its touches of high color common among the local peasants; and his vigorous, dimpled chin. She smiled to him through the dusk of all those years—wait, how long has it been, it must be ten years now, or maybe even more.

"Don't be afraid," she said softly to herself and to him there under the rust-colored sod. "I won't abandon you. I'll be true to you to the end."

While whispering those words, she thought that such fidelity was probably of no use to the dead, but immediately admonished herself. Miss Helena often had strange thoughts which caused her shame and which she could not confide to anyone.

"I must work more," she said softly, immediately thinking, But for what, and for whom? "We all have our duties." But once again some evil spirit prompted evil thoughts: What obligations, obligations to whom? "And what about my country?" whispered Miss Helena.

She had the feeling that there was someone beside her laughing furtively. But it was only a wild dove settling down to sleep in the branches of an old oak that bent solicitously over the old graves.

"Grant him eternal peace, O God, and may perpetual light shine upon him. Amen. Piotrus, Piotrus, my love, I'm ten years older than you now."

And suddenly she recalled Plater and his farmhands bringing Piotr back at the beginning of that summer. They didn't let her have even a glance at him, though she had seen bodies that had lain all spring in the woods and been eaten by wild animals. He must have been hit by a bullet, but did not die at once. Wishing to evade the Cossacks, who were in hot pursuit, he had crawled until he found shelter under the thick branches of a young spruce tree, and there he had remained.

She shuddered, crossed herself with a broad sweep of the hand, as if wishing to drive away evil spirits or bad memories.

"I've got to get back," she said with a sigh. "But back to what? Where's my real place?"

Later, in the woods, she asked Konstanty, who could not be seen in the darkness of the night, "Do you believe in that Schicklgruber? Will you swear that you do?"

The driver slapped the reins against the horses' flanks. The sun had already set beyond an unseen horizon, and only in a few last places were the trees splotched with the sunset's afterglow.

"I met him once, but I didn't know it was him. Nothing special to look at. He's got a little black mustache. They say he's from Courland, or maybe even from Prussia. There always has to be that sort, trying to kill off whole nations."

"But why?"

"So there won't be too many people."

In the far distance a locomotive blew its whistle. They both turned their heads in that direction.

"It's the train. Sounds carry today."

"What do you mean, it's the train? It's the earth sighing. It doesn't like the night."

They drove in silence for a while. Faint, vanishing in the mist, the first stars had already appeared in the night sky. Like the lights of a remote village lost in the marshes. Where's all that thunder and lightning that was supposed to clear the air, she thought.

The carriage came to a sudden halt. One of the horses started to snort.

"Easy, boy," said the driver gently.

"What happened?" said Helena, returning to her senses.

"Look there," said Konstanty, pointing with his whip.

She looked where he was pointing and saw that the carriage had drawn up beside a boy, seven or eight years old, who was standing by the side of the road. His clothes and the cap on his head were the same light-brown color. Seeing Helena, the boy removed his cap and bowed politely.

"And where are you off to, little boy?" she asked.

"Bujwidze, my lady."

"Then you're heading in the wrong direction."

"I am?" said the boy, downcast. "And I thought I was headed right."

"Who are you?"

"Ziuk," he said with embarrassment.

"Fine. But whose boy are you; what's your parents' last name?"

"Pilsudski. My dad and I went to Bujwidze for the feast day. He left to play cards. At his estate," the boy added, seeing Helena's surprise.

"And what are you doing here?"

"I wanted to see Uprising Hill in the forest."

"And did you?"

"I did. There's a cross there."

It was only then that Miss Helena noticed that her parasol

was lying open uselessly on the floor of the carriage. She picked it up, shook off the dry needles that clung to the white batiste, and rolled it up with an air of deliberation. Then she came down from the carriage.

"Konstanty, this boy must be driven to Bujwidze."

"Thank you, but I can make it on my own."

"Get in, would you please. I'll wait for you here, Konstanty."

Konstanty scratched his gray head. "You shouldn't stay all alone here in the woods."

"Nothing's going to happen to me. Get in, boy. Drive as fast as you can. I'll be waiting here."

She began helping the boy into the carriage, but he slipped nimbly from her hands and hopped up onto the coach box beside the driver, exactly the spot the young man with the red hair had chosen. Without saying a word, Konstanty turned the horses around; and he was about to utter another word of caution but only clicked at the horses while fiddling with his whip. The carriage set off at a lively pace on its way back to Bujwidze.

Helena was alone. What am I doing, she thought in a panic. The night was emerging from the heart of those endless woods whose darkness concealed evil people and evil spirits. It's fate. She glanced up at the darkening sky. More stars now. Just then one star began streaking at an angle toward the earth. But Miss Helena did not know it was meteorites falling, nor did she know that a comet was also flying somewhere above in icy space, later to vanish in one of the Milky Way's infinite ruts. I forgot to make a wish. But what would I wish for today? A long life? Mr. Plater? Or maybe a great love?

"Oh, what nonsense," she said, flicking her parasol against her skirt. "What do I need love for? What nonsense my head is full of today. Such a strange day. And why should it be strange, of all things?"

She stopped by a juniper bush. A fine warmth, like that from a cooling bread oven, still rose from the sandy road. She seemed to remember that about thirty paces from there the two forest roads converged.

Once again she shuddered.

"It was here. It wasn't far from here they found Piotrus. I wonder what the last hours of his life were like. And how many frightful hours it all lasted. And if he had survived . . ." she whispered, suppressing a shudder. "It's cold. The dew's coming out. There won't be any storm. And what if he had survived and we'd lived together? Ten years. Ten unknown years. But perhaps this wasn't the place. The woods look the same everywhere."

Finally, when it was pitch-dark, she heard the hollow rumble of the carriage and the snorting of the horses. She began waving her furled parasol as if apprehensive she might not be seen.

"Konstanty, is that you?"

"Whoa, whoa, you beasts." She heard the old driver's hoarse voice. The carriage stopped right by the juniper bush.

She hopped up into the carriage, whose interior was cold and damp with dew.

"Schicklgruber didn't try to scare you?" asked Konstanty good-humoredly from out of the darkness.

"All right, drive quicker now. We've dillydallied terribly today. Did you bring the boy to his father?"

"Hoho, they even gave me a ruble," boasted the old man.

He clicked at the horses and the carriage set off on its way to Bohin. The old man's back stood out vaguely against the night sky. To Helena he seemed to be crossing himself again and again. Or maybe he's just dozing—it was the hour when old people slip into their first sleep.

Finally, she saw a glowing light rocking evenly back and forth. After driving closer, they saw it was Michal Konwicki, who had come out to meet them.

He got into the carriage without saying a word and placed the lantern at his feet.

"I'm sorry, Papa." She bent down and kissed his warm, dry hand. "We had all sorts of adventures."

Konstanty turned around on the coach box, the lantern's faint light flickering on his face. "A boy was lost in the woods. We had to bring him to his father's estate. He's a Pilsudski—they're the ones who had that steam engine brought in all the way from Warsaw."

Michal nodded. He sat stiffly, in his usual straight-backed way, as he listened to the sounds of the forest.

"Is everything all right?" asked Helena softly.

Once again he nodded silently.

"Have you eaten anything all day?"

He raised his brows.

"I'll fix you a little something the minute we're home."

They drove for a long while, the still-warm sand sifting audibly through the carriage's wheels. Somewhere nearby a dog began barking, and in that stillness, it seemed that the barking would travel through the woods and over the waters all the way to America.

Suddenly she took her father's arm. "Papa," she said softly, "it looks as if I'll be marrying Mr. Plater."

8

Michal Konwicki ceased speaking one day after the failure of the uprising. All of a sudden at dinner he announced: "There's nothing more to be said. I'll start talking again when my country is free." And, indeed, from then on he had not said a single word, though that's not quite true either, because every so often he would say something when forced to by extraordinary circumstances. But in common, everyday life, he was doggedly silent; his decision became an addiction in the end. And other vices were to appear by and by, like the fasts he kept on a great many days during the year and, in particular, on that day in mid-August when his wife, Maria, had died unexpectedly while bringing Helena into the world.

No one could remember why she was buried in the woods along the road to Daugiele, and no one dared ask Michal Konwicki, out of respect for his eccentric oath. And I don't know the reasons behind that unusual decision either—it must have been Maria's own decision, her will—just as I know nothing and will never know anything about her background, life, and character. She just appeared one day at Milowidy, lived there a short time, and died, leaving behind an orphaned infant and a grief-stricken husband.

What did Michal Konwicki look like and is what he looked like important? When I strain every nerve, I begin to discern in the darkness a Lithuanian yeoman, not tall but strong of build, with a small, graying head, an aquiline nose, bushy eyebrows, and a mustache with its ends twirled up. Beneath those brows I see faded blue eyes looking out dispassionately—actually, with a certain cold severity—at the world of his time, a world one step away from the twentieth century, which was to give people space flight and the crematoria.

Miss Helena was just returning from the farm, brushing chaff and thick dust from her old dress, when Emilka came running out of the orchard behind the manor.

"Miss, some man's here waiting to see you."

"Who is it?"

"He says you know him."

"Where is he?"

"In the front hall. I wouldn't allow him any farther, he didn't look like much of anyone to me."

"I know, I'll go in through the kitchen."

The two of them went quickly along the path that had been worn through the tall wild sorrel and the nettles, which were quite thick that year. They passed the long-neglected orchard and the collapsing fence, skirted the old park at a run, and dashed into the manor, which smelled of old whitewash and fresh herbs.

Helena quickly changed into her best dress and straightened her hair in front of that elegant old mirror horribly specked with tarnish like an old man's face pitted by the pox. Then, with some curiosity, she headed toward the broad and gloomy front hall, the largest space in that manor which was never really home to them.

The door was wide open behind him, and Helena could not distinguish his features, which were obscured by the deep shadow. But when he bowed with an odd laxity, Helena was seized with impatience.

"I'm listening. What is it?"

"Good day, ma'am," he said, bowing again with a sweep of his foot in a boot that had a military look to it. "Please forgive my boldness."

"What do you want? We don't need any workers, the harvest's nearly over."

His head blazed with a cold yellow light against the brightening courtyard. She couldn't see his face but would have sworn there was an insolent smile on it.

"I would like to ask you if you would teach me how to read and write, ma'am. I'm hoping to find work in the Niemen revenue office."

"I teach the village children. Who sent you here?"

"Begging your pardon, ma'am, but nobody sent me. Good people just advised me to come see you."

"And why are you acting so cap-in-hand?"

"A person must always show his respect to his betters."

All the while she was troubled by the suspicion that this raw youth was mocking her ever so slightly. She hesitated for a moment.

"Come along, then, into the front room."

He followed her and they found themselves in a small sitting room whose low, buckled ceiling was supported by cracked larchwood beams that were full of dark knots. The room contained a settee and an armchair both slipcovered in coarse cloth.

"The same as they use on horses' ears," he said merrily to himself.

But she didn't ask him what he had said. She was now clearly having misgivings about this inopportune intimacy with that redhead in the faded cap of the sort worn by the young insurgents who came from dirt-poor hamlets at the back of beyond. Large rectangular patches of blazing sunlight lay on the well-waxed floor.

"The heat's terrible and the air's awfully heavy. Am I interrupting something? I could come another time, even though it is a bit of a way," he said in that tone, seemingly polite yet oddly free and easy, that so irritated Helena.

"What's your name?"

"Elias."

"Elias? What a strange name."

"I wish I had been named Tadeusz, but my parents decided otherwise."

Just then voices and irregular hoofbeats could be heard from outside. Helena looked out the window, recalling that there were cobwebs on the panes, which had not been cleaned for a long time. Just past the porch she saw two horses. Konstanty and Ildefons were helping Mr. Alexander Broel-Plater down from the better of the two, which had white fetlocks. Plater grimaced and seemed to moan softly. Miss Helena dashed through the front hall to the porch abuzz with bees besieging a forgotten sugar bowl full of fine, pale-blue sugar.

"What happened?" she cried.

Without saying a word, they carried Plater up the low stairs to the porch. Attempting to bow, he could only gasp with pain.

"Careful not to move his legs, Ildefons."

"I wasn't about to."

Helena began bustling about the porch. "Do please come in. The sitting room might be best. But for God's sake, what happened?"

"It's nothing, nothing. A trifle," groaned Plater through lips compressed and drained of color.

"A fine trifle," said the rifleman lugubriously. "He passed out twice on the way."

"Quiet, you dolt, and keep your eye on the door!" cried Plater as they plunged into the airless gloom of the hall.

They carried him into the sitting room and placed him on the settee with the coarse cloth covering. Plater wiped the sweat from his forehead. "I seem to have broken my leg," he said with a smile that cost him some effort.

Just then the man with the red hair appeared out of nowhere, walked over to the settee, and lifted the injured man's right leg up into the air.

"Careful, you fool!" shouted Plater.

Paying no attention to the count's protest, Elias pulled over the armchair and set Plater's leg, already swollen in its expensive box-calf boot, on the seat of the chair.

"Now it'll hurt you less."

Plater sighed, feeling immediate relief. "It really does hurt less."

"May I bring you some water, Count?" asked Helena.

"Bring the water later. What I need right now is a knife," interjected the redheaded Elias peremptorily.

"What's the knife for?" asked the rifleman.

"Don't ask questions, just give it here," ordered Elias.

"You're taking too many liberties," grumbled the rifleman, but he removed his hunting knife from his belt and handed it to Elias with alacrity.

Elias slashed the leg of the boot open in one vigorous stroke.

"Holy Virgin of Ostra Brama!" groaned Konstanty. "Are you out of your mind?"

Elias pulled off the sock, mumbling in recognition, "Oho, English," then delicately began probing the foot and the area around the ankle. Plater gasped and groaned but did not resist being examined by the self-appointed physician.

"I'll need a basin of cold water, some cloth bandages, and two small wooden slats," commanded Elias. Emilka, who had appeared in the doorway, darted away into the darkness of the hall, followed by Konstanty.

"The bandages are in that little alcove; you know where, Emilka!"

"I know, I know" came a shout from the other end of the house. "They've been in that chest there ever since those days."

Everyone knew which days Emilka meant. Just then they heard the rumble of a wagon. It was Michal Konwicki returning from the fields for his lunch. He was wearing a linen coat to protect him against the August dust that rose from the thinning fields. He strode toward the porch with a weary gait.

"So, what really did happen?" asked Helena in a whisper, because for some reason the sitting room had suddenly grown hushed. Only the flies buzzed lazily near the ceiling, auguries of a storm that somehow was unable to arrive from the north.

Plater's breathing had become deeper and a little color was slowly returning to his cheeks.

"My horse bolted, Miss Helena. He got scared by some forest animal. Maybe a deer, or maybe a boar. He flung me off toward a beehive, but, my luck, I hit a pine stump. And ever since, my leg's been dead as a doornail, I can't lift or move it at all."

Ildefons the rifleman cleared his throat reluctantly and said, "That was no animal. To tell the truth, it was Schicklgruber, blast him. He came flying naked out of the marshes and scared the horse, and we never made it duck hunting."

"Pay him no mind, my good woman," said Plater more merrily now. "What is all this Schicklgruber business anyway? I don't believe in him. That Osiris is a flighty beast. He once bucked the groom and almost killed him too—he hit a big pine."

"And I say it was Schicklgruber naked, Count. He came flying out of the marshes, fire spouting from his nostrils, and then he just disappeared," repeated the rifleman insistently.

Her voice calling out, Emilka came running from the other end of the house. Konstanty was already tapping two golden-colored slats together when they all noticed Michal Konwicki standing in the doorway.

"Hello, neighbor," said Plater in a somewhat pained voice. "I apologize for the intrusion, but I've had a little mishap. My horse was scared by an animal and threw me."

"By a naked devil," grumbled the stubborn rifleman.

Michal Konwicki nodded and took a few steps toward the injured man. Emilka had just knelt at Plater's feet with the basin and strips of cloth.

"Leave him to me," said Elias decisively, and set to work.

They looked on admiringly as he moistened the bandages in the ice-cold water and wound them around the injured leg, which he then set with the wooden slats.

"It's nothing terrible, Count," he said in the end, wiping his wet hands on the count's jodhpurs, which had just come into fashion. "You've torn the synovial capsule. You need three weeks of bed rest. The most important thing is to keep the leg raised. Best with a pillow."

"And how do you know all this?" asked Plater, his voice normal again, the cold compress having afforded him definite relief.

"I know everything."

"What's your last name?"

"Szyra."

"Szyra. Didn't you people have a mill outside Worniany?"

"No, we didn't."

"That may be even better," said Plater with a smile. "Come see me at Woloki and I'll give you your reward."

"I thank you, sir."

Once again Helena thought she detected an unpleasant tone of voice in Elias, a tone of some inconceivable superiority.

"That's all well and good, but a surgeon should be brought in from Wilno. In the meantime, our house is at your disposal, isn't that so, Papa?"

Her father nodded silently, whereas Plater laughed with even greater merriment. "I am grateful to you both for your advice and for your hospitality. Ildefons, run over to Woloki and tell the steward what's happened."

"But I'll be coming back," said the rifleman menacingly.

"There's room for you in the barn. Everyone sleeps on the hay here. They like it like that. But please don't be worried, a bed will be found for our good neighbor."

"Oh, and might it be yours, my lady?" said Plater with a laugh that at once became a scream of pain, because Elias had begun adjusting the splints on the count's leg.

9

She stood there and looked at him, thinking: What does it mean, what does it all mean? Anxiety spread slowly through her breast, her throat, her hair. The roe deer Malwinka approached at a leisurely pace from out by the ponds covered with the green velvet of duckweed. Along the way she sniffed at herbs, nibbled leaves from bushes, demonstrating to all and sundry that she was the true mistress of the farm. It's terribly stuffy, there'll have to be a storm in the end, thought Helena with despair.

He was standing casually before her; the sun, as usual, was behind him. Strange that he always grimaced instinctively. But the hair on his head blazed like a brushfire and something in his eyes, a sort of acumen or restless intelligence, kept flaring violently and dying down. The closeness bothered him too. She could see an anxious pulsing at the base of his suntanned neck.

"So what have you decided, ma'am?"

Miss Helena was disconcerted, feeling an odd annoyance again, or perhaps it was simple anxiety. "You're playing some game, isn't that so?"

"No, I came here to ask you a favor. I want to learn to read and write."

"And when were you thinking of beginning?"

"Tomorrow, if I could."

She stared at him hesitantly. What am I doing all this for, she thought. "I don't even know you, boy."

"It'll come back to you. People remember me here. I didn't leave here of my own free will."

"When did you leave?"

"Toward the end of 1863."

"Aha," she said. "I see." Malwinka had walked up behind him and had begun butting the small of his back in a friendly way, as if wishing to push him closer to Miss Helena.

"Git, git," said Helena, moving her hand as if to strike Malwinka.

"You know, animals always intercede for me." The flash of his teeth was a striking white.

Mr. Plater's rifleman came out of the manor, and as he passed them, it suddenly occurred to Helena that Ildefons was oddly and unnaturally handsome and wore those good looks as if they were old clothes. With absolute abnegation and indifference. His jacket unbuttoned, he walked lazily over to the horses, which were hitched to a post. He wore no hat on his thick brown curls, and he cast furtive glances with his violet-colored eyes, his eyes truly violet in color, intense, with a certain uncanny luster. The slight stubble on his cheeks only lent him an additional nonchalant elegance.

He jumped lightly up onto his horse, and it was only then that she noticed that his trousers, rather fashionable and no doubt a gift from Plater, were worn at the knees.

"We'll send a carriage for the master tomorrow afternoon," he said casually, saluting with his whip.

"And who decided that?" asked Miss Helena with sudden anger.

"The master and I." He turned his horse around abruptly, spurred it, and darted off down the old tree-lined allee toward the gate, or rather where there had been a gate in better days. Plater's horse followed at a run, obedient as a dog. A great red sun hung over the horizon.

"So," said Helena softly, "what was I about to say? Aha—

bring a tablet and a slate pencil with you tomorrow. Can you borrow them from someone?"

"I can do anything." Once again he smiled warmly.

"All right then, you may start coming by."

He bowed low and walked away in the direction Ildefons, now out of sight, had taken. He had his own way of walking, like a man who'd had to do a great deal of walking in his life; precisely that: walking, not marching. He wheeled around, surprising Helena, who was still standing in the same spot and pensively scratching Malwinka behind the ear.

When she was on her way back to the porch, that deep, haunting sound rang out again, seeming to issue from the depths of the earth, and for some strange reason, it caused her heart to miss a beat. I must be having delusions, she thought. It's the heat. The storm's passed us by. Everything's passed us by. She stopped for a moment between the small columns. You mustn't talk like that. It's a sin. But a sin against whom?

"Papa, may I go in to see Mr. Plater?" she asked her father, who was sitting under the grape arbor, a rosary in hand. There was a vague aroma of flowers, or perhaps of ripening wild apples.

Her father nodded. Heading toward the manor from the ponds, a stork flapped its wings when it was over the lawn, as if to greet the household before alighting in its nest on the roof.

Helena sighed and went into the house. Alexander Broel-Plater was lying on the settee in the sitting room, covered by a saddlecloth despite the heat.

"I had the shivers," he said. "It was from emotion."

"I had them yesterday. The days just before the end of the world will be like these."

"Why do you put it that way?" he asked, opening the lid of his pocket watch.

"It's been a strange year. Not normal at all, right from the start."

"Every year's been strange for quite some time now. Would you care to rest? Please sit here beside me, if that wouldn't make you uneasy."

She sat on the armchair at the head of the settee where Plater rested in a half-sitting position. His leg, like a gray rag doll, reposed on a pillow.

"My accident was a sign from God," he said softly.

"Why do you say that?" said Helena, swift to blush.

All of a sudden, he placed his hand on hers. She was about to pull her hand away, but he clutched it in his soft, delicate fingers. Yesterday, the other one had grabbed her hand the way a dog grabs a bone, she thought.

"Forgive me for repeating myself, Miss Helena, but we are not as young as we used to be, and thank God for that. The days of mad passion are behind us. I can offer you many calm and serene days. And I for my part will do everything to make you happy."

He paused for a moment, then added, "If there is any such thing as happiness."

He withdrew his hand to click his watch lid shut. Sparrows were squabbling under the eaves, while there in the sitting room a mosquito had come to life and begun whining in one corner. Every so often the contracting floor would creak dryly.

"Yes. And I so want peace. I feel so very tired."

But to herself she thought, What's made me so tired, where's my appetite for life? What does this all mean, and where's it leading? Plater closed his eyes. The cheek beneath his left eye twitched almost imperceptibly.

"We owe you so very much. If it hadn't been for your help at the time Milowidy was seized . . ."

"Oh, let's not talk about that, that's over and done with," said Plater softly. "I feel that I'm to blame here. Perhaps I should have asked for your hand earlier. But those were troubled times and I was traveling the world looking for something, with no idea what to do with myself."

In the distance, the cows returning from pasture began lowing. The cry of birds, a high, metallic clangor, mounted out past the ponds, where great flocks gathered each evening for a convocation before flying away to the south.

"So, what's it to be, my dear Miss Helena? Can I count on your consent?"

She bowed her head as she collected her scattered thoughts.

"I apologize for not using finer words," Plater whispered softly. "But I'm afraid it would have sounded artificial. You must feel my sincerity, you must know I have the best of intentions, don't you?"

She nodded silently, without raising her eyes.

"Thank you, my dear fiancée."

Seeming to hear genuine emotion in his voice, she jumped from her chair and was running toward the kitchen when she was brought to a halt by the rumble of wheels and the sound of voices at the front entrance. She looked out to the porch and saw her father standing silently between the columns and, beyond him, Mr. Korsakov and the police chief in a carriage.

"I apologize for the intrusion," said Korsakov with a thick Russian accent. "But our throats were parched and so Mr. Dzhugashvili and I took the liberty of paying you a neighborly call. Might you have a little cold milk for us? It can even be sour so long as it's cold."

They were sitting in a sumptuous carriage and wearing leather aprons as protection against the dust. Since they had not been invited onto the porch, they began smoking cigarettes there in their elegant vehicle.

"Emilka, go get a pitcher of milk and glasses," Helena called out. Her father stood beside her, fingering his rosary in silence.

"What commotion today," said Korsakov with forced liveliness.

"We heard that Mr. Plater dislocated his leg, and Mr. Dzhugash-vili's little one-horse rig got wrecked in a rut. So I have to give him a ride home; you have to live in peace with the police, after all."

He began laughing boisterously, but his mirth was uninfectious. The chief of police regarded the people of Bohin Manor with a baleful eye while weighing something in his mind.

Fortunately, just then Emilka came running up and began serving milk, first to the guests, then to Michal and Helena.

"Oh, what good milk," said Korsakov with somewhat feigned delight. "Milk tastes like this only in Lithuania. Mr. Konwicki, you know what I sometimes think—why don't you come by Milowidy one day for a game of cards?"

He paused, peering intently at the two of them. But how am I to blame? I bought the property without ever laying eyes on it.

You got it as a present, you villain, thought Helena, while politely saying aloud, "My father doesn't play cards. He stopped going out when my mother died, and he makes a special point of avoiding gambling."

"What do you mean, gambling? We play for kopecks, just to spice things up. What people tell me is that Michal only bets with people he trusts, kin."

Korsakov's laugh was somehow unpleasant. "Forgive me, dear neighbors. Sometimes I like making little jokes. Oh, what nice milk, just like malmsey. Well, I thank you, and now I'll be on my way."

The chief of police was, however, holding the reins tight. "I'd like to take this opportunity," he said in Russian, his voice harsh and hoarse, "to use this chance to ask you good people to keep an eye out for strangers. There could be disturbances in our province. And it's up to us which way things go."

They looked without moving at his gray, dusty-looking face, which was covered with pockmarks.

"Do you understand what Mr. Dzhugashvili is requesting of

you?" asked Korsakov and, just to be sure, went on to explain: "He's requesting that you keep a lookout for strangers, people passing through, suspicious people."

Then they drove off into the sun's bloody afterglow, while my grandmother Helena stood on the ordinary porch of an ordinary house, herself involved in ordinary situations and circumstances, the commonplace events and conflicts which, in those ordinary days and nights, made for the ordinary life of those times, which has been recounted, described, and painted to the point of boredom.

1 0

On the other side of the river, the tall pines with crowns of wispy dark green had begun turning red. That day those majestic trees stood motionless, as if collecting their thoughts before some mad and reckless act. For madness was in the air, in the settled, ashy, distended heat. A hawk, the only creature to have bestirred itself in that universal stasis, flew in large circles over the edge of the old forest and the quiet, humble river.

As far back as I or my ancestors could remember, the Wilia was always a tidy river. Drowned men did not float on its surface, nor the bodies of animals that had strayed into its waters; it was never clouded with blood, nor did it ever bear the corpses of fallen insurgents or Cossacks. On occasion, and for a short while in the spring, it would be troubled by floodwaters and for a few days be swollen, bulging, covered by a slimy, turbulent foam full of bark, grasses, and broken branches, like some river in South America. For the rest of the year, and particularly in summer, and especially toward summer's end, its surface would become gray-blue and its depths the dark green of old glass. And it was transparent as glass too. Its depths afforded you the pleasurable sight of miniature forests, groves, and shaded allees of algae. You could follow the rhythmic dunes of golden sand at the bottom and see rare, mysterious stones overgrown with mussels. People used to say that, years ago, at the point where the Uzla flows into the Wilia, the insurgents' wagon train bearing the treasure of the National Government had found a clear and watery grave. Many boys had dived there, but no one had ever found anything—except once, when a vagabond came up with a silver horseshoe, then disappeared, horseshoe and all.

Miss Helena let the slow current bear her along. She was not so much floating as reclining on that velvety green water, moving her hands slightly, the current rocking her gently back and forth, as she cast a melancholy gaze at her body covered by the thin, transparent cloth of river water. Like the other girls and women, she always wore a long shirt when she went swimming, but that morning, for some reason, she had taken off all her clothes and entered the river shamelessly naked, even though someone could be spying on her from the other shore, that other shore which Miss Helena had feared since she was a child and on which she had never set foot, though it was no more than thirty yards away.

She looked up at a sky gray and dense where the sun had faded, insistent in its prophecy of a storm that somehow could not reach those endless secluded forests, and that river battling its way through them to Wilno.

"Maybe I should let the water just take me away," she whispered to herself.

She stopped moving her hands, her feet began falling toward the murky bottom, some imperceptible eddy turned her gently on her axis. She caught a glimpse of the shore on their side of the river; it was much steeper, overgrown with bushes and weeds. Malwinka was grazing peaceably there, raising her head from time to time to look at the river.

Will I still be free, wondered Miss Helena. But have I ever been free? What does freedom mean for an ordinary person? What kind of independence can I have? You have to work. And trust in God. No one's ever seen my body, the thought flashed through her mind. She was about to cross herself out of fear, but only swallowed a mouthful of the cold and slightly bitter water.

Afterward, she took a roundabout way back to the manor to have a look at the farm's fields. The peasant women were already reaping the sparse and paltry oats, which had been flattened in places by the July rains or wild animals. The women sang a drawn-out, plaintive song which rose and fell between long silences.

Then she caught sight of Father Siemaszko dozing in a one-horse carriage that was approaching at a leisurely pace. The sexton halted his horse at the sight of Miss Helena. His surplice rolled up on his lap, Father Siemaszko suddenly lurched and woke up, blinking his eyes.

"And where has God sent you today?" she asked.

"I've been with a dying man. It was a long way too, my child. There and back took the whole night."

"Would you like to stop by the house for some breakfast, Father?"

"Ordinarily I wouldn't refuse. But today I can't. I've got to get back. I've been on the road so many hours."

The sexton clicked at the fat and lazy horse. The gelding set off reluctantly, snorting, with its head hung low. Helena walked behind them, holding on to the carriage's rolled hood.

"Look how high the sun is already," said the priest in surprise. "I had nightmares all last night."

"Must have been from hunger."

"No. But I am in for a spell of fasting right now, child. Like the Jews, I'm ending one year and beginning another. I do my reckoning in September, like they do."

"I'd like to do mine too, but I don't have anything to account for," said Helena with a sigh.

"Maybe it's better that way."

"But how could a holy man like you, Father . . ."

"Don't talk nonsense," he grumbled, and was about to cross himself, but abandoned the idea and let his head fall.

Once again her eyes were lashed by that whiteness like summer lightning. What's happening to me, she thought. What's happening to us all?

She continued walking behind the priest's carriage, waiting for something. But the priest had sunk back into thought, his dark eyelids covering his eyes. He'd forgotten to take off his wire-frame glasses last night. He must use them when he's reading the prayers for the dying. Now the glasses flashed silver on his deeply creased forehead.

The peasant women in the oats straightened their backs and gazed avidly at the priest. That would give them something to talk about for the rest of the day. Where was the good Father just back from, whom had he just seen off to the next world? Shielding their eyes with the palms of their hands, they stood in the middle of the field devouring this sensational development.

"This is as far as I'll be going, Father," said Helena, letting go of the edge of the carriage.

He had already covered a good stretch of road when Father Siemaszko returned abruptly to his senses and had the sexton halt the horse.

"Come here, child, come here!" he called.

Helena ran to the carriage, her feet sinking in the hot sand, which sifted into her purple slippers.

"Did you want to say something to me, Father?" she asked.

He looked intently at her, as if seeing her for the first time. "Do you believe in God?"

"Same as everyone," she replied in confusion. "But there must have been something else you wanted to say."

It was only then that he noticed that his glasses were still needlessly on his forehead. He took them off, folded them up carefully, and placed them in a pocket of his well-worn cassock.

"It's not the right time for it," he said with a sigh. "Oh, is it sultry. My best regards to your father."

The sexton clicked at the horse and they rolled away toward

the woods, raising scanty clouds of dust. He's just given someone last rites. A terrible duty.

Then, feeling a strange rush of energy, she began heading back for the manor that loomed amid old trees. One of those trees was a tall, slender larch whose lower leaves had already begun turning yellow, a sign that fall was nearing. A stork the farmhands called Maciej was circling with deliberation over his nest on the roof of the manor.

Her father was sitting on a small, rotted bench green with mildew, to one side of the old park. He was leaning on a double-barreled shotgun which he had not used for a long time. Now he was content to track animals and observe them in the wild. He was breathing heavily as he looked with narrowed eyes at Bohin's fields parched by the August sun.

Miss Helena paused by the trunk of an old maple tree. "The priest was just with a dying man," she said.

Her father nodded. Now they both looked at the gray and empty fields.

"Papa, I'm going to marry Mr. Plater."

Without looking at her, he nodded as a sign that he had understood.

"Are you pleased?"

He flipped the safety on his gun and spread his hands far apart. Malwinka appeared from behind a bush. Standing fairly close to Helena and her father, she gazed with wise and understanding eyes at them.

Miss Helena sighed, then headed for the manor sunk in lilac bushes, clusters of wildflowers, and nettles that were tall as trees. She suddenly felt that, in some other life perhaps, she had already once walked like that among the trees and warm scents of summer's end, walked like that to some horrible fate. Now her heart began racing and she spoke to herself in a reassuring whisper: "Doesn't matter now. It's all over. Long gone. It's obligations that await me now. But obligations to whom and to what? We all have our obligations. My mother had them, my father had them—and he still does; Piotrus had an obligation and he fulfilled it. There's a terrible storm coming, bigger than anything we've ever seen."

Then, after tidying herself up a bit, she walked into the sitting room. Alexander Broel-Plater was on the settee with his jacket unbuttoned and, his head against the armrest, was either lost in thought or dozing with half-shut eyes. The floor creaked under her foot and he awoke, buttoning the top of his jacket with shame and speed. A gray rag doll, his leg rested comfortably on the chair.

"Go back to sleep, sleep's the best medicine," she said.

He smiled and looked intently at her. "I was doing some thinking, just to pass the time. The horses will be by for me before noon."

"You could stay here a whole week if you'd like."

"I thank you most sincerely, but I do have obligations to attend to."

He has obligations too, she thought. How handsome he is, with that gray at his temples; he may even be handsomer now than he was before. Yes, that strange and alien man's looks have improved with age. God, what am I saying. He's my fiancé.

"I was thinking about us, Miss Helena," he said, and began looking through his pockets for a cigarette.

"Good thoughts or bad?"

He paid no attention to her question. He took a drag on the cigarette, then exhaled long streaks of blue smoke from his soft red lips. "I used to think my mother would live to see the day, but she didn't."

She wanted to say, "You should have moved with more haste, then," but she didn't say anything. He's going to be my husband, after all. A sudden fear made her blood run cold and she stopped in mid-step.

"You know, I loved my mother very much. I sacrificed a great deal for her. She tyrannized me my whole life. That helpless, bedridden woman."

"Perhaps you regret the offer you made yesterday?" she asked out of the blue.

"Miss Helena, for God's sake, what are you saying?" he said, tossing on the settee.

It was only then that she noticed that the settee's black wood trim was decorated with carved oak leaves and acorns. She smiled gently. "I apologize if I hurt your feelings. But oughtn't we to be honest with one another?"

"Of course we will always be open with one another. What a pity that I cannot get up and kiss your hands."

"How do you feel? How was the night?"

Coming to life now, Plater put out his cigarette in a stone ashtray.

"At first, my leg gave me some pain, but it died down after a time. I even slept a little just before dawn. I dreamed I saw you come into the room."

"I really did look in on you just before sunrise."

He broke into laughter, glancing merrily at her. "I don't know what to say myself. I've never been engaged before."

Blushing, she turned away. "I don't have any great experience either."

"Everything's going to be just fine, Miss Helena. Don't pay attention to what people say."

"And what is it that people say?"

"What they say about me."

"I haven't heard anything."

"Please don't listen to people. Will you promise me?"

She glanced off to the side, at a wall with a horrible water stain. "I promise."

"Well, now I can have the banns read with an easier heart."

"Shouldn't we wait till fall?"

"Fall's not that far away. This is the last of the heat waves. There'll be a terrible storm and autumn will come in after it."

"But why rush?"

"Autumn is coming. Your autumn and mine. Our autumn."

She could see that his expression and tone of merriment were forced. Suddenly she was seized by fear. What is married life? What does it mean to share a bed with someone for the rest of your life? But he's afraid too. For no reason at all, she ran over to the window and looked out at the day, airless, motionless, just like yesterday. She and Piotrus had kissed all of three times when he asked for her hand. Then he was killed. They hadn't really kissed, they were just learning how. He'd pursue her and she'd run away, as good manners dictated. What am I thinking about? Am I going to spend the rest of my life thinking about something that never came to pass?

Just then the door squeaked and Emilka appeared. She glanced over at Plater, then covered her overly exposed breasts with the palms of her hands. She had clearly just come running from the kitchen, where, summer or no, the bread oven was lit every day.

"Excuse me, my lady," she said confidentially, lowering her voice, "but that Jew is here."

Helena felt even hotter now as she let go of the edge of the muslin curtain. "What Jew?"

"The one from Bujwidze."

That was the last question Helena asked. She went straight out to the front hall where the redheaded Elias stood, tablet and slate pencil in hand. He bowed, but without any particular ardor and with even a hint of defiance, though his eyes were cheerful and sincere.

"Good morning, ma'am."

Flustered, Helena began moving nervously about the front hall.

Like bits of seed grain, brown dust floated up from the floor in shafts of sunlight. Emilka was already back in the kitchen and singing.

"You're in a hurry to start studying. You didn't even give me time to prepare the lesson," she said, still in a state of confusion.

"But it was you who told me to come in the morning."

"That's so, but I didn't expect you right away. But that's my bad luck."

He remained silent, not going to her aid. Once again she began bustling helplessly about the hallway. "Where would you give some-one a lesson here anyway?" she asked herself. "Not on the veranda, Papa will be taking a rest out there. Mr. Plater is in the sitting room. Well, where am I supposed to receive him?"

Elias waited without a word, his red hair blazing like the glow in a blacksmith's forge.

"Well, there's no other choice," she whispered in resignation. "Let's go to my room."

She led him from the front hall down a small corridor, whose walls were covered with sacking, to her room, which did not re-semble any of the others. Elias looked curiously about that room, darkish because its windows looked out onto the old and shaded park.

"What a beautiful room," he said sincerely. "And your choice of things for it is beautiful too."

Once again Helena blushed slightly and began angrily moving an old armchair over to her round table, where a splendid modern oil lamp rested on a lace doily.

Indeed, the good-sized room was full of flowers, fresh and dried, bunches of herbs, stones of unusual color, abandoned books, multicolored ribbons fastened to rusted nails, drawings begun but never finished, holy pictures from the feast days in Bujwidze hung wherever there was a place for them, rowan branches, and, on the small table by her bed with its tattered silk canopy, resting against a nickel-plated crucifix, was a large gingerbread heart with the words *Love Me Forever* written in icing.

Miss Helena walked over to the table and, without knowing why, turned the heart so that the inscription faced the crucifix— even though her guest was unable not only to write but to read.

"Sit at the table," she ordered.

Obediently, he pulled back the chair, whose sea grass stuffing protruded from the upholstery, and took a place opposite the lamp. Helena was about to sit down on the bed but, since that did not seem fitting, instead walked over to the window. Enormous yet timid rooks with large, scratched beaks were hopping about with what seemed a limp on the bare ground among the trees.

"How old are you?" she asked, taking the offensive.

"Twenty-eight. You don't remember me?"

"No, I don't. And you're a Jew from Bujwidze?"

"A Jew boy from Bujwidze, if you like."

"And you really cannot read or write?"

He glanced at her from the corner of his eye. His shock of red hair was not so vivid there in that darkish room and grew dimmer all the time. But what do I care about that Jew, she thought, drawing the half curtains on the window. The windows have to be washed, they've gotten all dusty, it's been such a dry month.

"I can read and write Yiddish. Now I'd like to be able to in Polish."

"Why did you choose me to be your teacher?"

"It was because of you that I joined the uprising."

"What does that mean? What are you talking about?"

"I was with a group of insurgents in Belorussia. Right up till the end. Till the winter of '64."

"Shhh, quiet. What is all this nonsense? And who sent you here?"

"Please, don't be afraid."

"Do you know what went on here in those years?"

He fell silent, lowered his head, and looked at the floor or at his boots, which were not the sort Jews would be expected to wear.

"Please trust me. Perhaps I can give you more proof that I am worthy of your trust," he said softly.

Helena sighed and walked over to the table. For some reason she shifted the position of the lamp, causing the golden oil to slosh slightly.

"What's your name?"

"Elias. I told you, but you forgot."

All of a sudden she smiled. "Oh, that's right. And you wished you'd been named Tadeusz. Like Kosciuszko."

"I didn't know anything about Kosciuszko back then."

"Something tells me I shouldn't give you lessons."

"It was fated. Since I've come back after all these years, it means that you have to teach me how to read and write."

"All right, put the tablet in front of you. Don't lean your elbows on the table. We'll begin with the letter *a*."

But just then bare feet could be heard stamping down the corridor and Emilka, red in the face, flew into the room like a fireball. "Miss, miss, you must go. The count's leaving."

Helena walked through the hallway, now redolent of fresh bread made from new flour, and out onto the porch, where her father was already bidding Plater farewell. The count was on a pair of crutches, old and blackened but padded with velvet, no doubt an inheritance from one uncle or another. The rifleman was waiting in the front drive by a small cabriolet that was polished, stylish, truly lordly.

Helena could sense Elias's presence behind her and was displeased by it. But she hadn't time to send the young Jew on his way. Besides, Plater was either pretending that he didn't see him or hadn't yet looked his way.

"Michal," he said a bit too grandly, "allow me to treat you like a father from now on."

Michal Konwicki nodded and, a bit at a loss, twirled one end of his mustache. Plater bowed and kissed Helena's hand with great ceremony. "My dear Miss Helena, I thank you with all my heart for your hospitality."

"But you were in your own home, after all."

"This is your home and your father's until Woloki becomes your real home."

Elias began coughing because of the dust drifting with the wind, though there really was no wind, only the hot air stirring lazily in that stock-still world.

Despite themselves, they all glanced down the allee lined with old lindens which led to the highroad. There was a rider at the end of the allee. Though he reined his horse in firmly, the dark mount with the white patch on its chest kept shifting its thin legs uneasily.

Plater narrowed his eyes and stared for a moment into the light.

"It's the chief of police. He flies through the district like a demon," said the rifleman Ildefons.

"Muravyov the Hangman takes an ordinary policeman and appoints him to a post like that," added Plater. "The man sniffs around like a pointer. Well, it's time to get going. Thank you and goodbye, though I hope not for long. Will you allow me to send you at least one little note a day?"

"Naturally I will," said Helena with feigned delight. "And we'll always be most pleased to have you as our guest."

Michal Konwicki nodded silently, and his severity made it difficult to tell whether he was happy or unhappy. Konstanty walked over from the coach house wearing a linen dustcoat. He stopped respectfully at the edge of the long-dead lawn and glanced once at the chief of police's halted horse and once at the household which had gathered in front of the manor to bid the limping count farewell.

"Until we meet again."

"I'll look forward to it."

"And thank you again."

"We thank you."

He hobbled over to the cabriolet, set his crutches aside, and, rejecting the rifleman's help, used his arms alone to hoist himself up into the vehicle. Ildefons hopped in after him and flicked the horse with a handsome whip that had a scarlet tassel.

"Did he propose to you?" she heard Elias ask softly behind her.

"And what business is that of a Jew boy from Bujwidze?" she snapped without turning around, continuing to watch the elegant cabriolet vanish in the shade of the allee.

1 1

"It's too big. But it came out very nice. Now try to make it smaller. See, the way I did it." She handed him the slate pencil, which he clasped carefully, examining it closely as if searching for the warmth of her hand or the magical trace of a finger.

She walked over to the window and again looked out at the dark trees in the old park, their trunks twisted, more dead than alive, their crowns meager manes of thinning green. Between the trees she could see the distant fields, and the wagons full of grain, streaming in the gold of a sunny afternoon. She suddenly realized that she never used to look out windows before. Of course, sometimes, without thinking, she'd glance at those small panes of glass and the blur of green beyond them, but never had she peered so intently at the scant yet mysterious life of that neglected park.

Coming abruptly back to her senses, she walked over to the table with the beautiful lamp that had been shipped there all the way from Wilno. He straightened up and put his hand over the tablet.

"What were you drawing?" she asked in surprise.

"Have a look, if you'd like."

The white face of a woman, hair pulled tightly back, stared out from a border of black.

"Who's that supposed to be?"

"Oh God, can't you tell?" he said unhappily.

He began drawing a halo of tiny *a*'s around the woman's face, then said with a sigh, "It's you, of course."

"Me?" she said, jumping back from the table. She had a premonition, not necessarily of ill, but a strangely piercing and painful foreboding that took her breath away and chilled her bones.

"You can't read or write, but you can draw?"

"I can't read or write Polish. I learned how to draw from a lithographer in Paris."

"What are you talking about, young man? Why have you come to Bohin? Who sent you here?" she said with anguish in her voice.

He looked at her, his light-blue eyes wide open. There's something noble about his face, she thought unhappily. He should leave and never come back here again.

"I've already told you that I joined the uprising because of you."

"You're making up stories again. You couldn't have been more than sixteen at the time."

"That's right. I had just turned sixteen. And I joined the partisans because of you. First I was in Colonel Mineyko's detachment, but the Rooskies smashed us right away. Then I served under Kalinowski, and in the end I formed a detachment of my own."

"You're out of your mind." She suddenly ran over to the table but didn't know what to do next. "I knew right away there was something wrong with you. Who told you all those stories about the uprising?"

"I could swear to it, but you still wouldn't believe me. In the end I went back to the Nalibocka Wilderness, where we, meaning Colonel Borowy's division, had been smashed by the Russian infantry. Then I retrieved the weapons which I had hidden very carefully after the battle in some uprooted trees, right by where the marshes start. I gathered a few people—stragglers, bootleggers, foresters, runaway peasants—and we kept at it right up until the early spring of '64. Then the Cossacks caught up with us and there was nowhere to run. One soldier nailed me to the frozen ground with his bayonet. The bayonet broke and stayed in me, which saved my life. The steel prevented internal bleeding. Later on, in the summer, I was sent to Siberia, on foot. The nobles went by wagon, but me, a Jew, I went with the peasants on foot, even though I was a noncommissioned officer."

Somewhere far away a woman was singing plaintively, perhaps out in a field or in one of the farm buildings. There were not many things, events, or people there, not much of anything, not many of all those quirks of human fate worthy of an enduring place in mankind's memory, not much of anything at all in that secluded region north of the Niemen River, which marks the start of forest and marshes that never end because they are without end. And I am unable to warn my grandmother Helena Konwicka; I don't have the power to restrain the course of events; and I cannot avert the finale of which I am thinking even now, concealed in a horrible solitude, gnawed by the fears of old age, racked by a sense of doom that can suddenly cause a person to shudder and shove him blindly into the black abyss of the unknown.

"Now you listen to me," said my grandmother Helena Konwicka. "Leave, and never come back."

"But why, my lady?" asked Elias. "Did I say something wrong?"

"It's better that way. Maybe Father Siemaszko or someone from Bujwidze can be your teacher instead."

"You asked me about the uprising and I told you. It's all true. All the boys were joining, and so I joined too. To please you."

"Don't praise yourself to others, mind your tongue. The police chief is going around the province on the lookout for strangers, trying to ferret out suspicious people. Go back to Bujwidze and forget you were ever here."

He looked at her for a long moment, his spirits gradually dimming. His hair had lost its glow, his face was gray and even seemed to have shrunk. Voices could be heard speaking in normal, everyday tones, either in the kitchen or out on the porch steps. Helena stood with her back to him, never looking away from the window she had suddenly discovered that day and which was in definite need of cleaning.

Rising from his chair with a sigh, he gathered up the tablet and the slate pencil attached by a string to a wooden stick, and straightened a few rumples in the lace doily. He opened his mouth to say something, but then clearly changed his mind and began heading for the door without another word.

Helena stood unmoved, looking out the window, seeing nothing. But when she heard the drawn-out groan of the bone-dry door, she said softly, "Wait."

He halted obediently in the doorway.

"Do you really want to learn how to read and write?"

"I swear to God."

She smiled with sudden relief. "Jewish oaths aren't to be believed."

"And why is that, may I ask?"

"Because the Jews have their own morality and laugh up their sleeves at ours."

Then he turned around and smiled as he had before.

"Did I say something foolish?" asked Helena, immediately angry with herself for asking the question.

"All I want to do is learn how to read and write. Then I can make my way in the world."

"You did mention the Niemen revenue office."

He smiled again, this time with something that approached impudence. There was a transparent yellow glow around his tousled hair again.

"Oh, so you do remember."

She returned to the table, shifting the lamp pointlessly from one spot to another. She frowned, her eyebrows drawn low over her eyes, one of which tended toward the blue and the other to the green.

"Well, all right," she said in the end, "I'll teach you to read and write, because I can see learning comes easy to you. I think two or three weeks will be enough. But watch out, be careful, you can spoil the whole thing at any moment."

All the while she was thinking, God, what am I saying, and why am I saying it? Suddenly she regretted speaking with such familiarity to him, a slight humiliation which he endured patiently. But there was no changing that now. Everything will be out of kilter right through to the end—but what end?

"Thank you. I understand," he said softly.

Somehow, that irritated her. "What is it that you understand now?" she asked in an impersonal tone.

"I'll be coming here no matter what."

"Listen, did you graduate from the talmudic academy in Mira?"

He made a vague gesture and said, "The world's been my school."

"All right, get going now, there's plenty of other work to be done around here."

"When can I come again?"

She hesitated for a moment. "Come tomorrow, in the morning. The sooner we get started, the sooner we'll be done."

He looked at her and said nothing. She avoided his gaze. It's all so tiring, she thought. And I'm so weary.

Then suddenly he turned and walked out of the room without closing the door behind him. She waited for a long minute, then walked at a slow and careful pace to the porch. But there was no sign of Elias. He'd vanished.

She stood by one of the small columns, putting her arms around it like a friend, resting her cheek against the rough surface, which smelled of old whitewash. She heard someone nearby clearing his throat. It was her father sitting on a wooden bench with a mug of sour milk in his hand.

"It's nothing, nothing," she said to herself. "Papa, you know I've agreed to give lessons to that Jew from Bujwidze. He's trying for a job with the assessors."

Her father cleared his throat again, staring into his mug of milk.

"He helped in the uprising," she added, lowering her voice.

1 2

They ate supper in the cluttered dining room, which had not been redone for a long time. Half-empty sacks stood in the corners, sieves hung on the walls between lithographs, and the sideboard, on which dark flour had been carelessly spilled, showed traces of hen or bird tracks. This disarray was offset by the lush red demijohns on the crooked windowsills in which forest and garden berries fermented vigorously.

The setting sun bathed the entire ceiling in a ruddy glow. Helena's father ate slowly and with moderation. Every so often he would clear his throat and cast a quick glance at his daughter. The thud of flails carried from the barns, where a test was being run on the already overripe rye.

"It's awfully stuffy inside, Papa," said Helena. "Shouldn't we have our tea out on the porch without lighting the lamps?"

Her father nodded his consent and Helena called for Emilka to bring the samovar outside. They went out to the porch. Her father took a seat on an old, slippery bench while Helena sank into a small, unsteady armchair. The samovar hummed and rumbled, and every once in a while it spat red sparks as if through clenched teeth. Bats were already flitting among the trees and over the lawn. A distant, muffled shot rang out in the depths of those immeasurable, monotonous, uniform forests.

Mosquitoes had already begun circling them, reminding Helena that soon a haunting summer stillness would fall in which the only sound would be their intrusive whine. I'm so afraid of the night, she thought. I'm afraid of summer nights, and winter nights. I'm afraid of every night.

The clatter of hooves carried from the allee, someone spoke with excitement, another voice cried "Whoa." A lantern with a steady yellow light flashed on in the distance, then began drawing nearer the porch, skirting the lawn in a broad semicircle.

Finally, they could make out an old man wearing a white alpaca jacket and a Russian shirt, a *kosovorotka*, its side-buttoning collar left sloppily undone. A footman was standing beside him, holding a basket covered with a white towel in one hand and a sooty lantern in the other.

The imperfectly buttoned old man doffed his battered Panama hat and bowed almost to the ground, peasant-style. "Good evening, dear neighbors."

Miss Helena peered intently into the early dusk. "Good evening. And whom has God sent us tonight?"

"You mean you don't recognize your own neighbor?"

Helena had a moment of apprehension. "Could that be Mr. Korsakov? And to what do we owe this honor?"

Korsakov looked about uncertainly, then put his hat back on his head. "Are you going to ask me to rest, in the shade of your porch, so to speak?"

She glanced over at her father, who was slurping his tea from a glass. "Our luck," she whispered, then said aloud with forced politeness, "Please. Please do."

She rose, pulled another old armchair out from a corner, its rusted springs twanging. Accompanied by his footman, Korsakov had already begun mounting the porch stairs. There was now a strong smell of alcohol in the air.

"Put it on the table," ordered Korsakov, his eyes indicating the white-covered basket the footman was holding. "Why's it so dark here? Run out of oil?"

"We don't want to attract moths," said Miss Helena. "The air over the river is quite damp. They breed the size of sparrows here."

Korsakov began ordering his footman about again. "Set the lantern down on the grass but leave the basket here. I'm paying a visit to my very nice neighbors. I keep meaning to visit, I've been meaning to for years, and, at last, here I am."

The footman set the wicker basket down on the table, and water immediately began streaming out of it.

"It's all right, won't do any harm," Korsakov assured the Konwickis, who had been taken aback. "Presto!" He whisked the white towel from the basket. "Here you are. Direct from Paris."

Konstanty appeared out of the night, which was still transparent as dry smoke, and came to a stop on the lawn by the lantern and the motionless footman.

"What's all this supposed to mean, Mr. Korsakov?" asked Helena uncertainly.

"Korsakov, you call me Korsakov? Do you mean to insult me?" said her guest with a sudden frown.

"But that's what everyone calls you."

"You and your noble father should call me Mr. Korsak. I came here to apologize, to bow down to the ground. What am I talking about? Why should I bow, that's not our way. Let's drink champagne, that's the thing."

Reaching into the damp interior of the basket, he withdrew a few tall glasses and a slender bottle clinking against the last of the ice.

"Perhaps some other time, I beg you, neighbor. We're very tired today, it's harvest time," she said, on the defensive now.

"And aren't I a landowner too? We're also harvesting. But champagne's the best medicine for the harvest, for your worries, and for the humidity." He held up the bottle for them to see, then sat down so heavily in the armchair that the springs groaned.

Bewildered by it all, Michal Konwicki kept clearing his throat and stroking his mustache. Somewhere behind them Emilka broke into a quiet giggle. One of the kitchen maids looked out the kitchen window.

"We don't drink," said Helena helplessly.

Korsakov had been fiddling with the cork, but now let go of it and cast a quick glance at Miss Helena. "You've taken the pledge, then, have you? Still in mourning, are you? For the uprising, is it?"

It suddenly became very quiet. Everyone was still, as if touched by the icy breath of an open grave. Bats flew in zigzags over the lawn, evidently enticed by the lantern's faint light.

Mr. Korsakov bent back over the bottle and industriously began unwinding the wire around the large cork. Without lifting his head, he said in a suddenly matter-of-fact tone, "That's just why I'm here."

And he fell to silently tinkering with the bottle again. Helena's heart leaped. Her throat had gone dry, and meanwhile he was plainly waiting to see how they would react.

"We don't understand what you mean."

"Please don't be afraid." The old man, who was really not that old at all, smiled a sly smile. "It's just a very lucky thing that it's me who's involved, not some outsider."

Pricking a finger, he gasped and gave it a sloppy lick. The smell of alcohol emanated from him again. Helena's fingers closed around her teaspoon.

"I'm having a new wine cellar dug, the old one's too small," resumed Korsakov, examining the bottle in the faint and flickering light of the drowsily wheezing samovar. Then, his stubbly face showing the effort, he began prying the head of the cork with his thumb. "And the workers dug up a surprise for me."

The cork suddenly shot away, ricocheting off a windowpane behind them. As the champagne flowed in a white stream, Korsakov filled their glasses with uncommon agility.

"To the health of my good neighbors and the well-being of their home," said Korsakov, raising his glass.

They held theirs indecisively, in wet fingers.

"Please drink this wonderful champagne while it's still fresh from the bottle. It's the drink of kings, you know."

"What is it you were about to say?" asked Helena uneasily.

Korsakov took a sip of the champagne and licked his lips, which were as red as if inflamed by a fever.

"Nothing important, even though it is confidential. My farmhands over at Milowidy dug up a little chest full of documents. Receipts, accounts, lists. The names of certain local citizens are mentioned. Somebody buried the National Government's documents when the uprising was quelled."

"And why are you telling us about it?" said Helena, finding it difficult to speak.

"Because, my good neighbors, Milowidy used to belong to you."

"But the chest could have been buried after we were no longer living there."

"Well, of course," said Korsakov with a jolly laugh. "I could have looked through all the papers carefully, but for what? Just to be on the safe side, I opened the door of my wood stove and poof! right into the fire. I did do the right thing, didn't I, Miss Helena?"

"That's your business."

"My business, your business, the business of us all. There's no need to be afraid of me. I took a Russian name, but my heart's still Polish." He struck his fist against the lapel of his alpaca jacket, then quickly began filling the glasses again. "*A la votre!* I directed the uprising from Paris for a year. If it hadn't been for my efforts, it would all have been over ten months before. From England, I dispatched arms, ammunition, and money—and what money, in gold—on English and German ships. You don't believe me, Miss Helena? I could swear, but what would it be worth? I have witnesses in France, and in Italy, and in England. Prince Adam, God rest his soul; General Mieroslawski; I corresponded with Garibaldi; I gave the socialists money to set up printing presses. Yes, I did disavow my own people when I was young, I did serve the Rooskies eagerly, I disowned my good name, which had never been sullied before. There're many Korsaks, but each one's taking the straight path to heaven . . . But the path that I've taken . . ."

He lowered his head and began slurping champagne.

Out past the park two people were singing together. A water bird fluttered its wings on one of the ponds. Helena mechanically raised her glass to her mouth. All at once her throat went dry.

"The hour's getting late, sir," said the footman in the flicker of the fading lantern, his voice timid.

"Shut up, you oaf. People don't respect me, because they think I took Milowidy away from you by force. But you tell them, Miss Helena, you tell them, Michal Konwicki, what really happened. How was I to know what really happened? Our Most Gracious Sovereign the Tsar gave Milowidy to me, and I accepted. Hadn't I suffered enough in the Caucasus and during the war with Turkey? And isn't it better the estate ended up in Polish hands . . . ? Shh, not a word of this to anyone, but we're all like family here and I'm one of you: Korsak, a Lithuanian noble. I changed my name, but I didn't change what I believe in. I can always get rid of those two little letters at the end of my name, and my children can repudiate them too, even though they live in Petersburg and it's not easy to live among strangers. Mr. Konwicki, Miss Helena, forgive me, absolve me, vile worm that I am, I have sinned greatly, but I want to atone for my sins, I've come here to ask your forgiveness. Have mercy on me." He collapsed to his knees, groping blindly in the dark for Michal Konwicki's hand, which he then began covering with kisses. Michal Konwicki jumped to his feet, trying to tear his hand free of Korsakov's grasp. They knocked against the table, sending sparks and gray flecks of soot flying out of the samovar.

"Quiet, easy, why make a spectacle of yourself in front of the servants? Emilka, go see if the girls have gotten everything washed up in there."

Emilka shifted from one foot to another and, as was her habit, covered her overly exposed breasts with the palms of her hands. "I got it all done. The girls went off to sleep. I just want a little air. I spent the day, the whole day, by the stove."

Now Korsakov was weeping bitterly, hiding his eyes with the brim of his Panama hat. He was on his knees in front of the table and from time to time would attempt to strike his forehead against the edge of the tabletop.

"And why doesn't anyone ask why I sinned, why I sold my soul to the devil? It was because you all spurned me."

He suddenly staggered to his feet and wiped his eyes with the hand holding his hat. "I was insulted by my own people. But over there, people respected me. That's right, that's the truth. The Russians held me in esteem and Our Most Gracious Sovereign awarded me a high rank. I played cards with grand dukes. I was sent to France on a secret mission. What am I saying . . ." He was suddenly sober. "We've been expecting a storm and it'll come one of these days. Don't be so cross with me, Michal Konwicki. I give you that advice out of the goodness of my heart."

"My father's tired, he spent the whole day in the fields," said Helena in a weary voice. "We're not used to this."

"Not used to what—not used to me? You have contempt for me, but you're glad to drink tea from Plater's samovar. But do you know who's waiting for me in my carriage?" he said, thrusting a finger at the darkness over the lawn. "I'll call him right now and he'll come too, because he's my friend."

"Please don't be angry, dear neighbor," said Helena in a persuasive tone. "We've grown unused to being with people."

"Then I'll show you who drinks with me and goes visiting with me. Call Mr. Pushkin here!" he cried to his footman, who dashed off toward the allee. "Now you'll see Pushkin in the flesh."

Emilka giggled, leaning against the recessed doorway. The sky was studded with stars, as it usually is in August, especially toward the end of the month. From somewhere in the vast stillness came the tinkling of a dulcimer.

"God, let him be quick about it," whispered Helena to herself.

"Did you say something? I'm sorry, but I'm a little hard-of-hearing."

"No, I didn't say anything. I was sighing, we're all so tired here."

Korsakov looked closely at her for a long moment. "Could those papers have been of some importance? Did I make a mistake in burning them?" he said with deliberation.

"Who knows? Only the person who buried them," said Helena. "It might have been anyone, even someone just passing through. They say that sometimes even the police do such things."

"Does that mean—how can I put it—that you're prepared to suspect Monsieur Dzhugashvili?"

Helena made a gesture of denial, but Korsakov broke into laughter and began tottering slightly by the wall of the manor.

"No, no, it was just a joke. Nothing beats a good laugh with friends every so often. One time, I lost a lot of money to a grand duke. In one night, there went my whole estate, everything I'd inherited from my father. I had to go look for a job with the government."

Michal Konwicki had finished his glass of tea and now cleared his throat with a meaningful sound. Suddenly, Korsakov leaned close to him and shoved a finger against his Adam's apple.

"And how come all you do is clear your throat, huh, neighbor? Why do you all think you're better than other people, why do you all turn up your noses and play the martyr?"

He swayed back and forth for a moment as a thought came to mind. Standing by the lantern, Konstanty was fighting off the mosquitoes. Emilka could not suppress an unwholesome giggle.

"In Paris, those rogues, those clowns, those common swindlers said—how can I put it—that I was a traitor and a tsarist agent. And so, a citizens' court was convened, and Prince Adam and many generals, the cream of the emigration, so to speak, issued a verdict saying Korsakov is innocent."

He began drawing nearer to Helena, who took a half step away in fright. "I kept the uprising supplied for a year," he said in a strangled voice. "If you don't believe me, say so. What will it cost you?"

"We don't know about anything, dear neighbor, and we haven't heard about anything," Helena was quick to reply. Her lips had already begun to tremble. And what if I just slapped that face of his, she thought. Lord, grant me patience.

Then, escorted by the footman, Pushkin emerged from the darkness. Plainly, he had been asleep in the carriage, concealed by the night. Yawning slightly, he covered his mouth with his hand; a signet ring gleamed in the scant light.

To Helena he seemed taller and stouter than in the pictures of him. But he had the same curly hair and negroid lips.

"I have the honor of introducing Mr. Pushkin, my friend and confidant, and future good neighbor to us all."

"Welcome to our home," said Helena. Not much more than forty years old, he bore himself with a certain obtrusive elegance. Pushkin bowed his head smartly.

"Thank you for the honor, but perhaps some other time," he said in something neither quite Polish nor quite Russian.

"He's looking to settle near Wilno, to find some peace after all that intrigue in Petersburg and Moscow," added Korsakov.

"Yes, a fine thread of sentiment binds me to that city." Pushkin smiled, revealing teeth that were all still white. "My great-great-grandfather, who later became famous as the Nigger of Peter the Great, that forefather of mine was baptized in Wilno."

"For God's sake, why didn't you tell me that before!" cried

Korsakov. "Such an extraordinary occasion calls for a drink. Isn't that so?" he said, addressing Helena. "Shouldn't you have the servants bring us something to drink?"

"Don't get excited, Korsakov," said Pushkin gently. "Can't you see that these people can barely stand on their feet? I humbly apologize for my friend who, as soon as he's had a glass to drink, wants to embrace the whole world. Come on, Korsakov, let's go to your place, like you promised, come on, I've got something to tell you, come on, it's late already, all right, come on, come on, that's a good fellow."

And Pushkin lured him on so, and gestured at him so invitingly, and spoke so persuasively, that Korsakov put on his Panama hat and began walking down the porch stairs. Just when he had reached the bottom, he suddenly had second thoughts.

"Why go gallivanting around in the middle of the night! It's fine right here at my neighbors'. Why, we've got a marriageable woman and a noble host who—how can I put it—is famous for his patriotism. Come here, Pushkin."

It clearly afforded Korsakov pleasure to utter the great Russian poet's name. Fortunately, just then Korsakov stumbled in the dark and ended up sitting on the grass, which was damp with dew. Pushkin and the footman rushed to help the old man back to his feet. Once again a shot rang out in the forest, hollow, muffled by the great distance.

"Let's go home, brother," appealed Pushkin, taking the old man by the arm in the dark. "Otherwise that Schicklgruber of yours will attack us on the way."

"You know, I met up with him seven years ago, right when I'd just moved here."

"So what did he look like?" asked Pushkin with a laugh. "Was he breathing fire?"

"He's an old wolf. An ogre; he eats people. He's a hundred

years old, but big and full of life and lust. There was a certain young lady outside Oszmiana that he . . ."

"Stop it, Korsakov, the young lady can hear you."

The footman picked the lantern up from the lawn and began walking behind the two of them. When they had taken a dozen steps or so, Pushkin, barely visible in the dark, turned and cried out in Polish with a thick Russian accent: "We apologize for the intrusion and thank you for your hospitality! Hope to see you soon, either at Bohin or at my place in Markucie."

"Go to hell, both of you," whispered Miss Helena, and began cleaning the table, which was sopping wet with water, tea, and champagne.

Later, when kneeling by her bed, she crossed herself quickly and began reciting the words of the prayer: "Our Father who art in heaven, hallowed be Thy name . . ."

Then all of a sudden she thought, And what if God is evil and Satan only his good brother?

1 3

All her morning tasks done, Miss Helena sat on the shady porch, sipping wonderful cold water from the small stream that gushed out from under a rock in the old park, then with speed and alacrity flowed into the Uzla, which in turn fed into the Wilia a short way from there. Wearing her finest frock, Miss Helena was taking tiny sips of that water, which could hold its own with those of foreign spas and was in any case renowned throughout the district. While sipping that water, she kept glancing with what seemed reluctance toward the allee lined with lindens, or rather maples, that led out to the highroad. But no one had appeared in that corridor of shade.

The sun was already high and the milkmaids were on their way to the nearby meadows to milk the cows. From somewhere in the parched and lifeless distance came the rhythmic clank of scythes being sharpened on whetstones. Every once in a while, a two-headed hammer would begin banging away as someone straightened out the edge of a damaged scythe. These were the sole echoes of the sleepy life of that farm, so far removed from the other human settlements which God had scattered quite sparsely along that capricious river.

Miss Helena finished her water, then called into the house: "I'm going to visit Mama's grave!" No one replied. She descended the porch slowly, haltingly; then, without apparent cause, she walked to the yellowing flowering shrubs which were planted along the manor wall and had already been overwhelmed by the nettles multiplying with great audacity.

It was then that she saw her father through a closed window. He was in his room, which she never entered even though he had not forbidden it. Through the small windowpanes, she could see a stretch of the wall; a part of the desktop, on which there were bills and a candlestick pinning some papers to the green cloth covering the desk; and a severe prie-dieu, not padded with anything to comfort the knees and worn slippery by constant use. Sheets of paper with her father's elongated handwriting on them had been tacked to the time-darkened wallpaper; those sheets might have contained household instructions or been fragments of important letters or documents. She had never looked at them, out of respect for the deliberate solitude her father had chosen.

Just then in that murky room referred to as the study she noticed her father kneeling in shadow. Then he rose from his midday prayer, the Angelus, the prayer for dead relatives, close and distant, rose from his prie-dieu and began removing his shirt. She could see his thin and yellowish body, the ribs in dramatic relief, and was about to run away, for she knew what would happen next. But she remained there awhile among the dahlias, fighting back tears. By then Michal Konwicki had taken his whip down from the wall, and his grizzled head bent forward, he began lashing himself in a regular cadence, as if he were performing an ordinary household task. Miss Helena pressed her lips together and ran off toward the tree-lined allee. She knew of her father's strange practices, but they had never discussed the subject and she had never before witnessed her father doing his penance for sins unknown to her.

She walked out to the highroad and turned left, toward Daugiele, which lay in the opposite direction from Bujwidze. Malwinka came running out of the brush and began following her mistress like a dog, but along the way, Malwinka would also stop from time to time to nibble a flower or a tasty leaf.

The forest was motionless and, for that reason, frightening. From behind Helena heard a noise that sounded like the muffled echo of a chase. She stopped and turned around, blinking as she peered down that sandy road strewn with black pinecones.

A runabout came rolling around a bend in the road. And in that runabout, his uniform unbuttoned, his cap sitting askew on his bristly hair, was Chief of Police Dzhugashvili. Drawing up beside Miss Helena, he tugged at the reins and brought his lathery horse to a halt.

"You're not afraid of the woods?" he asked in Russian, with a thick Georgian accent.

"Why should I be? These woods are home to us," she answered in Polish.

"And I know what you use the woods for," said the chief of police with an ambiguous laugh. When grimacing, his gray and horribly pockmarked face became even grimmer. "But you might make a mistake and run into someone you shouldn't. The world's getting more dangerous all the time. What happened to those days when a man could stay home in the city and run things peacefully from there?"

"The world is far away. The world's forgotten us."

"But people that nobody knows are even starting to turn up around here. These are the western provinces of the empire. We have been instructed by the highest authority to tail strangers and prevent disturbances."

Helena kept walking, not saying a word. Her heart was striking against her ribs so hard that, despite herself, she pressed her hand to her chest. It's awfully hot, not a breath of air, she thought. It turns out even I have a heart.

Dzhugashvili clicked at his horse, overtook her, and asked, "Can I give you a lift somewhere, Miss Helena?"

"No, but I thank you for your kind offer. I'm not going very far, just to my mother's grave," she said, to rid herself of him.

"Well, it's a shame I couldn't have been of any service to you. Goodbye. And please give my regards to your father."

Dzhugashvili suddenly lashed his horse, and his runabout, which had been repaired by a blacksmith in the Niemen district, went racing off.

"But I'm not really going to Mama's grave," said Helena in despair. "What's happening to me? There's so much to do in the house and in the fields. And on top of that my heart's starting to act up. Thank God I have one. Maybe it'll put an end to my suffering someday."

Malwinka ran after the chief of police but stopped by a turn in the road, beside a large stone, and waited there for her mistress or, rather, her friend.

"What's happening to me?" repeated Helena. "I always wanted to be free. I am free, and what of it? I gave my word to Plater." All of a sudden she couldn't get her breath. She sat down on a rock around which large forest ants were swarming. What if they bite me, she thought. Let them.

"I'm an old woman," she whispered, rising from the rock, brushing pine needles and quick, restless ants from her skirt.

In the distance she could see a cross made of white birch—that's right, come to think of it, it was made of wood, not iron—marking a grave that had once been covered with bare earth. Now forest flowers grew on that grave and even a cluster of still unripe boletus mushrooms had chanced to grow there. But why is Mother's grave there by the side of the road like some vagabond's, she thought, as she had so many times before. What's all the mystery about? What's behind that caprice of hers? Did she take some vow? I never knew my mother, my friend who follows my steps from heaven and protects me and keeps me from evil.

She knelt, made the sign of the cross, and was about to recite a prayer, but the words grew jumbled in her mind. She started again from the beginning, but kept losing the thread of that prayer whose words she knew by heart. In desperation, she raised her head to see the sky through the tops of the towering pines—and what she saw was him. To her horror, she found that she was not surprised to see him standing before her, leaning against a tree, his coat unbuttoned, and, as always, a living light playing on his hair.

She rose from her knees. He stood without moving by the reddish trunk of the pine.

"Where are you coming from?" she asked.

"Bujwidze."

"From Bujwidze by way of Daugiele?"

"I took a roundabout way."

"And why didn't you come for your lesson, Szyra?"

After a long, silent look, he said softly, "You speak to me as if I were a tavernkeeper."

She lowered her head, pushing aside with her foot a large spruce cone that was in her way. "How am I supposed to speak to you? I don't know that myself."

"I didn't come for my lesson because I didn't know if it would be worth it."

"You changed your mind that quickly?"

"You know what I mean."

"I don't know a thing," she said in alarm. "If you want a lesson, let's go back to the house. Do you have your tablet and pencil?"

"I have everything," he said, reluctantly withdrawing his writing implements from inside his jacket.

Saying nothing, she turned back in the direction of the house. He walked behind her. Malwinka was frolicking up ahead of them, flustered by some timid, solitary breath of air, some gentle breeze.

"Better call me by my first name, then, would you please," said Elias, finally breaking the silence.

"You don't feel like studying?"

"That's right," he said hesitantly. "I'm discouraged."

"And why is that?"

"I don't know. Maybe I feel I'm intruding."

"Why's that? I have a little time. I still haven't started teaching the village children."

His good cheer suddenly returned to Elias. He caught up to Helena and seemed on the verge of taking her arm, but restrained himself and only matched his step to hers.

"You're a bold one. Life hasn't taught you any humility yet."

"Life's not so bad as they paint it." He laughed in that way he had, a little lighthearted but a little insolent too.

"Were you really in the uprising?"

"And then five years in Siberia. I escaped during a prisoners' revolt near Lake Baikal and I made it all the way to the Volga. I was the only one whose escape succeeded. Maybe it was because I was so young. To the young the sea's knee-deep, as the Rooskies say."

"And you really are a Jew?"

"Real as they get."

She walked for a long while without saying anything. All of a sudden he was in front of her, blocking her way.

"And is that so very bad?"

She shrugged her shoulders and walked past him, down to a spot at the edge of the forest that was covered with dry, silvery moss that rustled like vellum. Once again, from somewhere very far away, probably the depths of the gray and fleecy sky, came that strange, deep, all-embracing sound, as if planets were grinding against each other. No one hears it, she thought. No one hears it but me.

She knew that path from somewhere too, though not from her daily walks, and not from her childhood either. Back then, that path had somehow been humbler, and hadn't had any of those flowers which wound like bindweed around the trunks of the pines, or any of that moss, luxuriant, fleshy, almost predatory. And it had never been so hard to breathe back then; now the air was like that in a large crock covered with a heavy lid.

"I came back here for you," said Elias, approaching from behind her. He plucked a withe from an alder bush and lashed it against the grass, which was tall and slender but had already begun to die, even before autumn.

"What are you talking about?" she said pensively.

"I came back because of you. And I left because of you too."

Suddenly she stopped and turned around. He was standing three paces behind her.

"Do you understand what you're saying to me?"

"Yes, I do. I understand spoken Polish very well."

"Do you know who I am?"

He smiled uncertainly, striking the withe against the tops of his dusty boots. "Oh, I could have been someone else. It's really just a matter of chance that I was born in Bujwidze to a Jewish family."

She set off in silence toward the allee now visible among the thinning trees. I meant to pray at my mother's grave, she thought, but he hindered me. He hinders me. That redheaded man is becoming a hindrance. Her heart beat wildly against her ribs.

Later, when he sat down at the table in her room, she positioned herself at the window once again. The door squeaked, and her hair combed smooth, Emilka's head appeared in the dark crack. She mouthed the word "dinner" a few times.

"Later. I'm not hungry," whispered Helena from the window, gesturing to indicate she was not to be disturbed.

Elias set the tablet down on the lace doily and moved the lamp a little to one side.

"I've already taught myself a few letters at home."

Helena turned from the window and walked over to the table.

In the next room, the clock struck the hour heavily, laboriously, its works clanking, but again they failed to note the hour.

"Well, aren't you the studious one. Show me what you can do."

He stuck out his tongue like a schoolboy and began making a capital *H* with his slate pencil, then a small *e*, then an *l*, until he had written the word "Helena." After a glance at his work, he raised his eyes to hers.

She didn't say anything for several seconds. Someone was shouting in a far corner of the house, most likely the kitchen. A woodpecker flew up and lighted on the trunk of a dead tree by the window. The woodpecker hadn't set to work yet; it was still looking curiously about. Elias was waiting, staring at her face through narrowed eyes.

"It's better if you don't get ahead of the study plan," she said at last, ironically. "Now I'll show you how to make the letter *b*, which is a difficult one, then we'll move on to *c*, which is much easier."

A cry reached her through several walls. Helena thought it must be her father, and once again her heart pounded. Sometimes during the night her father would cry out in his sleep and sometimes during the day when there was no one around. This may have been an instinctive way of compensating for his many years of silence.

Helena made a capital *B*, then a small *b*. She could feel his cool breath on her hand and bare forearm with its trace of a tan. He smells of mint, she thought, cool mint.

Then the door squeaked dryly again, and red with excitement, Emilka's face popped into the room.

"Excuse me, miss, excuse me, but the count's arrived. With four horses, the coachman, and the rifleman."

Helena set the pencil aside and walked over to the mirror. Speckled as it was, it was still favorably inclined to her beauty, which was now showing its first flaws, the result of time passing faster and faster, like a stone rolled from a steep hill. She sighed, touching the tortoiseshell comb in her hair, then the pink down beneath her nose, whose bridge was slightly freckled.

"Wait. I'll be right back."

"I wouldn't want to be in the way." He jumped up from the table.

She pointed with one hand, categorically ordering him to resume his seat, then she set off down the dark corridor to the gloom of the front hall and out to the porch with its bright green grapevines and impetuously chirping sparrows.

Beside the polished, gleaming carriage, which had a coat of arms on its door, Plater stood conversing with her father. That is, Plater spoke respectfully while her father listened, every once in a great while nodding in agreement. He's the only one who pays attention to detail, she thought. Nowadays no one polishes harness fittings, no one fixes up old sofas, no one even makes new dresses or clothing. Everyone seems frozen in motion like the carvings on gravestones. But he pays attention to detail.

Tall, elegant, an ash-gray top hat in one hand, Plater turned from her father. All the marriageable young ladies in the province would be thrilled if they were in my place, but I'm not thrilled, she thought.

"Hello, and I do beg your pardon for the intrusion," he said, gallantly kissing her hands.

"Good Lord, how utterly unexpected," she said with a blush, while thinking, Why am I saying such things and acting the little provincial goose?

"That may be the best way with you, my dear Miss Helena. Despite the weather and the time of day and everything else, we're off for a dash, perhaps to the Niemen district. Or perhaps even to Wilno. For coffee and cake and, if you so desire, ice cream as well."

Even her father brightened. Konstanty walked over to the

carriage and with respect touched the fittings that truly were fit
for a lord. Helena lowered her gaze and fussed with the sash on
her dress like a well-mannered young lady.

"I'll be snatching you away, Miss Helena!"

"Forgive me, but I cannot."

"And why is that?"

"I'm just giving a lesson."

He let go of her hands and, suddenly becoming serious, took
a step back.

"To whom? That Jew from Bujwidze?"

Unexpectedly, Helena raised her eyes. "Yes, he's the one."

Plater said nothing, giving her a significant look as he took her
measure.

"He walked four miles for his lesson," she added.

Plater smiled. "Well, I must say, your discipline is commend-
able. In your place I wouldn't have been able to resist such an
enticing prospect. I applaud your firmness of character."

As if it were to the Queen of England, he bowed and began
backing away toward his carriage.

"As you can see, Mr. Konwicki, I've been turned down. But,
I hope, only as far as the coffee and ice cream are concerned. Is
that so?"

He's so strange, she thought. He's so strange and I have the
feeling I knew him in some other place and time. This is the start
of an illness, an illness of the mind or soul.

The carriage was already on its way, raising a thick veil of
brown dust. The rifleman Ildefons was on the box beside the driver
and, for no apparent reason, was looking back into the drab greenery
around Bohin Manor, which had once served the Platers as a hunting lodge.

Michal Konwicki raised his eyes to Helena and, saying nothing,
nodded in what was neither quite approval nor quite reproach.

1 4

I keep fighting my way back over the dunes of time past, through
the quagmires of days and the wilderness of hours, back to my
grandmother Helena Konwicka, whom I never saw. And I never
knew anyone who had met her, looked into her eyes, touched her
hand, or spoken a kind word to her. Yet I pursue her across the
terrain of intuition, lakes of longing, and through dense mists of
uncertainty. But why now, when I have outlived all my nearest
relatives, when I am as old as they get, and can hardly wait for my
hour, my own end to come, why do I pursue a ghost, a specter,
the apparition of a young woman running through an ordinary
August meadow toward an ordinary white manor house watched
over by a solitary larch that was slowly changing into a golden torch.

"Today," she said, panting for breath as he rose from his chair
at the sight of her, "today we'll be working on the letters *i, j, k*,
and *l*. Have you been waiting long?"

Elias looked at her face for a long time, an unnaturally long
time, and there was something utterly shameless about that look
of his which made her suddenly drop her eyes.

"All right then, sit down and write."

He did as he was told.

"Emilka didn't want to let me into your room."

"I hope you haven't violated my privacy."

Now he grew embarrassed, his ears flushing dark red. It was
only then that she noticed that he had ears to hear what people

said and God commanded, large, protruding ears, though nicely formed.

"How would I even dare?" he said uncertainly.

"You Jews have your own morality."

"You've already said that."

"I have?"

"Yes, at the very beginning."

Once again the clock struck the hour and once again they failed to count its strokes. Helena was standing in her usual place by the window. It has to mean something if a person stands by the window so often, she thought.

"Have you been practicing your letters?"

"Yes, I have. I taught myself a few words at home. And now I can write a word that begins with the letter *l*."

"It's still too early for that. You have to learn the alphabet first."

The old stork whom the people of Bohin called Maciej flew from the meadows over the old trees of the park. He flew unhurriedly, followed by his mate, a strange stork, all white except for a few black feathers that appeared to have been dipped in tar; even her feet were strikingly white, bloodlessly white. They were on their way back to their nest.

Those trees are broken, sick, and crippled, she thought. Like people.

"And so you escaped from exile and got as far as the Volga. Then what happened?" she said out of the blue and to her own surprise.

"I was in Simbirsk, which is quite an old city. I found a place to live where nobody asked me any questions and I entered the service of a family. I worked as a driver for a man named Ilya Nikolaevich. An important person. Province superintendent of elementary schools. We drove all over in a sort of wagon they use there. He was very demanding of people, a strict man, he kept order. We drove around to every last school, ones under construction, and ones under repair, and ones that had to be closed because they were falling apart, they were so old. On the road, always on the road. Snow, rain, or scorching heat. We'd be away from home for a couple of months at a stretch. One time, I remember, Ilya Nikolaevich received word by telegram that his wife, Maria Alexandrovna, had gone into labor. What a ride that was! The horses could barely keep their footing, the road was so bad—it was the beginning of April, must have been 1870, there was still snow and mud and God knows what else. Then our way was blocked by the Sviyaga River, which was still frozen over. Anyway, I tried driving across the ice, but it started to crack and break; the water was coming up through it, the wagon was sinking, the horses were up to their stomachs. We were looking death in the eye, and it was late in the day. But we got through it. There was a city right there on the high bank of the river—I mean the western shore of the Volga—and it had a fortress and an old city. And we had made it in time for the father to see his son give his first cry. Later on he was baptized Vladimir. Everyone liked the boy and called him Volodya."

Helena looked out the window, listening to his story as if to the sounds of a blizzard or a river. He grew lively when he spoke of distant lands and the people who live there, people who will die someday and all trace of them will vanish from this sandy road whose beginning and end are unknown. Oh, what does it matter, she thought, while saying aloud, "I'm listening, I'm listening. Why did you stop?"

"I thought it might not be interesting to you. I really did come to love that family. I still think of them and sometimes I even send them a postcard to remember me by, so they'll know I haven't died and I'm still alive, though why I'm alive I don't know."

"What makes you so pessimistic when you're cheerful by nature?"

"Yes, I am cheerful," agreed Elias. "But I speak like that to get attention. After all, it was because of you that I returned to Bujwidze from the ends of the earth."

Miss Helena frowned. "Now listen, you . . ."

"You Jew boy . . ."

"Now listen to me, you Jew boy, or I'll be sending you packing."

"Aren't you interested in what happened next?"

"And what did happen next?"

"I saw a good piece of Russia. Maria Alexandrovna liked speaking German with me; she was German herself, her maiden name was Blank. At the beginning of her pregnancy, I used to drive her to the provincial capital, Kazan, to see her father, Dr. Blank, who had a small estate called Kokushkino. He took a liking to me too, but somehow I think he was more a Jew than a German."

He fell silent and began making a row of letters, the tip of his tongue stuck out like a schoolboy's.

"Why did you leave them?"

"People were starting to get interested in me. I ran into a man who'd been in the army. And he'd been one of the guards who marched us to Siberia. So, it was time to get lost. Ilya Nikolaevich and his wife were good people and the children were very nice. Two girls, Anya and Olya, and the little boy, who was still breast-feeding."

Helena turned from the window. "I listen to you, I listen to what you say, and I think, What's all this playacting?"

"Me, playacting?" he said with genuine surprise.

"You pretend to be a simple person, you act like a small-town Lithuanian Jew, but there's something restless and false about you."

She turned back to the window. The view hadn't changed in the least. The old black trees stood motionless, with their tops reaching for the sky. It'll never rain now, she thought. The whole world will dry up like a fly on a windowsill in the fall. He didn't say anything. She was waiting for him to speak.

She cast a stealthy glance at him. He had lowered his head to the table, his forehead resting on the lace doily. And that hair of his seemed absolutely on fire. He didn't stir.

"What happened?" she asked.

He neither moved nor responded.

"I'm asking you, are you all right?"

She walked over to the table which had been separating her from him. "Do you feel ill?"

She noticed a ladybug trudging across his thick, dry hair.

"Stop being such a baby," she said in a severe tone, as if speaking to a child.

But he didn't react.

She grabbed his hair and pulled his head up a little. His eyelids were shut tight, but even so she could see his eyeballs twitching beneath them. She didn't know what to do, whether to keep holding his lifeless head like that or to shake it vigorously. Just then he opened his eyes, piercing, light-blue eyes, which now suddenly smiled, and she thought: How strange, when the area around his eyes is so dark. Suddenly he threw back his head and pressed the palm of her hand to his forehead. She was on the verge of screaming, of jumping away, or even of striking him, but at that very moment someone began banging at the door. Helena tore her hand free of its trap, hiding it behind her as if it were unclean or crippled.

In walked Chief of Police Dzhugashvili, his cap on his head and his left hand on his saber, which knocked against the rolled top of his boot made of the soft leather Georgians love. Michal Konwicki, Konstanty, and a mustachioed gendarme appeared behind Dzhugashvili.

"You'll excuse me, ma'am," he said in an official tone, "but it's my duty to check to see if any strangers are on the premises."

"Please do."

Dzhugashvili had immediately spotted the inconspicuous white door that led into an adjoining alcove. Saber rattling and spurs clanking, he opened that door and entered the dark room with the rest of them trailing behind. From the alcove he went to the sitting room and to the former library, where winter apples were now stored between layers of straw. Then he went back and checked the dining room, glanced into Michal Konwicki's study, but examined the kitchen closely. He even climbed the old stairs to poke his head into the attic, but seeing the curtains of ancient cobwebs and the dust particles floating in thin shafts of hot sunlight, he shrank from his duty and came back downstairs. Then he went to Helena's room, where everyone was standing in uncertainty except for Elias, who was still at the table, pencil in hand.

The chief of police took off his cap and wiped the band with his handkerchief. His pockmarked face twisted into something of a smile. "It's just a formality," he said. "I know you people."

"Someone must be informing," said Helena.

Dzhugashvili looked at her with new interest. "Yes, people will do even that. All right, then, we'll be on our way."

Dzhugashvili headed for the door, followed by the middle-aged gendarme. When he was at the door and reaching for the handle, he came to a sudden stop, as if having just thought of something— as police commissioners always do in stories. So he stopped, turned around slowly, and jabbed a finger in Elias's direction. "And who's this one?"

They all froze in silence.

Helena swallowed, her throat dry. "He's a Jew from Bujwidze. I'm teaching him how to read and write, because he's been promised a job in the revenue office."

The chief of police looked silently at her, then shifted his gaze to Elias. "And what's your name?"

The young Jew rose slowly. Michal Konwicki cleared his throat angrily.

"Elias Szyra."

"This is the first time I've seen you around."

Helena walked over to the chief of police as if to shield Elias.

"Oh, who can keep track of them all," she said, speaking quickly. "But we know him and his parents. They used to buy peas and feathers from us."

"Let him speak for himself, miss."

"He speaks terrible Polish and Russian."

Elias nodded ardently, his hair red as flame.

"Interesting, anyway," said Dzhugashvili hoarsely. "But I trust you and I trust your father, even though your father has played it more ways than one."

Then he turned to Elias and added, "You and I will get down to brass tacks some other time. I'll be on my way now."

He saluted, then went through the door followed by the gendarme. They could be heard as they went down the hall, across the porch, and into their runabout. Hooves clattered on the flat stones that paved the front drive by the porch, then the dry old wheels of Chief Dzhugashvili's runabout began squeaking softly.

Helena's father nodded, lost in thought. She cast a quick glance at Elias. He was standing, pale, his hand inside his shirt, as if he were hiding a pigeon there. When he met her gaze, he smiled through his teeth and whispered, "Thank you, my lady."

1 5

After dinner, she walked down the porch steps. An enormous number of stars were flickering, flashing, and glowing above the motionless trees and she seemed to see them in three dimensions, to see the glassine stretches of infinity between them. Every now and again a star would streak downward, a drop of cold fire burning out in the treetops or the pale-green band of the horizon. She stood and looked at the night sky as she always did in August, as she had for so many years now. A sudden sadness overcame her faltering heart. This is how everyone must feel when they go outside at this time of day, she thought.

Then the glow of Konstanty's pipe flared from amid the black lilac bushes that grew wild there. A brief ruddy glow illuminated his ageless face for a second, a face as tightly drawn as darkly creased leather.

"Do you want to see the dawn?" he asked.

"What dawn?"

"The real dawn. Sometimes it can be seen here too. Come over here."

He led her to the back of the manor, where the morning star shone through a break in the trees.

"I don't see anything," said Helena.

"It comes little by little. You have to wait. It'll start when the time's right."

The darkness was dense where they stood. Helena felt cold,

she began to tremble, then her body shook suddenly. She could feel her linen slippers being soaked through. Someone ran toward the manor, a window clanked open or shut, someone called out softly.

"Oh, look," whispered Konstanty just then.

And there was a pale blue-green glimmer rippling among the trees, making them resemble gigantic reflections of the icicles that hang from roofs in late February. The glimmer would die out after a moment, as if someone had shifted the dull mirror that was sending night beams into the northern sky, and once again the stars were in sharper focus—but only for a moment, because the aurora borealis had reappeared, stronger now and more widespread, flickering timidly over the horizon.

"I saw more than enough white nights in Petersburg, God help me. But, as you see, ours are pretty good too."

"Who was that walking around in the night?"

"That's Antoni Sieniuc. He works with the blacksmith." Konstanty chuckled and sparks flew from his pipe. "He visits Emilka in the evenings. He's not young, but he's honorable," he added after a moment's thought.

She hugged herself for warmth. It's time to go to bed, but I don't feel like sleeping.

"The master was hollering something awful today," continued Konstanty.

She sighed and, skirting a nettle bush, walked back to the porch. Her father's window was dark. She strained her ears. The terrible country silence was reminiscent of death. Soundlessly, a particle of light streaked across the window of the night.

"I loved her!" She could immediately tell it was her father, his voice muffled and unclear. "I loved her as best I could."

A chill ran up Helena's spine. Maybe he's talking in his sleep. Or maybe he's awake. He must be crying, if he can still cry. She stood there for a moment, fighting off a sudden attack of the shivers. A piercing cold came from the vines, stiff and still. It'll be nice

weather tomorrow, she thought. That big storm will never come
now.

She sighed again and went into the house. She groped her way
through the door to the little hallway, where she stopped for a
minute to listen to the sounds of the house. Her father had quieted
down and was no longer crying out. All she could hear was the
beating of her own heart.

Back in her room, she went to the window without lighting
the lamp. She undressed in the dark quite often, as if she were
afraid of herself, though it was really her body that she feared. She
would fling her clothes off quickly and slip into the cool bed, where
her linen nightshirt would be waiting like a faithful friend. And
lying in an awkward position, she would pull the nightshirt up over
her warm body.

But on that evening she walked over to the window and drew
the half curtains. The section of the park nearest her room stood
in a shallow lake of fog. It all comes from the Uzla, that quiet
stream that meanders and zigzags on its way to the Wilia. Those
vapors are from the Uzla, they're entering the park and coming to
inundate the house.

I'm so awfully tired, she thought. And I'd so much like to rest.
Why don't I know anything at all about my mother? Why doesn't
anyone ever want to tell me anything about her? It's too soon for
me to be tired. What would have happened if Piotrus Pieslak had
lived? What would our life have been like?

She crossed herself and began saying her prayers, never taking
her eyes from the window. Then Konstanty emerged from the night,
shaking his watchman's rattle. He closed the shutters and Helena
locked them from inside. The slats made strips of the August night
sky, where a single star flickered. And for some strange reason that
star gave her heart.

Helena sighed, then began undressing in the dark, by blind
feel alone. Once again the clock struck and once again she failed

to count the hour, that is, she counted the strokes but wasn't sure if there had been eight or nine. Didn't matter. She crossed herself and got into bed.

She turned her face toward the wall and tried to think about what she had to do tomorrow. From time to time she would drift off and see Plater with a beautiful smile on his face, which people had still called girlish not all that long ago, but whose proportions now seemed to have altered, becoming darker and coarser, covered with a delicate web of wrinkles. Now he's set on getting married because he isn't afraid of his mother anymore, she thought. She made an effort to think about Plater and the distant past, so that crazy Jew from Bujwidze with the cold fire around him would not come slipping out from any of the nooks and crannies in the dark.

At some point she fell asleep, and at some point something began to work long and hard at waking her; and she almost awoke, only to plunge back into the far distance of sleep; then once again she clung to the shore of consciousness and once again fell away into oblivion. At last she did awake, aware of the beating of her anxious heart. Everything was still. Except for a tawny owl that cried once, then immediately fell silent again. Something woke me up, she thought. I probably did it to myself. I didn't get off to sleep right. And now I won't fall back asleep until daylight. Feeling hot, she kicked off the covers.

Just then a fist began knocking at the shutters.

"For the love of God, open up!" cried a strange, inhuman voice.

She jumped out of bed and began running blindly toward the corridor, sending a chair banging to the floor. My heart can't take it, was what flashed through her mind as she fumbled for the doorknob.

"Mr. Konwicki, open up, have pity on a person in trouble!" the plaintive voice cried out again.

She ran into the hallway, where her father stood, an old dressing gown thrown over his nightshirt. She noticed at once that he was holding his shotgun and felt relieved.

Now the banging was coming from the kitchen shutters, followed by the sound of bare feet as Emilka fled the specter that had descended on Bohin Manor at midnight.

"Open up, people, it's me, you know me, I've come to visit! I've got presents for everyone. And I've brought good news."

Catching sight of Helena, her father turned toward her and placed a finger to his lips. Now the invader was walking along the front wall and pounding it with a stone or a rifle butt.

"And where's Konstanty disappeared to?" she whispered.

"Miss Helena, Mr. Konwicki, have the kindness to let me in! I just want to say hello and then I'll be on my way. Don't drive me to extremes. I can see you through the slats. Do you want me to put a curse on you? My curse is something to fear!"

They could hear him kneel on the porch and strike his forehead once, then once again, against the manor's oak door.

"Mr. Korsakov," said Konstanty, his voice shaking slightly, "this isn't right. The hour's late. People are sleeping."

"Get away!" shouted the unseen guest sullenly. "Get away from here or I'll blast your eyes out of your head." There was a metallic click, Korsakov's shotgun being cocked. "Mr. Konwicki, I'm down on my knees before you, I'm begging for mercy. I came at night because I have to tell you what's eating away at me and gives me no rest and keeps me from sleeping. You can have Milowidy back, if you want. I don't give a damn about your estate. I didn't want it. It was a gift of His Most Gracious Majesty the Tsar, who even allowed me to kiss his hand. I don't want anything. I just needed to come back here. I dragged my bones back here in my old age. I was kicked out of here. Because of people's meanness, envy, contempt, ignorance. Oh, the coarseness of it all! They insulted me, humiliated me, and sent me packing to hell." He began weeping and beating his forehead against the door until the great rusted key fell from it.

"This is disgraceful, Mr. Korsakov, it's not nice at all, coming around here drunk and waking your neighbors up at night," said Konstanty in an effort at persuasion.

"Away, get away!" Clearly, Korsakov had jumped back onto his feet, because the floorboards of the porch began creaking. Then a shot rang out.

Michal Konwicki began moving toward the door with his gun under his arm, but Helena grabbed him by the elbow.

"Don't, Papa, he'll collapse in a moment and fall asleep. Everyone around here knows how he is," she whispered, her teeth chattering softly.

They heard Konstanty beating a retreat into the park. Korsakov returned to the front door.

"I can't fall asleep at Milowidy. I keep moving my bed from one room to the other. I try it with my head facing east, facing west, this way, that way. Who put a curse on that house, do you hear me, who?"

Just as he began sobbing again, the clock sounded and Korsakov suddenly fell silent. They listened as it struck the hour, its old works barely able to move.

Then all was still. He got tired and left, thought Helena. But just then the door began to groan horribly, Korsakov was striking it with his whole body.

"I'll have you all sent to Siberia. What do you think, Korsakov is deaf, Korsakov's lost his sight and his wits? I know you're all in a conspiracy against His Most Gracious Majesty the Tsar and against Mother Russia, I know you have meetings at night in the forests and marshes. I have lists of names. Tomorrow I'll have the whole goddamn lot of you sent to a place where your spit freezes in the air."

"No, no, Papa. He'll pass out any minute. He can barely stand on his feet," whispered Helena, clasping her father around the waist.

"Do you hear me?" said Korsakov quietly from the door. "Now I can try out those new matches they sent me from Moscow."

Evidently he began searching his pockets, having first set aside the shotgun, which fell to the porch. Then, as he bent over to grope for the gun, he must have fallen too and lay still for a long time before starting to cry again. First he whimpered like a child, then he began sobbing and wailing alarmingly.

They were stunned to hear the old man weep and wail. Just then Helena noticed that she was digging her fingernails into her father's elbow. She let go of his arm and covered her ears with her hands.

"Michal Konwicki," groaned Korsakov, "come out to the porch and shoot me, wretch that I am. I can't take the suffering anymore. I can't take it, there or here. A curse on the day I was ever born. There's devils there, and there's devils here too. The devil took me from my cradle. So that you'd all be swallowed up by hell along with me."

This he said more softly and more slowly, then he grew completely still. For a long time they stood in the hallway, not knowing what to do. A mosquito was droning somewhere in the dark. It would draw near, then move away, searching for something close to the ceiling that smelled of smoke. They stood in the middle of the hallway, fighting off sleep. Helena thought she had even dozed off for a moment a few times. Then, finally, they heard the sound of Konstanty's rattle again, far away, perhaps out in the allee. He'd been suffering from insomnia for years now and so kept watch during the night.

"He drove off," whispered Helena. "Or walked off. Or maybe flew off."

Her father cleared his throat, and his hands outstretched, he set off through the series of rooms toward his study.

"Good night, Papa. Forget all about it," whispered Helena, and returned to her room.

The next day they found boot prints around the house. Korsakov had torn up the flower beds and trampled the grass like a wild boar. One member of the Bohin household found the shell casing from the shot he had fired on the porch. It had been winter the last time Korsakov had invaded Bohin Manor. But the attack had been brief; it was bitter cold and Korsakov quickly grew hoarse, then lost his voice entirely.

The sense of alarm passed swiftly and they all went about their work, of which there was a great deal at that time of year. Helena spent the whole morning at her chores, glancing often at the allee that led out to the highroad. But no one appeared in that tunnel of shade, no one at all came by the manor that morning, except for Malwinka, who strolled over the lawn that had gone to seed and nibbled on the herbs she knew would be there.

All the better, thought Helena. There's no time to waste on nonsense. Who ever heard of teaching the alphabet to a grown man. He's not coming here to learn how to read and write. She felt hot and was aware of tiny beads of sweat tickling her lips. It's better that he didn't come. He finally must have understood that it wasn't proper. There's no time to waste on playacting.

All the same, she kept glancing at the allee. What she would actually do was cast a glance up at the sun over the allee, then slowly and deliberately lower her gaze to the horizon, in the direction of Bujwidze, which lay on the other side of the great woods.

Still, after lunch, when her father had gone to rest in his study, Helena changed into a better dress, issued Emilka her instructions for the afternoon, and went out to the porch.

"Probably won't be any rain today either," she said, looking at the sky. "I'll go to Bujwidze and see Father Siemaszko as I promised."

"Should I hitch up the carriage?" asked Konstanty from the bushes.

"No need to. I'll be happy to take a walk there myself. Maybe someone will give me a lift back."

"That'd be better," said Konstanty approvingly. "All the horses are out in the fields today."

Then, with seeming indifference, even reluctance, she began walking with a light step past the lawn and by the ponds overhung with clouds of bored flies until she found herself in the dark allee where the air was cooler and even drafty, as in a cellar.

Out on the highroad, she turned to the right, toward Bujwidze. She paused only for a moment on the bridge over the Uzla's flash of peaceful green. Maybe it was wrong of me not to go with Mr. Plater yesterday, she thought. The matter's been settled, my word's been given, there's no reason to shilly-shally.

Oh, never mind about Plater. She began walking angrily down the highroad hemmed in by the endless woods. But those were not good Polish woods. The lives of people and animals were ruled there by those enormous forests, full of strange trees and eerie bushes, and by terrible herbs whose very smell inspired dread. Now Miss Helena was walking briskly, energetically, among ferns that were taller than a man, a forest of ferns, though the real forest only began above the ferns, where the red-black pines dipped their tops into the moist gray of the August sky. Every so often there'd be a birch tree, paper-white, contorted in pain, seeking help from every side of that sacred grove which ended on Uprising Hill.

Back in the fifties, Mr. Alexander Broel-Plater's father had been killed in a duel in France under mysterious and, most likely, foolish circumstances. The young heir to Woloki had been raised by his mother, an energetic and imperious grande dame. His inheritance was not a very large one, because, as often occurred, his father had taken a large portion of the estate with him to sweet, enchanting France in the form of gold imperials. Alexander grew up at his mother's apron strings. And under her heel. Tormented by her peremptory love.

What do I care about Alexander Broel-Plater, thought Helena. Tomorrow I'll change my mind and that'll be that. But why should I change my mind? For what reason? After all, there's nothing standing in my way. She quickened her step. Casually, she removed her hat, since she was now passing through forest shade; only rare shafts of sunlight, lost in the dense woods, played timidly on her skin.

Yes, I am accompanying my grandmother Helena Konwicka through those old, those age-old woods to Bujwidze. And I am slowing down all those events of a century ago, drawing them out, prolonging them, breaking them down into pieces, in order to elude fate; but that fate is already approaching, drawing near, flowing broadly from horizon to horizon like a great river, the vast river of time whirling with eddies of individual destiny, sudden waves of human suffering, and the foaming waterfall of inevitable catastrophe. My grandmother Helena is out walking in a small land that is like ancient Greece. Every little town, every backwater, every crossroads belongs to the history of humankind. Everyone knows each other here, everyone is related, and everyone is also creating a new history, a new mythology, a new cosmogony which later on will be spread throughout the world by pilgrims and exiles. New machines were not invented here, none of the known chemical elements was discovered here, nor were better social systems established here. Here, invisibly, hidden from the sight of the gawking crowd, a great concentration of the human spirit took place; man grew inwardly here, his animal qualities were filtered out, and he underwent a gradual apotheosis before embarking on his great pilgrimage into space to meet with his fellow gods.

When Miss Helena entered Bujwidze, she stopped near the

first store, which was called The Golden Apple: there was a gold apple painted on the front of its signboard. She had stopped there to fan herself with her hat, the heat unbearable at that time of afternoon. Everything had grown still, trees, birds, and people. Miss Helena was on the outskirts of the little town, on the shoulder of the road that went down to the market, or rather the church square, overgrown with gray and crumpled grass that had withered in a few places. But Miss Helena was also fanning herself to avoid recognition, and though she was not looking from side to side, she was waiting; but had she been asked at that moment what she was waiting for, she wouldn't have known what to say.

The orchard was empty; even the Jewish children had gone to sleep, and the dogs had taken cover in the shade. A thin, swirling stream of smoke spiraled up to the misty sky from the church concealed on a rise by motionless trees.

Miss Helena set off for the church with a determined step. She peeked into the church, whose interior was redolent of incense, then walked past the cemetery, making the sign of the cross near Piotrus Pieslak's grave, finally to enter the shade of the orchard by the rectory. The doors were wide open and there wasn't a soul in sight. She went up to the porch, where she coughed once, then again, but no one came out. A faint smell of herbs emanated from the rectory, and the desperate buzzing of flies caught in a glass trap baited with whey.

Then she spotted a figure in white floating in a gray cloud in the middle of the orchard. It was Father Siemaszko himself.

Wearing white clothing and a hat with netting over his face, and holding a smoking smudge pot to scare off the bees, he was going from hive to hive, lifting their shingled roofs, looking inside, and straightening something among the droning, aggravated bees. Spotting Helena, he lifted the netting from his face and began walking toward the porch.

"I couldn't sit at home," she said by way of greeting. "Something's been eating at me since this morning. I had to come see you, good Father."

"Oh, and right you were to come," said Father Siemaszko approvingly. "Come here, child, take a seat on the porch and I'll bring you the little snack I prepared in case any good people came calling." The smoking smudge pot still in hand, he walked briskly into the rectory and was back a moment later carrying a firkin of honey and cucumbers piled in a shallow basket. She looked at his plain, broad face, his funny glasses with their wire frames, his head covered with a thick bristle of very gray hair. She was looking at him as if only now seeing who he was. What did I come here for? What will he think of me? Maybe he won't think anything, he's a simple soul, not the suspicious type. He has worries of his own, his own sleepless spells at dawn.

"The chief of police was at our house. He looked around all the rooms and even climbed up to the attic," said Helena.

"When he was here, child, he even smashed in some of my hives."

"And what was he looking for in the hives?"

"Belorussians," said the priest with a laugh. "Take a cucumber and dip it in the honey. You might even say that's Dzhugashvili's honey."

He set the smudge pot beside the firkin of honey to keep the bees away. She watched an invisible current of air sweep the stream of blue smoke from the table and divide it into curling plumes.

"You're shivering, child," said the priest.

"No, I'm just a little tired. I ran and I ran, but I don't know why."

"Sometimes people have attacks of fear. You have to pray to God when that happens."

He said that without conviction, looking down at the many reddish knots in the table.

"The common people think the end of the world is coming."

"They always have. And they always will, till the end of the world," he said with a laugh.

"What made them dare search here, Father?"

"It's because I was transferred here from Holyszy, a parish outside Molodeczno. When I was there, I started collecting old Belorussian songs, fairy tales, dances, just to pass the time."

"What's wrong with that?"

"That's right." He wiped the lenses of his glasses on the flap of his cassock. "But the authorities in Petersburg say there's no such thing as a Belorussian nation and one must not be created artificially. That's why I was put in jail. Things looked bad. But then I ended up in Bujwidze."

The gentle slope of the square in front of the church could be seen out past the orchard. I've gotten myself into a terrible tangle, she thought. I'm so tired. Now I understand why people on their deathbed are happy they'll have some rest at last. What am I talking about? Why did I come here? He'll never guess. He has troubles of his own. Oh God, the Belorussians. Are they a nation or one part of society? I always thought they were just peasants.

"I'm a terrible sinner," she said all of a sudden.

"We're all sinners," said the priest with a sigh.

"But you're a holy man, Father."

He lurched back on his bench. A cucumber fell from the pile and rolled down the table.

"What are you saying! In the name of the Father and the Son . . . God have mercy on me, a sinner."

"What are we supposed to say, we're ordinary people, we don't have the grace to be able to commune with God at any time."

Father Siemaszko struck his large, smoke-stained fist against the front of his soiled cassock. Then he began crossing himself again and again with outlandish intensity, like a Russian Orthodox priest. Maybe he only pretends to be a simple priest. Maybe he even knows why I've come racing here to Bujwidze. But I haven't come racing here for anything at all. I've been in this little town a thousand times, summer and winter. Bujwidze is our salon.

Someone began walking around inside the house, causing the floorboards to creak. They could even hear that person yawning deeply.

"Looks as if our guest has woken up," said the priest and then, in a much louder voice, called into the dark interior of the house. "Come out here, please, Grigory Alexandrovich! I'll introduce you to the most beautiful unmarried woman in these parts."

Pushkin, Korsakov's recent companion, appeared in the doorway, buttoning his traveling coat.

"Look, child," said the priest, "it's our Russian friend. He's looking for a home here, he wants to settle among Poles."

Still, he looks an awful lot like his father, was what flashed through Helena's mind. But how do I know what his father looked like?

"I beg your pardon," she said aloud, "there's honey on my hand. We've been eating fresh cucumbers."

"That presents no problem, just an occasion to wax poetic about honey and your lovely hands. I apologize for daring to speak such poor Polish."

"You already know each other?" said Father Siemaszko, a trifle disappointed.

"Korsakov brought Mr. Pushkin to Bohin."

Pushkin made a dismissive gesture with his thin hand. "Oh, that Korsakov, he thrust himself on me to help me find some property. He drove me around everywhere, acting as a broker, and wouldn't let me out of his sight. But the good Father rescued me by offering me his hospitality, for which I am deeply grateful."

"Hush, Grigory Alexandrovich," said Father Siemaszko out of

modesty. "I'd be more interested to hear how you came to be with Korsakov in the first place."

"Someone in Petersburg recommended him. He said we've one of our own people out here, and that he'd be the best one to help me."

Everyone's dead in this little town, she thought. I have to get back home before nightfall. If only it were all over. But what does that mean? If only it were all over with Plater. Still, maybe things should stay the way they are.

Someone walked by on the other side of the square. But it wasn't he. This man had a heavy tread and walked hunched over. When he emerged against the brighter background of the fence, she could see that he was using a cane. It's an old man, and I thought . . . no, I wasn't thinking anything. I have to get back home. But why did Elias turn so pale and thrust his hand inside his shirt when the police chief was at our house?

"There's always been unrest around here," said the priest, finishing some thought of his own while driving the bees away from the honey. Smoke had ceased coming from the smudge pot, and the bees had returned to reclaim their property.

"Yes, there's always been unrest around here," repeated Pushkin. "And we admire you for that."

"Your father never expressed that admiration," said Helena with sudden anger, immediately regretting it.

Pushkin raised his large, dark eyes to her. "Yes, and I apologize to you Poles for my father."

God, what have I done, she thought with despair. It's the heat, this horrible, blistering, end-of-summer heat.

"Please forgive me," she whispered. "I don't know why I said that. That's not a woman's business."

"Yes, life is complicated. But I assure you, my father esteemed and loved the Poles. But he had to speak out during the uprising.

The freedom and the lives of many people in Petersburg were at stake. That was the situation the Petersburg intelligentsia were in. It's a pity that it happened that way, but what's done can't be undone."

"That's the truth," said Father Siemaszko with a sigh.

"I must be getting back," said Helena.

"Wait a while, Jozef will give you a lift." The priest looked into the rectory and began calling the sexton.

"No thank you. I'd rather go on foot. I need to cool off. I don't feel at all well today."

"But you came here for a reason, child. Though you didn't have the courage to tell me about it. Isn't that so, child?"

"No, no. Actually, I wanted to make my confession. I'd completely forgotten what day you hear confession. It doesn't matter, I'll come Sunday."

"Wait a while, child, I'll get my stole and we'll go over to the church. Why didn't you say so right off?"

"No, no. Another time. I'll suffer with my sins a few more days," she said with a forced laugh. "You have a guest, Father. He mustn't be left alone."

"Whatever you think. But I can see you're not at peace. Is it something to do with your father?"

"Not at all. He's out supervising the harvest. And they're threshing as much as they can in the evening time."

It was only then that she noticed that Pushkin's eyes were on her. Those eyes seemed strange, but she couldn't fathom what was so strange about them. So brown, so dark, you can't even see the pupils, she thought. And there seems to be a dark-blue line around the iris. I've seen eyes like that somewhere before. Yes, Malwinka has eyes like that.

An enormous flock of purple birds flew west across the sky. They all looked up pensively at the birds.

"What strange birds," said Helena all of a sudden. "I've never seen any like that."

"It's the sunset that makes them look purple," said Pushkin softly. "It's a pity you became angry with me over my father."

"But I'm not. The past is over and done with. People have to live with each other, isn't that true, Father?" she said to the priest in confusion.

"It's true," said Father Siemaszko. "It's the sunset that makes them look purple. Maybe a storm will blow in after all. You know, Grigory Alexandrovich, we haven't had a proper storm here all year."

Pushkin raised his drooping head. "I have my eye on some property outside Wilno, near Markucie. But I was also shown a lovely little estate called Mohylnia, beautifully situated on the river, and not far from the railroad. You must consent to advise me, Miss Helena, which the better choice would be."

"You should live here with us."

He looked at her for a long moment, a bit too long. Helena rose, gave the priest an old-fashioned kiss on the arm, and curtseyed to Pushkin, at once ashamed of that girlish gesture.

"Praised be Jesus Christ . . . Goodbye, Mr. Pushkin, and good luck to you."

Then she walked very slowly across the little town square formed by five or six houses. Someone was chopping wood behind a fence. From one house came the sound of an excited woman speaking Yiddish. Away in the meadows by the Wilia, a shepherd was playing an alder alpenhorn. Large swarms of flies appeared out of nowhere and began hovering over the road in front of Helena. That's it, she thought, another day. Another day gone. Part of the past now.

Helena was waiting for her pupil to arrive that morning as well. She didn't go out to the farm at all, selecting only those tasks that would keep her close to the house. She poked around in the kitchen, looked into the pantry, sampled the jams which had been put up in copper bowls, and, without apparent purpose, even went to the cellar near the ponds, where the last blocks of ice were slowly melting under layers of straw.

But he didn't come this time either. The allee had been empty since the morning. Not even a homeless dog had dashed through its abyss of shadow. Once again, for reasons unknown, he had failed to appear.

It wasn't so much that Miss Helena was waiting for him. That redheaded young man was not Miss Helena's main concern. She loved orderliness, and any violation of order—the failure to keep an agreement, impolite unreliability—had a way of upsetting her equilibrium.

Explaining her edginess in that fashion, Helena bustled about outside the manor, staring blankly into the house as if hoping suddenly to see that flaming head bent over his tablet, slate pencil in hand.

At one point she found herself standing in front of the window to her father's study. She could see the white slips of paper pinned to the wall, some of them faded, their corners curling. She could also see her father's desk with its papers and bills, and among all those odds and ends she knew there must also be a certain yellowed sheet of paper: a fragment of an improvisation in prose by Adam Mickiewicz that someone had jotted down one Sunday in spring when the Philomaths had made a trip out to Markucie, that village outside Wilno where Pushkin's son had his eye on some property as a home for his old age. On the wall there was also a dried and crumbling wreath, from which spilled the remnants of a veil black with age. She had a sudden urge to enter that dark room, rummage about the old books and documents, peek into the drawers and nooks, and at last to discover the secret of her mother, who would remain forever in her roadside grave, like one of Napoleon's soldiers who had fallen in battle.

She ran into the house with a racing heart and tiptoed very slowly to her father's door. A large, rusty key protruded from the lock. She pressed the latch and the door gave a piercing groan as it revealed the room, which smelled of dust. God, what am I doing, she thought. Seized by regret, she was about to withdraw, but she went in as far as the threshold. I'm just going to take a little look— no, I'll find a book to read. I haven't picked up a book for the longest time. A person has to think about the world, other people, God. But I do think about God often. If you can call that thinking.

Out of a sense of fairness to her father, she did not close the door behind her when she entered his room. She stood by the window and gazed toward the far end of the allee, which was so terribly empty that it seemed no one would ever again appear there where it intersected the dusty ruts of the highroad.

A large garden spider climbed leisurely along the fine netting of its web toward the center, where a fly struggled against its entanglement. The fly roused itself for battle, but quickly lost its strength and grew still for a moment. Then it began tugging at the bonds of the web again. It's all so meaningless, thought Helena. All creatures eat one another. A pyramid of cannibals. Life feeding on death. Life devours death, death devours life. Was it a benevolent

God who ordained us to walk this path to Him? She sighed and walked away from the window. It was then that her eye was caught by one of the pieces of paper fastened to the time-blackened wall with a cobbler's nail.

I don't love Poland, she read, *because there is nothing to love about her. But I do not think that I shall hate her either, because she is not deserving of hatred on our part—nor worthy of it.*

She walked over to the next sheet of paper, took it by one curling corner, and brought it up to her eyes.

Nationalism is Poland's weak point, and since the Poles are a light-minded people, all that's needed with them is a little talk about the Polish nation: adroitly sounding that note, Napoleon was able to lead them to the ends of the earth, and with weapons in hand.

It is not the sins of the kings but those of the subjects that bring doom on nations . . .

Yes, it was her father's handwriting. Her father had copied out those frightening passages from works written by Russian, Polish, and Lithuanian writers. How many years have these sheets of white paper been withering on the wall like a funeral wreath?

At that time, Diets and regional councils could be dissolved with impunity. And it was far safer to dissolve a Diet than a regional council, because the Diet, by choice of its members, had retained a modicum of modesty . . . The regional councils, on the other hand, were commonly conducted in tumultuous, violent, and drunken fashion, and sometimes were dissolved; and there might even be armed opposition to the majority opinion, on the pretext that someone and his handpicked helpers had gotten into the chancellery, signed the manifesto, and managed to make their escape from the place where the council had been convened before the drunken deputies had gone their separate ways. It was only then, once having seen the manifesto, that everyone was of the opinion that further regional councils could not be held without violations of the right of liberum *veto, which was commonly called* pupilla libertatis, *"the pupil of liberty." But if they could catch up to him and cut him down,*

or put him to death before he could deliver the manifesto, that pupilla
libertatis *would be safe and sound, even if it had been slashed open or
pried out of its socket.*

The desperate cry of birds rose in the distance. Helena looked
out the window again. Through the dust-specked glass she saw
large flocks of black birds appear over the forest; their flight flailing
and uncertain, they kept rising and falling as if they were fleeing
something in the eastern half of the sky. Must be a hawk, thought
Helena, and walked over to a side wall where, at different heights,
her father had pinned yellowed sheets of paper with maxims, re-
minders, warnings.

*At home you can beat them all you want, but treat them politely
when you have guests. I would say they were desirous not of glory but
of renown. Domestic happiness meant nothing to them as long as they
could win Europe's applause. Political Don Quixotes.*

*Kutuzov enters Wilno as its conqueror. The Poles throw themselves
at him, kissing his knees. "Levez-vous, messieurs," says Kutuzov to
them, "n'oubliez donc pas que vous êtes de nouveau des Russes."*

Helena touched her mother's frightening veil. There must be
some letters from my mother to my father here, all those letters
that in the old days preceded the nuptials, that awe-inspiring ceremony in which you bought a pig in a poke from blind fate.

*How can the Poles fail to realize that Europe will not even mumble
a few words on their behalf, and that Russia will deal with them just
as she would with a revolt in Kolomna.*

*I went to see Radziwill, governor of Wilno province; I beseeched
him, I said: Go to Warsaw, head the government! All Lithuania is yours!
Save the fatherland!!! He wept, he was so moved. I'll beggar myself, he
said, anything to save the country. But it's not a question of sacrificing
property or risking your life, just go sit in Warsaw and run the government! And do you know what he came out with in the end?—My dear
man, while I'm governing in Warsaw, Michal Rejten will be killing off
all of my bears in Naliboki.*

Really, I should tear all this stuff off the wall and burn it in the stove, thought Helena. Why has he been torturing himself all these years? And what haunts him more at night—the memory of my mother or the thought of his country drawn and quartered?

The cities in the Polish provinces are exactly like Rome. All is dust, all is memory, albeit not so eloquent. All you will learn from them is the lesson that a nation without character and a government without laws, which always go together, can have no hope of surviving.

Wishing to afford the Prince pleasure, the King of the Gypsies taught several bears to pull a carriage in harness. A Gypsy served as footman to this team of six, and the driver was a monkey. And the absolutely unexpected sight of the King of the Gypsies pulling into the castle courtyard so utterly surprised and delighted the Prince that he treated the Gypsy like a true king and danced attendance upon him, saying: "Gracious King, you are my guest, a guest unique in all the world. Your visit does me honor and its glory will go down in history!"

Her father's double-barreled shotgun hung in the center of one wall. He had used it for hunting, which he most preferred in spring and fall, though he had often hunted in winter too. Both barrels were full of dust and rust-eaten. When was the last time he'd fired the gun? Must have been twelve years ago, during the violent months of the uprising. Later on, he carried the gun with him out of habit—it wouldn't be fitting for a nobleman to appear unarmed in the forests or the fields. But he had never cleaned the gun since, out of some sense of vengeance. Yet who was the old man avenging himself on? She touched the butt, whose wood had been worn shiny. A small beetle with glossy, chitinous wings crawled out from under one barrel and darted giddily into a dark corner. The whole world's a botch. From the clouds in the sky to the hell at the center of the earth.

Then, from far, far away, there arose a hollow rumble that sounded like cannon crossing a stone bridge. She stopped in the middle of the room. I'm hallucinating, she thought. I'd better hurry, Father could come back any minute.

We lived so well, we might have forgotten our country, were not Poland so sweet to a Pole that he never ceases longing for it. The Muscovites know how to be obliging when they want to, and for that reason, foreigners are drawn to their service and render the people as much harm as they render the government assistance.

The principles of political justice, accepted so that at least appearances were preserved until Napoleon's cause was reversed and destroyed, demanded the reconstruction of the Polish state, which for a very long time had served Europe as a spittoon, the proverbial Makar on whose shoulders all misfortune falls.

And we have before our eyes many examples of grandfathers not permitting the Diet to levy taxes and increase the size of the army to resist Moscow; and now that selfsame Moscow has taken the whole of the estate of which the grandfather did not wish to sacrifice a small part. And now the grandsons are doomed to spend their whole lives bearing arms in Moscow's armies because the grandfather did not wish to allow a few of his subjects to serve the republic for a few years. Thus do innocent sons and grandsons atone for the crimes of their fathers and grandfathers.

By chance she glanced out the window and was amazed by what she saw. The first storm clouds in several days had now appeared over the forest in the western half of the sky. The clouds were moving rapidly, spinning waltz-like, low to the ground, like autumn leaves whirled by the wind. The air'll finally clear, she thought. Why weren't there ever any daguerreotypes or miniatures of my mother? After all, before the wedding they did go to a man in Wilno who made daguerreotypes. Perhaps Father destroyed them or Mother instructed that they be placed in her coffin.

If Poland had not had the Emperor's support, the country would certainly have collapsed and been oppressed by the Jews, who were already seeking to rake in the majority of trade as well as the fortunes of many a landowner, the lifeblood of the state.

Prince Hieronim was one of the richest Radziwills, but, a thrifty man, he increased his enormous estate from one day to the next. The only thing for which he did not begrudge his money was the maintenance of his personal army. Apart from the garrisons, he had six thousand infantry properly uniformed and drilled. He considered himself almost a sovereign monarch. He obeyed no orders, neither those of the hetman nor those of the King. He paid no taxes. "I have more troops than the republic," he used to say. "I'm ready to use them to serve the fatherland, or to give them to the King, but I will pay no taxes." To be sure, warrants were sent him and sentences passed, but they were never carried out, because who would dare to attempt such a thing with a man who not only had a regular army but a few thousand Cossacks and fusiliers as well.

With Poles one should be mild in manners and firm in dealings. Offer a Pole your hand and shake his with polite courtesy, but squeeze that hand hard enough so that he feels your strength. They are incapable of gratitude, only of enthusiasm. So dear to them is their reputation for being noble and valiant that the very words "courage" and "valor" excite them beyond measure. In their theaters every high-flown phrase that has even a semblance of the heroic about it meets with applause, and their virtues are theatrical as well . . . They are forever exchanging the sun for fireworks.

Helena sat down at the desk. She lifted up the roof of a Swiss chalet masterfully carved in wood. The interior flashed with green velvet and the music box began to play an old polonaise by Oginsky. Then she opened the top drawer of the desk. A few yellowed bills, bits of crumbled tobacco; seeds for peas, wheat, and fodder grass. Christ God, what I am rummaging through my father's pitiful secrets for, she thought. And why am I haunted by the ghost of a mother I never knew, but who still feels close, dead so long and yet always here with me, with Father?

Oh, my young fellow countrymen, I shall never see Poland again, for I am an old man, but if you should live to see that day, mark what I tell you: Place no trust in any man who served Moscow for even a year; be he field marshal, judge, or professor. Drive him from your land, for he will never have the makings of a true Pole; and if you allow him to remain, be assured that you are giving the enemy an open door.

Agreed that Poles are reckless people, still one cannot imagine an entire nation going voluntarily to its death and inevitable ruin. For what else could Poland have expected when rising up against Russia?

The cause of his religious madness lay in the fact that first the Prince believed in reincarnation and then, like Vladimir, the ruler of Kiev (now St. Vladimir), decided to search for the best religion. His choice fell on Judaism. He had teachers brought in to teach him Yiddish and Hebrew. Soon he dismissed all his Christian servants, with a few exceptions, and formed a court composed nearly entirely of Jews. Jews served him, Jews managed his wealth. His chief advisor, cashier, and the executor of his instructions was a Jew by the name of Szymon. Every Friday, the Jews would gather at the Prince's for baruchas, lochen, pike, and kugel. The Prince was scrupulous in his observance of the Sabbath and kept kosher. On the Sabbath he would wear an old tattered jacket with the Order of St. Hubert around his neck.

The wind picked up in front of the window. Clumps of hay, whose last drops of moisture had dried up, began rolling along the ground. Fine wrinkles appeared on the pond where the water was free of duckweed. But the air was still stuffy and hot as a bread oven as it came in through cracks in the window frame. With an unpleasant sense of futility, Helena opened the other drawers, which were nearly empty and in which she found nothing in particular apart from a few bits and pieces of the forgotten past. In one drawer there was a ribbon, perhaps from a dress or a hat, and some flower petals, preserved out of love or more likely dried as ingredients for medicinal infusions to be taken on a winter's night. Nothing's left of her, she thought. Nothing but a sadness that is always in the air at Milowidy, which now belongs to strangers, and at Bohin, which still isn't home to us either.

By nature, a drunkard is little different from a madman, for when drunk he is mad entirely, wrote Prince Karol Radziwill, governor of Wilno province. *Malachowski killed people with wine, as described above; Radziwill killed them with arms. It was nothing for him to shoot a man in the head like a dog, but such behavior was considered ordinary enough in the Radziwill home and family. Thus did his uncles and his brothers, but not his father, a great Lithuanian hetman who was by nature very sluggish, both when sober and when drunk, and thereby did not distinguish himself by drunken murder. He, however, did distinguish himself by the most execrable acts, committed in public while he was accompanied by a great, drunken mob. At Radziwill's burial, he massaged his genitalia and ordered the honor guard to open fire. Decency will not permit me any more than to mention his jocularities on the risen and the dead.*

Yes, Poland would allow herself to be hacked into pieces, but would never give any sign of her suffering.

Among the still fresh examples of our magnates' lawlessness is Mikolaj Potocki, the subprefect of Kaniow, notorious for his cruelty in our part of Ruthenia, who killed forty men with his own hand. In Poland proper, Czapski, the subprefect of Knyszyn, was so ferocious that he would have people he did not like, or thought had wronged him, thrust into a barrelful of floor nails; and he ordered that barrel rolled in front of him for his amusement. For those atrocities, the hetman Branicki had him banished so that he could take over Knyszyn, which bordered Bialystok. In Lithuania, Radziwill, the standard-bearer of his country, lived in Biala and loved to listen to the groans issuing from his cellars, the groans of those he supposed guilty of wrongdoing against him and whom he called his favorite singers. All these brutes lived at the same time and were one cause of the dismemberment of a country which had slid into anarchy.

She tore that slip of paper from the wall and began crumpling it up in her hand, looking out the window, seeing nothing. She lifted the roof of the Swiss chalet once again. And again she heard the strains of that polonaise, probably called "Farewell to the Fatherland," thumped out to a rough and brassy waltz rhythm. Father will be coming back any minute. Let him. She was there for a book, even though she had never gone there for a book before. Still, she might have run in there once as a child. I do have a vague memory of something like that. Running through room after high-ceilinged room, and at the end of them all, Father at his desk. But that was at Milowidy.

She took a Bible with a tattered spine from a small shelf. She opened the cover and on the first page saw the crooked letters she had penciled there a quarter of a century ago. I'm so awfully tired of my life, she thought. My empty life which wouldn't even tire out a cat.

She looked out the window. An unusual, spindly shadow was moving down the allee. Oh, it was just Malwinka hurrying home from one of her expeditions into the forest. The sky was growing gray but was still bright. Once there was a man named Piotrus Pieslak, and now he's gone. Once, or at most twice, her heart had trembled when, as she was introduced to a distant neighbor or a passing traveler, she had touched a man's hand. And now there was Mr. Alexander Broel-Plater, who also seemed a stranger. There was no joy, no excitement, and no sense of expectation. The banns would be posted next Sunday. Why had she told Father Siemaszko that she wanted to make her confession? It's the worst time to make my confession. And it might also be a bad time for granting absolution.

She lowered her gaze and saw one end of a piece of yellow vellum. Yes, a page of vellum thoughtlessly torn from an old book. She pulled it out from the pile onto some keys half eaten by rust lying on one section of the desk. It was the improvisation Mickiewicz had done in Markucie when he was still a young boy and did not speak Polish well. She began reading the fine, slanting handwriting and for some reason first one eye then the other grew moist, the letters began to blur, and a warm, foolish tear rolled down her cheek.

How beautiful is the valley by this stream, which still has no name but which someday, perhaps not far in the future, will have more names than one, because a railroad will be built on sandy rises above the water and connect the two capitals of the empire with the world of the West, the world of Latin, the world of endless hostility, and along the roads by the railroad and the stream, which we can see down below through the alders as it steals along toward the city, accompanied by the merry cries of boys fishing in waters lush with vegetation and with large stones implanted in its bed, along those roads armies and throngs of refugees will pass, floods will surge, fierce epidemics and cruel pestilence, and people will flee from there to the ends of the earth, to America and Australia, taking with them our melodies still murmuring in the conchs of their ears, shouldering the burdens of our restless minds, our delusions, rolling the boulders of our sins and of the anathemas hurled at us by the giants who abandoned our planet and may now be living somewhere in icy intergalactic space, or else may have perished long ago, only their groans wandering through oblivion reaching us from time to time, for only we can hear and understand them, and only those who come after us, born of us and inspired by us, poets, scholars, madmen, and that boy who is driving a cow along the sandy road by the railroad tracks and who in a second will cross those tracks and go down to the meadow with his cow, or maybe a cow belonging to someone else, a woman's kerchief wound around his head, shamefaced, frightened by his future, tormented by hallucinations, that boy who has just stuck his feet in fresh cow manure to warm them up, and that young man will make this valley holy, and though it perish, vanish, fade away, heaped over with time and history, it will yet live, borne over the earth in the particles of our body, in the cells of our memory, and in the vestigial relics of our sacrilege that shall roam infinity above.

Helena had time to go bathing in the river again before the storm. By then everyone knew that a big storm was on its way: people, animals, and trees were all waiting for the hurricane to strike its first blow. But the air was still suffocating, heavy, flashing with gleams of light.

She swam for a little while in the strangely warm, calm water. The woods on the other shore were motionless. A bird was flitting anxiously back and forth over the treetops, as if searching for a nestling lost among the still branches. She also had time to give herself a good soaping and felt sorry for the white froth of soap bubbles which the water greedily snatched away and spun in small spirals, bearing it toward the bend where the world of Bohin ended.

Then, dressing quickly, she glanced nervously at the western sky, where vast black waves of storm clouds were streaming in from the shallow horizon. It wasn't only the storm that made everything grow darker and darker, dusk was also falling.

Then she ran as fast as she could to reach the house before the rain started. A wind had picked up, but it was irregular at first, its gusts bending the young alders low and, on the other side of the river, lifting and hurling whole sheaves of grain that had not been brought in from the fields yet. Flying low to the ground, the birds fled to the secret hiding places where they ride out storms; and people were running from field to farm.

The sky was flashing more all the time, having started when

Helena was still bathing in the river. Those sinuous ripples of pale-blue light cut silently through the dark blue of the sky and might have seemed only the thunderless summer lightning that is so frequent on airless nights, some errant reflection of a distant storm killing other people's animals in the fields and setting other people's houses on fire.

But then, after one of those mute flashes, a rumbling seemed to rise from the ground, and finally lightning struck somewhere near Milowidy, their very own Milowidy, which they hadn't seen for years, hadn't so much as visited for years, and hadn't thought about for years.

Then, her throat gone completely dry and unable to catch her breath, Helena raced into the park, which was as choppy as a sea. The old trees with their black trunks had sprung to life, soughing and sighing. At times a branch or dead trunk would crack, making a miniature thunder for gnomes. Then she heard the first spatter of rain on the leaves, raindrops the size of cherries mixed in with huge hail.

She ran into the house, familiar and homey, yet not home at all. She was struck by the heat of the walls and the searing air that hung motionless in all the rooms. Somewhere a cat was screeching; someone was stamping his feet by the house; and far from her rain-washed window a horse was galloping heavily, having broken free. And so began the greatest storm she had ever experienced.

Through a half-opened door she caught sight of her father standing at the window, or rather, close to the window, for he was using the window frame to shield him against bolts of lightning which could pierce the windowpane and against the fireballs which could come shooting in out of nowhere and strike people down, then vanish before you knew what happened. Her father was looking out the window at a world grown dark and gray, the little world of Bohin to which the end of the world had indeed come.

After a moment's hesitation, Helena went into her father's

study. He was not surprised by her entrance, naturally accepting his daughter's impulse at a moment like that. The lightning kept illuminating the room with its wretched slips of paper on walls that should have been used for pistol practice, that desk covered with the paltry remains of a tenant and almoner's moribund affairs, and that shred of a veil, a memento of her mother, who might never have existed.

"I'm sorry, Papa," she said, trembling slightly with emotion. "But I was afraid to stay alone in my room."

Her father nodded without turning around. He looked straight out the bare window and waited. A rose-colored glow was now spreading from the heart of the forest. A little backwater or dying, resinous woods was ablaze.

Then, from behind, they heard a plaintive voice. It was Emilka going from window to window, holding up a holy picture, blessing the infuriated elements. She was followed by Antoni Sieniuc, the blacksmith's assistant, who was lighting her way with a candle consecrated on Candlemas Day to be used during storms and at the bedside of the dying. Antoni clearly felt embarrassed and awkward making the sign of the cross with a wax candle thick as a wrist.

Father and daughter stood in the room without looking at each other. A slow fear overcame them, an animal panic at nature's mysterious powers, the dread of God's wrath. She was not aware at which moment she began praying, her lips moving soundlessly. Her father too had lowered his head and was beating his breast.

"Father," she whispered in the sudden stillness between thunderbolts, the only sound the hail rapping the window glass and a piece of sheet metal rattling in the attic. "Papa, I went into your study today without permission. I was looking for something having to do with my mother. I want to know what she was like and what I'll be like. Papa, don't be angry with me, I don't know how to live. I don't know if I'm living as I should. Papa, why don't you say anything?"

Then her father raised a hand to his eye seemingly to remove something from the lid, a stray ladybug or a bit of a rye husk. But he didn't say anything.

Suddenly she could see him, as if in a flash of magnesium, transparent against the spectral, transparent background of the wall, and she thought she had gone blind in a split second. But at that very moment she caught sight of a torch bursting into flame in the violently darkening world outside the window. A lightning bolt had split a huge maple on the other side of the ponds and a column of cadaverous-green flame rose from within the old tree.

She was unaware precisely when she took those two small steps and put her arms around her father, feeling his tendons and dry bones under the cloth of his jacket.

"Papa, I'm so frightened," she whispered.

He was still motionless, though she could sense that he was hesitating, as sudden feelings which he could not himself understand brought a lump to his throat and battered his ribs on the side where his heart was. She stood by him for a moment, waiting for some gesture from him, but he was waiting too, a prisoner of his obstinacy. A shame about that tree, she thought to console herself, and began slowly withdrawing toward the door.

And I'm blundering along after my grandmother Helena Konwicka, through those sacred and secluded spots, those wildernesses, there at the end of the nineteenth century. In my imagination, I was always stealing after my father; I wanted to know about his life, I craved knowledge of his secret, which he succeeded in hiding from me and taking to the grave with him, a grave in the cemetery that dominates a broad rise above Nowa Wilejka, the small town where I was born and which today is called Nauja Vilnia and is a district of the Lithuanian capital, Vilnius. No doubt my father's grave is unattended and may now have collapsed into the ground; maybe someone else is lying there in my father's dust. But perhaps from the heights of that rise my father's spirit locks out onto the

Wilenka, that small river which winds and meanders capriciously past cliffs of golden sand, then careens, dashes, races headlong through alders, aloof pine, sudden groves of oak. He looks out at a river whose shores I shall never walk again.

My father was baptized in Bujwidze; that fact alone is certain in his scant life story, which is why I am fighting through the obscurities of oblivion, mists of impossibility, clouds of sudden painful memory, to make my way to my grandmother Helena Konwicka, to spend a little while with her, near her, within her soul, even if that be but a few weeks at the end of summer and the beginning of fall in that year when my father was conceived. I set out on this journey a long time ago, but it's not an arduous one, because I am no stranger to those final decades of the nineteenth century, I have lived in and on that time, breathed its air. Because in those Lithuanian backwoods, those desert islands of Central Europe, the nineteenth century lasted until the Second World War. And as I marched along one winter day and seemed to see some finality just over the horizon, I made an abrupt turn and sailed with surprising ease over the mountains and the valleys, back one hundred and ten years to Bujwidze by the Wilia.

Along the way I saw many other pilgrims returning as I was into the depths of history, the shallow niches of the eighteenth and nineteenth centuries, in order to poison themselves with the terrible truth or to find a spurious, saccharine solace. But I am not seeking solace and I have no need of the truth, because I create my own truth. Inferior or superior, more believable or less, a truth that I compose myself out of memories, imagination, longings, and forebodings, so that I can leave behind a gravestone, a little monument made of fieldstone, which will turn to dust one autumn or spring and vanish forever like my father's grave; but I will hammer that fieldstone, carve letters and signs into it, press my lips to it, and try to breathe spirit into that dead matter, a spirit that could have been immortal but is, after all, mortal, only mortal. Where is my grandmother, the grandmother I have created, the Helena Konwicka who is experiencing love along with me and who will one day die along with me.

Slowly the storm subsided. Lightning was still striking on the other side of the Wilia, while good-natured thunder rolled over Bohin, preceded by distant, gentle lightning. Helena went back to her room. Wanting to light her lamp, she began looking for the matches which should have been on the table. It was then she realized that Konstanty had not closed the shutters. The storm had driven the ancient Konstanty off somewhere to lie low. Now her window would remain vulnerable until morning. Automatically, she began moving toward the shining rectangle, when a sudden fear stopped her in the middle of the room. What's there to be afraid of, she thought. Who'd be out in a downpour like this? Probably only Schicklgruber, if there's any such thing.

Heavy raindrops spattered against the little windowpanes, which clattered meekly. She sighed and began undressing, though she had no great desire to. She took off her blouse and had begun unbuttoning her skirt when she thought she saw something dark streak past the window, and she immediately felt the flesh creep on her shoulders and bare arms. I must be seeing things, she thought. It's a terrible day.

But once again something loomed outside the window. It looked like a head huddling into shoulders that had been instinctively raised. Despite herself, she withdrew toward the door, ready at any second to cry out, even though the rain and the sparse but rolling thunder would probably have drowned out her cry.

Then someone knocked once at her window. She was about to dash blindly into the dark corridor that led to the front hall, but then the knocking started up again, still tentative. Yes, a hand was tapping softly and evenly at the middle pane. She could see a wavering figure vainly attempting to peer into her room. Her heart was beating violently now, because she had guessed who was there.

"Who's there?" she asked, barely able to swallow. "Who's out there in the night?"

"It's me. Please let me in." She could hear a man's voice fading in the sound of the rain.

"Who's knocking?" she asked again, even though she knew who the night wanderer was.

"It's me. Elias Szyra." He pressed his nose and lips to the damp glass.

She walked over to the window and raised her hand, as if wishing to check if his hair was wet.

"For God's sake, please let me in, I'm drowning out here," he shouted.

She hesitated a moment, looking distractedly about the room. Then she whispered, making distinct lip movements so that he could understand what she was saying, if, that is, he could make out her features at all.

"Go to the right, there's a door by the kitchen. Go into the hall and wait there."

He nodded to signal that he'd understood. Then, on tiptoe, her ears straining for every sound, constantly stopping short in panic, she ran through the large hall and down a small corridor to a room which had doors to the kitchen, the pantry, and Emilka's alcove.

Standing barefoot on the earthen floor, Helena pressed her hand to her heart to quiet it and discovered that she was in her corset, blouseless. But it was too late to run away. He was standing there against the half-closed door.

"Shut your eyes," she said. "I'm not dressed."

"I can't see anything anyway," he whispered conspiratorially. "My eyes were poked out by branches when I was running from the storm through the woods."

"Follow me," she said in a half whisper.

"But I can't see anything. How am I supposed to follow you?"

Once again she hesitated for a moment, then, suddenly recovering her self-possession, she became matter-of-fact, resolute. One of the final lightning bolts struck near the river. The next day, the farm boys would find a flint there from which they would strike sparks for a bonfire that fall.

"Give me your hand," she ordered.

They sought each other's hand for a moment in the dark. Finally, she found his hand, sopping wet yet strangely hot. She led him carefully to her room, shushing him constantly on the way. What am I doing, she thought. Where's it all going to end?

"Where it's supposed to," she whispered haughtily to herself.

Out of habit he sat down at the table, still shaking from the cold every so often. Helena groped along the edge of her bed for her shawl, which had long fringe like that on ears of wheat. She covered her bare arms and felt better at once.

"What happened? Why are you here?"

"Oh," he whispered, struggling against the chills, "I was on my way back from Sobakince and I was caught in that horrible storm. Your house was the closest. I knew you wouldn't refuse me shelter."

"And how did you know that?"

"I don't know how I knew, but I knew."

"You're wringing wet."

"Yes, I am."

"I don't have any men's clothing."

"Doesn't matter. I'll dry quickly. I've got hot blood."

That had a somehow unpleasant ring to it, and Helena fell silent. At a loss now, she sat down on the edge of her bed, gazing blankly at the spectral window.

"There're fires everywhere," she whispered. "The whole horizon's red."

"It's Schicklgruber's night. He loves to burn people. Especially Jews."

He said this in a rather light tone of voice, and unable to see his face, she couldn't tell whether to take him seriously.

"You believe in those stories?"

"There's always a grain of truth in folktales."

"You're shivering."

"Yes," he whispered meekly, "I'm shivering, though I'm trying to control it."

She rose automatically and walked over to his chair. As if against her better judgment, she reached out and touched his hair, which usually looked like kindling on fire.

"Your hair's sopping wet."

"Yes, it's sopping wet."

"You're mocking me."

"I wouldn't dare. I just don't know what to say. But I really am drenched to the bone."

"It wasn't right to bring you to my room."

"I'm not saying anything, I'm afraid to say anything."

"I did the wrong thing."

Suddenly, to her horror, she felt that she was shivering too. It's so cold after the storm, she thought. It's a good thing the grain's been brought in. But why am I thinking these foolish thoughts?

She noticed that she was standing right beside him. A sign of the coming autumn, the rain roared like a river. She was about to go back to her bed when he suddenly took her by the hand.

"Please don't go," he whispered.

Frozen in fear, she did not pull her hand away in time. That might encourage him, she thought, in the center of the enormous roaring that filled the entire room, and the two of them as well. I'm so tired, she sighed, as if in justification.

Then he rose from the chair and stood right beside her, a sort of damp warmth emanating from him. I'm shivering, she thought with despair. Attempting to tear her hand free of his, she stumbled against the leg of the table and at once found her breasts against his chest. Suddenly his lips were stinging her cheek like nettles. She wanted to turn her face aside, but he was holding her head with his hand and had no difficulty finding her mouth with his lips. She struggled and thrashed, but then, feeling faint, she ceased offering resistance for a moment, to keep from falling. Jesus Christ, what's happened, she thought in despair, sinking into a terrible yet enticing trance.

"What are you doing?" She could barely whisper the words.

"It's nothing. It's good. It's right," she thought she could hear him say.

"You mustn't. Leave here. And never come back."

"I came back to you from the ends of the world. From the next world."

"No, no, oh God . . ."

"It's too late now."

Suddenly she could feel his hand, terribly hot and trembling, as it plunged beneath her shawl, touched her neck, her collarbone, and began stealing toward her breasts. Then, in a sudden surge of strength, she tore her right hand from his grasp and struck him in the face with all her might. She hit him a second and a third time, but with much less force now, because he had let go of her and was standing as still as a tree.

"How dare you, you disgusting Jew!" she said in a fury.

He remained motionless, not saying a word.

"Get out this very minute," she added, without conviction.

"Please don't raise your voice, or someone will hear," he whispered in the dark, and she couldn't tell whether he was mocking or in earnest. There was a trembling in her body now and it kept throwing her off. By now he can hear my teeth chattering, she thought angrily.

She went back and sat down on the edge of the bed, wrapping the shawl tightly around her. He still hadn't said a word. The rain had let up a bit. Every so often blurred lightning flashed in the distance. That horrible country stillness was reemerging from every side. He wasn't moving and looked like a slim streak of shadow on the wall, on the other side of which the clock was softly striking the hour. Maybe he's died on his feet, she thought nonsensically.

"Why didn't you come for your lessons?" she said, regretting the question at once.

Elias drew closer, extending his hands in front of him as if afraid of banging into furniture invisible in the dark.

"I'm very sorry about that. I have certain obligations here. I had to do some traveling, by foot."

Cautiously he sat down beside her on the bed. Instinctively, she raised her hand. "Have you really gone out of your mind?" she cried.

He rose obediently and stood beside her, his wet knees almost touching hers through her thin petticoat.

"Shh, be quiet. Someone could still hear us."

"Where do you get your boldness?"

"From life."

Once again he sat down quietly, almost soundlessly, beside her. She pretended not to have noticed.

"I can remember from years back you and your father driving up to the church in Bujwidze in a splendid carriage. You were still living at Milowidy then. You always wore a white dress, but later on, when I would think about you, when I was out wandering the world, I'd see you in a white dress with a rose-colored sash at your waist. Tell me, is my memory good?"

"Not at all. I used to wear all sorts of different dresses to church. And in the winter, I'd even wear a long beaver coat."

Very delicately he took her hand in the dark. He did this so lightly that all she felt was a dry warmth. She wanted to tear her hand away, but not having done it when she should have, she now thought a deliberate gesture would seem somehow comical, even inappropriate. She held her breath and waited, without knowing what she was waiting for.

"Don't fight me," he said softly.

"And what if I start screaming and call the servants and my father?"

"Won't help."

"What makes you so sure?"

"It took me twelve years to make my way back to you. I escaped from Simbirsk to France on a French ship that called at Petersburg. So I arrived in Paris in time for the revolution, because that was just at the beginning of the summer of 1871. I fought under Commander Wroblewski. When the Commune fell, I had to go into hiding. Terrible mobs were rampaging in the streets of Paris, wanting to take revenge on foreigners, and especially Poles. I could barely speak French, and so, one night, they caught me and hung me from a tree in the Luxembourg Gardens."

He stopped there, turned his head toward the window, probably looking at the window's vague flickering glow. She almost laughed but only cleared her throat softly. "The French hung you?"

"That's right, but I'm never easy to deal with. I broke free of the rope, and that bloodthirsty mob let me off with my life."

"You do make up the most outrageous stories. Why do you do it, who's supposed to believe those absurd stories?"

"I've never told anyone about that. And please be discreet about it too. What difference does it make here and now, in the middle of the night far from anywhere, what difference does it make if I'm telling the truth or not?"

"Good God, what a tangle," she said with a sigh.

"No, it isn't, it has to be this way. It was fated by heaven above."

"This couldn't have been fated. Who ever heard of such a thing."

"And I could have entered this home and taken you by force, you know."

"Why are you talking such nonsense? What's come into your head?"

He squeezed her fingers delicately. "Please don't be afraid. I love you too much."

"I didn't hear a word of that, and I don't know what you're talking about," she whispered desperately.

He fell silent and she could not even tell if he was breathing. There in the dark he seemed a completely different person. At that moment she could not even recall what he looked like. What's this stranger doing in my bedroom, she thought. How did this all come to pass? And how will it all end?

"Please leave," she said in a muffled voice. "Please leave and never come back."

"I can't promise you that. I have to finish learning the alphabet, don't I? We stopped at *l*," he replied in an oddly light tone which alarmed her.

"Let's forget the whole thing ever happened," she said, rising from the bed. The idiotic, decrepit canopy shook overhead. "It's all because of the storm. The storm will pass and everything else will too. Follow me now, but on tiptoe please, my father is a light sleeper."

He took her gently by the hand. "Can I come for a lesson tomorrow?"

She hesitated, saying nothing, listening to the beating of her heart—or perhaps his.

"All right, you can come. But let's finish up by Sunday. After that, you're on your own."

In the darkness he raised her hand to the heat of his lips. She wanted to tear free, but told herself that wouldn't be right. He'll be walking all those miles in the rain at night. But that was his problem now.

She began moving briskly toward the door. His step was so soft that she had to turn around a few times to be sure he was still there.

She opened the door, which, fortunately, did not creak, and stepped aside so he could leave. I won't say anything, she thought. It's better that way.

He shook at the sight of the still heavy rain tussling with bushes of wild lilac. He went out onto the fieldstone steps, turned around, and looked at her for a long while without saying a word.

"No one sends me packing," he whispered, then walked briskly away, immediately disappearing into the night.

It's a bad dream, she thought. I've just woken up from a nightmare. This ambiguous charity has to end. I'll go to confession, and starting next week . . . starting next week, I must begin thinking about my new life, my future.

Just then the door beside her groaned softly and Emilka, still warm with sleep, appeared in the doorway in her nightshirt.

"He left?" she whispered.

"Who?" asked Helena, abashed. "Oh yes, he left."

"Thank God for that."

"The lightning was terrible out there," said Helena softly. "It wouldn't have been Christian to leave people out wandering in the woods."

After a moment's silence, Emilka finally said, "Sleep well, my lady."

"You too, Emilka."

"It'll be light soon."

"Yes, we'll be getting up soon too. A lost night."

Then, for some reason, she ran over to Emilka, kissed her cheek, which still bore traces of a button from a pillowcase or someone's shirt, then ran down the little corridor to her own room.

1 8

The next morning at breakfast Michal Konwicki cast his daughter a questioning glance, then furrowed his brow and bent over his plate. Breakfast at Bohin Manor did not consist of real coffee and fresh croissants but of buckwheat flour boiled in milk—which was why Michal Konwicki bent over his plate. But Helena kept looking away, at first in apparent confusion and then with irritation. She was slowly overcome with anger, dissatisfaction with herself, and a sense of grievance against her father or, rather, against his eccentricities, which seemed noble-minded enough but in the end had become a burden to those around him. Maybe now he'll finally speak, she thought. And at last tell me about my mother, why she died just after giving birth to me, and what was behind her wish to be buried by the roadside like a vagabond or a suicide. Oh, it's all because of that night and that terrible storm. That's why I'm so out of sorts. Enough sulking, there's work to be done.

She rose from the table, tied a large linen apron around her waist, and went off to do her morning chores. Her father cleared his throat as he watched her go. Disconcerted, he submitted to his daughter's anger. This time she had the upper hand in their silent duel of so many years' standing.

The day after the storm was on the cool side. The sky had cleared and soft white clouds, oddly sprightly and jaunty, raced across it. Maciej the stork had not returned to his nest on the peak of the roof, but perched on one of the withering trees in the old park; there he loitered, opening and closing his wings, cleaning his feathers with his beak, shifting his weight from one foot to the other. Malwinka, who may have spent the night with Konstanty in some shelter, or may have spent it elsewhere, was now grazing with dignity by the ponds.

The performance of her customary tasks did not, however, bring Miss Helena any peace of mind. What insolent people those Jews are, she thought, glancing automatically to the far end of the dark allee which led to the highroad. Jews are impossible. Lots of revolutionaries are Jews, and plenty of informers too. They start the fire, then they put it out. They build a Tower of Babel, then tear it right down. It's a good thing I laid down the law to him. What are things coming to these days? Before, it would have been unthinkable for some Jew to come creeping into a manor house, to a woman's bedroom, in the middle of the night.

Slowly the morning hours passed, and the sun rose higher and higher, leisurely approaching that point above the allee which signified noon. Miss Helena worked with a will that day and it was a good thing that no one crossed her path. But finally she did spot Konstanty, who, with a scythe over his shoulder, was on his way to cut some aftergrass for his beloved horses.

"Konstanty!" cried Helena from the porch. "Hitch up the carriage, please. I may be going to the store in Bujwidze."

Anger surged through her again at that moment—why was she explaining herself to that old man? Konstanty stopped, thought for a moment, shifted the scythe to his other shoulder, and headed back toward the farm.

"Hitch up the horses, would you please, even though I might not go to Bujwidze. Why should I? Who's there to shop for?"

It was then that Plater came to mind and she suddenly felt cold and short of breath all at once. Christ God, what have I gone and done, she thought. Why did I agree to that contract; that's what it is, a transaction. He's buying me like a foundered mare.

Neither of us is as young as we used to be, that's what he said. Christ God.

Does nothingness exist? Can something arise out of nothingness? Were we all brought forth out of nothingness? To disappear into nothingness. To find rest. But I'm not really tired. It's just a lassitude that gets heavier all the time. What's in store for me here? And in the hereafter?

She crossed herself stealthily and tried to whisper the Angelus prayer, because the bell must be striking noon now in Bujwidze. An immense cloud of rooks rose over the fields at the edge of the woods.

A clatter of wheels preceded the carriage's emergence from the bushes. Konstanty was on the box, flicking his whip near the horses' rumps without striking their lackluster hides.

"Wait a minute," she said, and ran off to change her clothes.

Helena surprised Emilka by saying she wasn't hungry, then ran out to the porch, where she nearly collided with her father, who had his gun on his shoulder—that gun which he had not fired for so many years.

"I'm going to the store in Bujwidze, I'll be right back."

Her father cleared his throat and furrowed his eyebrows, which hung menacingly low over his eyes that were either clear or had lost their color. He even opened his mouth as if about to say something, but did not speak this time either.

To be about her business as quickly as possible, she ran down the steps and hopped into the carriage. "Go."

The horses sprang eagerly into motion and the carriage rolled off toward the highroad, where it turned to the right, toward Bujwidze. The carriage's wheels rumbled on the little bridge over the Uzla, then grew quiet again in the wet sand of the road.

"I'm doing this for myself. I have to see some other people, some other buildings, even just hear the sound of a different wind. I'm going mad at Bohin," she whispered to herself.

Konstanty was sitting a bit to one side of the box, as if wishing to hear her monologue, but in fact he always sat like that, as people who are hard-of-hearing will do. The horses were farting merrily. Blades of grass, bushes, and low-slung branches all shone golden with great drops of moisture.

Still, something might have happened to him. Why was that Jew wandering around in the middle of the night? Where was he going in that deserted neck of the woods? What business drove him out of his home, if he even has a home? What do I care about any of that? Why did I let myself get involved with those lessons? Christ God, it'll all end badly.

In Bujwidze Konstanty halted the carriage in front of The Golden Apple, which sold groceries and just about everything else. Miss Helena went up the stairs and into the gloomy store—but gloomy in a pleasant way, because its darkness had a light-blue cast to it and was saturated with odors: herring and soap, raisins, freshly tanned hide, butter and lamp oil, even some vague perfume. The store was empty, but a bearded Jew came right out through a narrow door, his beard flaring red in a shaft of sunlight. He bowed low.

"May I pay you my respects. And how may I be of service?"

"I just wanted to see if you were open."

"How could our store be closed when you've come all this way?"

"Good, I'll be back. First I'll go to the rectory."

"Very well. We'll be expecting you, ma'am. We have lots of time, even too much, for the amount of business we do. I'm sorry for talking so much, but there's so much time and so few people."

From the store she went across the empty square to the church. She intended to go straight to the rectory, but something drew her to the half-opened church doors, from which a light warmth emanated. The thick church walls were now releasing the heat that had built up over weeks.

She went into the darkness of the nave, where she had to

narrow her eyes to see anything at all. Far overhead, sparrows chattered rancorously. A jay flew diagonally through the church and took cover among the Baroque angels on the altar.

It was then that Helena caught sight of Father Siemaszko, who was wearing his cassock but not his surplice or stole. He was kneeling in front of a black catafalque on top of which was a humble, unadorned coffin of plain pine marked with reddish knots. The priest was praying from a tattered breviary, frequently raising his head to look up at the birds frolicking under the vaulted ceilings.

She knelt down in the first row of benches. The priest went on praying, mumbling ardently at times, until finally he marked the page with a colored ribbon, kissed the edge of the book, and closed it loudly like the lid of a chest. Then, showing no surprise, he turned, rose heavily from the prie-dieu, and walked over to Helena.

"Praised be Jesus Christ," she whispered.

"World without end."

"And whose coffin is that?"

"An old crone's, a beggar woman's. She came here to me from over by Molodeczno, out Holyszy way. And so I have to bury her. Right now I'm praying for her sinful soul."

"I came in to do some shopping and while I was here stopped by the church. Did the storm do any damage?"

They began walking down the center aisle toward the door. The tops of the organ's pipes were streaked with a golden, almost autumnal sunlight.

"The chief of police is doing more damage than the storm. You saw yourself how he smashed my hives. And this morning too, first thing he was out flying around like the blankety-blank Antichrist and arrested that young Jew Szyra, the one whose parents left here for America."

"The Jew Szyra was arrested?" said Helena in surprise. "What, are they arresting Jews now?"

The priest looked around the church.

"People say he was in the uprising. And he's restless again too. He disappears for days, then all of a sudden he's back. I heard they searched his place for weapons."

Helena stopped by the door. "And did they at least find some?" she asked banteringly.

"Of course not. It's the Belorussian problem that has them most nervous right now," said the priest confidingly. "Everywhere I turn I see eyes watching me. Oh, my child, the surveillance they've put this old man under."

He turned toward the altar and knelt, crossing himself in farewell to God. But he doesn't believe in God, thought Helena with strange vindictiveness. He doesn't believe in the God he's been commanded to serve. Christ God, the things I think. She knelt to take her farewell of God too and began crossing herself with the fervor of an Old Believer. But you won't be saying farewell to those terrible doubts of yours, snickered a voice within her, causing her a horrible shudder.

"Maybe I was wrong to stir up the Belorussians," said Father Siemaszko with a sigh on the church stairs. He narrowed his eyes behind the lenses of his glasses, which only then did Helena notice were the color of bluing. "It's not for a priest to be mixing in politics. I'm a sinner, a terrible sinner. I can't sleep at night. And I've already said enough prayers to last me to Advent."

They walked in silence awhile and Helena saw they were headed toward the rectory. Torn, she came to a stop and didn't know what to say.

"You're all right, you're still innocent," said the priest.

"Oh God, my heart's in pain today."

"Come in the house, I'll have them put on the samovar."

"No, no thank you, I have to go."

"What's the hurry, child, you've got plenty of time."

"No, forgive me, but I must go." She bent to kiss his hand. He made a small sign of the cross over her and sighed, even more mournfully this time.

She was barely out to the square when she heard a loud clatter of wheels as Plater's cabriolet rolled in on the road from Santoka, the small railway station at the edge of the great woods. The count spotted Helena, who had a violent urge to hide. But there was nowhere to hide—the count had already caught sight of his fiancée and ordered Ildefons to drive toward her.

The cabriolet halted, its elegant black harness squeaking. The beautiful horses shifted their weight impatiently.

"What a surprise!" Plater jumped happily down from his carriage. He was addressing her affectionately in public, as if she were already his wife.

"I was with the priest in church, but I must get back home as quickly as possible, though I am glad I ran into you. Where have you been?" she asked, her heart skipping a beat unpleasantly.

"I'm just back from Petersburg, where I was doing some shopping." He smiled mysteriously. "More about that later. I'm going to see the priest now, to make the formal arrangements for the banns. Would you care to accompany me, my dear Miss Helena?"

With a dejected look, the rifleman Ildefons was toying with a beautiful whip, which he might have brought back from Petersburg itself. He was frowning at Helena and clearly impatient.

"I wouldn't feel right about it," said Helena, blushing. "Couldn't it wait until Shrovetide?"

"The matter's been settled, my lovely Miss Helena." Plater laughed, but his laughter struck her as somewhat unnatural, willed. He comes from a strange home, strange counts and countesses living strange lives. And are they really counts anyway, she thought. I could become a countess. But what do I care!

"Please don't be angry," she said in a polite whisper.

"I'll catch up with you, we can do that, right, Ildefons? I'll take care of my business in the rectory and we'll catch right up with you."

He hopped into his cabriolet with excessive briskness. "So I won't say goodbye."

The cabriolet turned toward the church and Helena rushed to her carriage almost at a run. Konstanty was standing in the cool shade flicking gadflies off the horses' rumps with the tip of his whip.

"We're going back. And let's be quick about it too, Konstanty. Or else he'll catch up with us."

"And who might that be?" asked Konstanty sneeringly. "That count who makes money off the Jews? He doesn't have a chance."

She barely had time to climb onto the carriage—not sparing his beloved horses, Konstanty had already put the whip to them, first to one, then the other. Like greyhounds, the horses dashed down the highroad toward the woods.

Konstanty turned around on his box. "This is what he'll catch up to." Konstanty's hand, gnarled by arthritis, rose with the index finger straight up.

They raced for a good mile or so before Konstanty slackened the reins. The horses were eager to slow their pace; a fine gray steam rose from them. Helena felt cold. She huddled against the carriage's uncomfortable upholstery of worn and badly cracked leather. Every so often Konstanty would turn around, look at the road behind them, and mutter to himself.

When the little bridge over the Uzla came into view, Helena said suddenly, "Konstanty, go to Milowidy."

The old man turned around, shaken. "Milowidy?"

"That's right. I have an urge to see it, from a distance. It's been so many years."

"Nothing but a whim," said Konstanty with a sigh and clicked at the horses, who were clearly surprised to pass the familiar allee and continue on the highroad, which soon forked, Milowidy lying to the right and Daugiele to the left. A moment later they passed the grave marked only by a birch cross. Growing sorrowful at once, Helena automatically crossed herself. How many more times was she going to pass by that painful mystery covered over with sod and thick, luxuriant grass? Someone takes care of the grave. Yes, Father does, he still remembers. He spends many hours here, rambling through the woods concealed by the bushes, the ferns tall as trees, the wild-berry patches, with no one ever calling his name; he wanders with that rusty old rifle of his. Helena crossed herself again. One day I'll learn the secret, if there even is one, she thought. I'll probably see it in a dream some winter night, when everything around is blanketed in snow and the world has lost all shape, feature, and color.

Konstanty had started urging the horses on again. An autumn wind was blowing in from somewhere, even though nature had regained its green the previous night.

"Konstanty, were you ever at Milowidy afterward?" she asked.

He shrugged angrily. "Never even drove past."

They had lived so near to their old home for so many years and had never driven by. For them it was dead and buried.

Now the horses were stopping of their own accord at the edge of the woods in front of a small hollow filled with a birch grove. Over the years the road through the grove had been covered by grass. So they stopped at the edge of that little chasm and gazed at the low rises from which poplars jutted skyward like green-gray clubs. Glinting and gleaming somewhere among them was the great old manor of Milowidy.

Helena's heart began racing again. She felt that she had come back in her old age from a distant journey and was standing by the gate to her home—known to none, forgotten by all.

"It's a beautiful location," said Konstanty with a sigh. "Not like over at Bohin."

"Bohin's pretty too."

"What are you talking about?" He gestured bitterly with his whip, which came back dotted with dried burrs.

Then, to their surprise, a runabout came racing out from the bottom of the birch grove. They could see two men in it, one in uniform.

The runabout soon reached them and came to a stop by the carriage. It was Chief of Police Dzhugashvili, his jacket half undone, and Mr. Pushkin, wearing a low top hat whose gray had a reddish tint. Seeming somewhat taken aback at the sight of Helena, Pushkin was quick to doff his hat.

"And where would you be going?" asked Dzhugashvili—as usual, in Russian, even though he did speak fluent Polish after all those years.

"I'm going home," said Helena with forced cheer.

"Aren't you taking the long way around?"

"It's easy to lose your way in the woods."

"I think I know who you're looking for."

"And who might that be?"

"Could it be that pupil of yours?"

Helena felt the blood rush to her face, but her honor as a woman would not permit her to turn her head away. "I have more than one pupil. I have the authorities' kind permission to teach the younger and older children in our district."

As she regarded the gray, dusty-looking, and darkly pocked face of a Georgian in his middle years, his small, slightly slanted eyes glanced probingly at her. "I let the Jew from Bujwidze go, though I might regret it later on," he drawled with that odd Georgian accent of his. "Mr. Korsakov stood bail for him."

"Oh, I see," she said in confusion—and angered by that confusion.

Pushkin took off his hat again, as if wishing to air his curly, woolly hair. Helena noticed that one of the first glinting strands

left by gypsy moths, and typical of Indian summer, was stuck to
his hair.

"I travel and travel, but I don't seem to get anywhere," he said
with a pleasant smile.

"Will you be staying on here with us?" she asked politely.

"Maybe here, maybe a little farther on, but always in the
neighborhood, isn't that right, Grigory Alexandrovich?" said the
chief of police from behind him.

Pushkin placed his top hat over his heart and recited in a
melodious voice:

> *There's no tsarina fairer than a Polish maiden:*
> *Happy as a cat beside a stove,*
> *Pink as a rose, white as sour cream,*
> *with eyes that gleam like two candles.*

Dzhugashvili's narrow brow furrowed. "Is that Pushkin, Grigory Alexandrovich?"

"No, it's Mickiewicz, Vissarion Josephovich."

"Oh, that rebel. Just look what different kinds there can be
in one family. Mickiewicz's brother was a respectable, loyal man,
spent his whole life as professor at the university in Kazan or
Kharkov, I don't remember which, but the other one, the bastard,
the criminal, fled abroad and engaged in illegal activities."

"Vissarion Josephovich, you should watch your language, you
might offend Miss Helena," said Pushkin with a courteous bow.

The chief of police was about to click his horse on and had
even settled back into his beloved runabout, which had soft leather
upholstery conducive to long journeys, but then once again he
turned his unpleasant face to Helena. "And why is it you don't
speak Russian, my good woman?"

"I didn't attend school. My father taught me at home."

"It's high time you knew the official language."

"He's only joking," interjected Pushkin, whose face was now a permanent red. The delicate aroma of alcohol had been hanging in the cooling air for a while now.

"Yes, I let that Szyra go for the time being." The chief of police slapped the horse with the reins. "But I can assure you it won't be for long. My best regards to your father."

Pushkin was about to bow elegantly, in Petersburg fashion, but the runabout lurched and he had to grab hold of the metal railing. The runabout raced away into the woods with the guest from Petersburg, or rather from Wilno, waving his elegant top hat.

They waited a good few minutes, then Helena sighed. "Let's go back."

What sort of allusions was he making, she thought. And could I have given him cause for such undue familiarity? What do I care about any of it? I'm so tired. Christ God, I keep saying the same thing over and over. Thank God, the end of the world's coming. But enough of these foolish thoughts. Enough thinking. Sin is born in the mind.

She did not even notice when they drove into the allee leading to Bohin.

"The sun's going down," she said to herself.

"What did you say?" Konstanty turned around with alacrity.

"I said it's almost sunset."

"It's getting there. That other Russian has good manners."

"He's the son of Pushkin the poet."

"What would Pushkin's son be doing around here? He's probably just a rogue who goes from one manor to the other cheating people at cards."

Emilka was waiting for them in the front hall. Antoni Sieniuc stood in the kitchen door smoking a pipe. When he puffed at it, he revealed his metal tooth, a token of his worldliness.

"Mr. Plater was just here," whispered Emilka with emotion.

"What did he want?"

"What do you mean? He was looking for you. He said he was trying to catch up with you but couldn't find you."

"I visited Mother's grave," said Helena with embarrassment, and was about to walk away when Emilka suddenly took her by the sleeve of her dress. Helena looked at her, startled by this gesture.

"I'd say something, but I don't dare to."

"Go ahead, say it."

"You won't be angry at me?"

It was very still all around except for a woodpecker rapping at a hollow tree in the park.

"They say he's not inclined to women," whispered Emilka, scarlet with shame.

Helena froze in mid-step. "What's that supposed to mean?"

"It doesn't mean anything. You know what it means. He's always with that Ildefons of his, day and night, winter and summer, just like a wife."

"Shame on you! How can you say anything so outlandish! Those are all nothing but stories from immoral books. In real life people live the way God and nature ordain."

Emilka crossed herself quickly.

"God willing, it's as you say, ma'am." She threw a quick glance at Antoni Sieniuc, who was tapping his pipe against the door frame.

1 9

Something woke her just before daybreak. She lay for a long while listening to the pre-dawn stillness, the dull roar of the Wilia seeming to reach her in slow waves of sound. A bird was flying from tree to tree, issuing piercing cries. Then the clock struck what must have been four times, though once again she had failed to count them.

I'll get up and get dressed, she thought. Maybe I'll pray awhile or take a walk out to the highroad and back. Best of all, I'll do both at the same time. I'll say my prayers while I'm out walking.

She lit a candle whose reflection acquired a flickering aura in the window. Pouring water into her washbasin, she thought of the old woman concealed within the large coffin beside which Father Siemaszko had been praying. Why had he been kneeling before the catafalque of that old beggar woman he didn't know and who had come to him all the way from Molodeczno? He too had his own little secrets, and maybe they weren't so little either.

After washing in ice-cold water, which made her teeth chatter, she dressed quickly and put on a warm jacket. Then, carefully groping her way along the walls, she went out to the porch. Everything was white with dew and it looked as if the first timid snow had fallen during the night. To the left, the sky over the farm buildings had turned opalescent. The horizon was making way for the newborn sun.

Like a firefly, a little patch of light emerged and slowly, quiv-

eringly, approached the porch. Someone coughed an old man's terrible cough through a corneous larynx permanently clogged with
phlegm.

"Is that you, Konstanty?" she asked softly.

"It's me. Come here, I'll show you something."

"What?" she asked reluctantly.

"Come here and don't ask questions."

As she went down the steps, he began moving through the old
park toward the river. Every so often a bird would dart up from
the dew-whitened grass and fly silently away. The route took them
a very long time, though by day it could be covered in just a few
minutes.

Finally, Konstanty came to a stop, listening for a moment to
the mighty voice of the river. Then he raised the glass in his lantern
and put out the light.

"Just don't say anything, or else something could go wrong,"
he whispered. "Follow a little way behind me."

They went down through the wet grass and herbs almost to
the very bank of the Wilia. The old man squatted by a bush covered
with droplets that had a glassine shimmer. He gestured for Helena
to kneel beside him.

He pointed toward the river. "Do you see?" he asked in a
piercing tone.

Helena looked for a long time at that spectral river, which
could not be seen moving in the darkness and from which came
the sound of autumn wind mixed with the splash of water against
tree stumps on the shore.

"No. I don't see anything."

"Over there, a little to the left. In the middle of the river."

"But what is it?"

"What do you mean? You're young, your eyes are good—and
you can't see it?"

"There does seem to be something there. A tree in the water."

"That's no tree."

"What is it, then?"

Konstanty turned and whispered triumphantly, "It's Tsar Alexander and Napoleon."

"The Tsar and Napoleon?"

"Just look. They're sitting in a little boat facing each other and both of them are rowing. Each one's pulling in a different direction. And that's why they're not getting anywhere."

"Maybe it's a tree trunk that snagged on a stone under the water. Whatever falls into the river after a storm gets washed downstream."

"That's no tree," said Konstanty derisively. "They've been sailing back and forth from the Niemen to the Wilia for half a century now."

"But why right here? Why would they haunt people here?"

"That I don't know," said Konstanty. "We have to get back, it's not good to be around them in broad daylight. Curiosity's cost more than one man his life, and his soul."

Slowly, he withdrew from behind the bush and then, grabbing hold of other bushes, he clambered up the bank on tiptoe. Shivering from the cold, Helena followed behind him.

"So, now you've seen the Emperor, haven't you?" he asked in a louder voice when they were back up.

"There was something out there, but God only knows what it was."

"I've seen them a few times already. They appeared before the uprising, and when the plague came from the east, and before the eclipse of the sun."

It grew brighter as they returned through the meadow and the park. Day had broken. It's too late to go back to bed, she thought. I'll say my prayers on the porch.

But she was hindered in saying her prayers by the smell of pipe tobacco drifting out from the front hall. She rose and in the gray light of the lazy early morning she went to her father's door. Yes, that's where the strong smell of homegrown tobacco was coming from. Konstanty grew the tobacco somewhere out past the ponds, dried it on the sly in a hay barn, then kept the brown-green leaves in a box, layering them with pink flowers that had a strong, sweet aroma; finally he cut the tobacco into large plugs, which he shared with Michal Konwicki.

Her father wasn't able to sleep at night either. He'd wake at daybreak, as old people often do, then flog himself, say his prayers, and, still on an empty stomach, smoke the long-stemmed pipe that lay among the papers on his desk.

"God, can you hear me, God?" Michal Konwicki moaned softly in the fastness of his study. "People are oppressed, nature's in torment, even the trees are suffering. You have sent an Antichrist down on us. He has cut us up into four parts, divided us, driven us from our homeland. He throttles us every day, weighs us down, grinds us under. And no one's coming to our help. And it will stay like this for centuries. Because of our fathers' sins and our own. Because of the sins of our children and grandchildren."

Then, causing the floor to creak, he walked away, no doubt to his window now filled with the glow of the rising sun. Helena went back to the porch and sat down on the bench.

"I have to collect my thoughts," she whispered to herself. "Everything's in a tangle. It's been a terrible year, but it'll be ending soon. The Jews' year will. And maybe mine too. Maybe some change is coming. But what kind of change, and from where?"

The porch was warm now. A reddish sun was rising over the woods and beginning to warm the chilled earth. The dense bands of mist over the ponds were filtering into the old park.

Emilka was already busy in the kitchen, humming "When dawn's light rises" in a chesty voice. Someone spoke lazily to her and Emilka interrupted her devotional song to reply.

Helena began mentally reviewing the day's tasks. There were

a lot of them, exactly the same as yesterday's, and tomorrow's too. Why do I have trouble praying, she thought, why do I keep starting over, trying to understand those old words which other people recite without thinking about them? Why do horribly blasphemous doubts come creeping out of every corner of my mind day and night? Yes, sometimes people believe, sometimes they doubt. How else could it be?

Then suddenly Emilka raised her voice in the kitchen, bustling boisterously about. "Stop asking me questions! What do you care? What business is it of yours?"

Who are they talking about, thought Helena with a shudder. Probably about me. But why me? It's probably about one of the farm people. But if the shoe fits . . . Oh, what nonsense I think. Christ God, just let me start growing old.

She jumped up from the bench. Malwinka was approaching from the farm with a light and graceful step. Cows were lowing, already put to pasture.

"And what if I run away," she whispered to herself. "Pack up a few things and go to the station at Santoka; no, better to Bezdany, get on a train, and then it's through the forests and out to the world and real life. I've got a headache from lack of sleep. I'll walk to the woods, then come right back."

She ran down the porch steps and set off down the allee that led to the highroad. Reaching the road, she stopped in indecision. She was about to head for Bujwidze, but restrained herself.

"No, no," she muttered. "I won't go running after anyone. And why would I anyway? It's all idiotic."

She turned to the left and after a while took the left fork in the road, which led to Woloki. For a time she was in the open sunlight, which dried her chestnut hair and the hem of her dress, which was damp with dew. Suddenly something told her to look to the right. With no surprise but with a certain anger, she saw Elias Szyra lying on dry, silvery moss. His hands were behind his head and he was sucking on a piece of sweet grass. He did not change his position.

"What are you doing here?" she asked angrily.

Without rising from the ground, he said offhandedly, "Look at these trees and clouds and birds. It's a strange land."

"Why strange?"

"Because, at one time, millions of years ago, the South Pole was located here."

"You're raving again."

"No, I swear to God, it's true. The earth changes poles every so often. Probably out of boredom. I've seen the South Pole. Why don't you rest here beside me? You don't have to worry, the moss is dry."

"And where did you see the South Pole?"

"In Australia. I escaped from Paris to Hamburg. There I got a ship to America, to go see my parents. But after we put to sea, it turned out that we were the captain's prisoners and he was taking us all to Australia as forced settlers. I was in Australia a couple of years, waiting for a chance to escape. I prospected for gold and traveled as far as Tasmania. If you've got good eyesight, you can see the South Pole from there."

She knelt down beside him on the creaking moss. "And did you find a lot of gold?"

"Excuse me." He jumped up and took off his threadbare, old-fashioned coat and spread it on the ground for her. "Sit here, it'll be better, drier."

Hesitantly she touched the brown cloth that still held some of his warmth.

"Don't worry," he said softly. "It's Australian material but the coat was made by a Pole."

"What about the gold?"

"I didn't find much at all, just enough to pay for a return ticket. I absolutely had to come back here."

There was a long silence on her part. The entire forest had come to life. Birds were chattering everywhere and a breath of forest air had strayed out over the road.

"But your parents are in America," she said, even though she knew she shouldn't say a word.

"I had a present to bring you. A keepsake from that other world. A talisman to last you all the rest of your life."

He reached into his shirt and withdrew a leather pouch that resembled a scapular. From that pouch he shook onto the palm of his hand a small stone that looked like a May bug and shimmered iridescently as May bugs do.

"What's that?" asked Helena softly.

"It's an opal. A strange stone. They come from Australia. Please take it. I brought you this little stone from halfway around the world."

She shrank back from his extended hand holding the opal.

"Australia is the Noah's Ark of the future. The most beautiful place on earth. God created it so people could find a refuge from people. So good could find a refuge from evil, and virtue from sin. And eternal life from eternal death."

She was moving away, across the lining of his coat, on her knees while he, on his knees too, moved after her, extending the hand that held the mysterious, otherworldly stone.

"Why did you deceive me? Why did you pretend you were illiterate?"

"How else could I have gotten close to you?"

"Stop. Wait."

"But I love you. And that love was with me through all of Siberia and when I was going down the Volga, and when I was in Paris and at sea. And I loved you when I was down under in Australia digging for opals. I've loved you for so many years, you see. As I remembered you in your white dress with the rose-colored sash at the waist—or was it light blue?"

"I don't want that stone. It will bring me bad luck."

Her back was up against a bush of alder and now there was nowhere to run.

"It'll bring us good luck. We're fated for each other. It's God's will."

He grabbed her hands, two fluttering birds. "Or maybe it's the will of hell," he added in a whisper.

"What are you saying? That's blasphemy."

"No, it isn't. Today is the Day of Atonement. Didn't you know? During the night devils will grab sinful Jews and carry them off into an eternity of black, frozen death. Don't run away, my love. There's no running away for us. I have nowhere to run, and you must remain here with me."

As he spoke, he drew her closer to him. In a panic, she tried to tear her hands from his, push him away as far as could be, hurl him into the abyss of oblivion.

But then she felt his lips on hers. She began trembling as if having entered a darkness. What's happening? This is terrible. The last of her thoughts flailed in her fading consciousness. Oh, my head is reeling. The dew is so cold. The sky will burst with lightning any second now. She could feel his warm hands as he grappled with her skirts. He lingered there, quivering like aspic. He whispered something in a broken whisper, then returned to her lips, her eyes, her temples taut from the cold or from fear. Then, at last, it began, fearful, unexpectedly painful, yet at the same time wildly delightful. But before she was able to explore this new continent of pain and pleasure, he froze at the edge of a crimson sea, and for a very long time, perhaps all eternity, she was on her way back to that woods, that road, and that sky crossed quickly by fleecy clouds, their undersides lined in blue shadow.

"What have you done?"

"It had to be. It was fated," he whispered hoarsely, his lips close to hers.

I can hear the distant roar of the Wilia. I can see the birds flying south against the crimson of the setting sun. Mornings pass, days, evenings. On every side, a quagmire of banality. Banal events, banal responses; banal landscapes. Life slowed down. Life strained of impurities. Life, like a specimen dried for use under a microscope. And I am sinking into that quagmire of banality while leading my grandmother toward a finale of which I am still ignorant. But I must hurry, because my arteries are bursting, my head is bursting, my heart is bursting. With my last breath, I must bring my grandmother to that finale, that place from which we can see the darkness of the past behind us and the dazzling brightness of the future ahead.

2 0

They took a shortcut back along the forest's edge. The fields were empty of grain and had been partially plowed. The sky had expanded above the earth and seemed larger than usual. Thrifty squirrels darted among the trees stocking their larders with hazelnuts and acorns.

He took her by the hand. She tried to pull free but he wouldn't let go. Shame kept them both silent, but he was trying to make the best of the situation.

Storks were descending in slow circles in the direction of the river, soon to hold their first parliament before flying off to warmer lands. Helena suddenly recalled the local superstition—if a young woman sees a stork in a meadow, it means that she'll become pregnant soon. What has happened, she thought. What have I done? But she was in a state of sleepy bliss. I'll think about it later.

He walked alertly beside her. From time to time the sun would break through the thickening clouds and set his hair ablaze, and he would smile tenderly with uncharacteristic timidity.

"We still believe that the sun revolves around the earth. If that's what people thought for thousands of years, it must be so," she said with sudden gaiety, raising her head.

He bent down and picked up the prickly fruit of a chestnut whose gleaming brown seed casing was visible through a crack. He peeled the chestnut from its green hull and handed it to Helena.

She pressed the cold, dazzlingly smooth chestnut to her cheek, which was on fire.

"Give me your hand," he said softly.

She hesitated for a moment. Elias stood among ferns tall as trees and waited with his hand held out.

"But swear to me that we shall never see each other again." She placed her hand in his warm palm.

"Why shouldn't we see each other again?"

"We did a terrible thing. God won't forgive us, and neither will people."

He came to a stop, making her stop too. She could feel the heat emanating from him.

"Come on, this is the end of the nineteenth century. The whole world is out there just waiting for us."

"My world is here, and it ends here, on the other side of the Ruska Wilderness, by the shore of the Niemen."

There were wild cumin bushes as tall as palm trees on the fallow in front of them. Once again that strange sound arose from the depths of the earth or the sky. Yes, she thought, my world is coming to an end. My world, our world, is coming to an end again. She had another fit of shivers.

Then he pulled her close to him. She tried to thrust him away, but his dry lips kept kissing a lock of her hair that fluttered in the slight breeze. In fact, he was only touching his lips to her hair, flitting from one place to another like a butterfly. She rested her head against his chest for a moment, then he found her lips and they began a desperate kiss. A cold wing of shadow passed over them. Elias threw his coat on a patch of ground that smelled of summer savory, and they slid slowly down to that bed. She thought she could hear the sound of the church bell in Bujwidze carrying on the wind through the woods—yet another warning.

Then he began forcing his way through her skirts as if through thick branches of young pine. He whispered, requested, explained, but what she heard was the beating of two pulses, her own and his.

"No! No!" she cried in a whisper, and with unexpected strength struggled out from under him and dashed toward the fields. Her feet sank in the freshly turned soil, where crows were already pecking at seed; then she began heading for the woods, breaking into a run when she was in among the cold bushes, yellowing birch leaves, and high anthills.

He raced off in pursuit, certain she was running away forever or would meet with an accident in some forest ravine. She fled in silence and he was afraid to cry out to her. They zigzagged through the forest, sometimes in shadow, sometimes in a downpour of sunlight. Wind-swollen clouds, autumn clouds, clouds born on the shore of the Arctic Sea were racing faster and faster to the northeast in the sky above them.

Finally, she grew tired and stopped by an old pine. Clinging to its black bark, she tried to exhale the immense fatigue lodged in her lungs like dry, spiky pinecones.

Slowing his pace, he pressed his hand to his racing heart and walked slowly over to Helena. They could hear each other breathing now. Slowly, timidly, Elias began to smile.

"Don't be afraid," he whispered, gasping out the words. "I'm scared too. We jumped from an awfully high cliff."

She looked at his forever-blazing hair, his lean face, and that smile of his, which she knew quite well from somewhere but which she couldn't have known from anywhere.

"You know what, you know what?" she said, still short of breath. "For years I've been having a dream about a huge city with tall buildings, much taller than the ones in Wilno. The trains go under the ground in that city and they make everything shake, they rattle the windows. In the sky over the city, there are balloons with cabins shaped like omnibuses suspended beneath them. People lean out the windows of those cabins and wave white handkerchiefs at the people out strolling the streets of the city. Every dream seems like a continuation of the one before, even though nothing special ever happens in any of them. I'm not running away from anyone, no one's chasing me. No evil forces have cornered me, and there aren't any moments of sudden happiness either. I am just there in that marvelous, unusual city, which exists for me alone and which sends trains under the ground and bright balloons up into the air, all for me."

"I was gone so long. But you didn't change. Don't you remember me? Don't you remember that Jewish boy who ran with all of his might after your carriage? When his strength was gone, he fell on the heath by the road, trying to catch his breath, as we're doing right now."

"But I was older than you were," she said softly and with embarrassment. "I never paid any attention to adolescents like you."

"I ran behind you all the way to Krakow, maybe farther."

He looked at her for a moment, then finally lowered his gaze. Then, quite clumsily, her hands still shaking, she began stroking his hair.

"You're looking at me as if you're saying goodbye," he said softly.

Not replying, she continued to stroke his hair, and in that gesture there was despair.

"Come on, walk me to the allee. We'll say goodbye there," she said in a whisper, with a glance up at the sky. "Christ God, the sun's so low already. What will I tell them at home?"

"You'll have to lie. To lie for my sake."

They joined hands and walked back along the edge of the woods. I'm doing the same thing people have always done, she thought. Is this the law of nature, or our own laws of passion? In a minute I'll say goodbye to him forever. And I'll go back; but back to what? To my hermit's freedom, which is no freedom; to Mr. Alexander Broel-Plater, who has some horrible secret lurking in his past.

They walked through patches of tall huckleberry ruddy as the ponds at sunset. Helena had to lift her skirt a little. He tried to take her by the arms to carry her to the other side of the patches, but once again she tore free and went on ahead of him.

Now they could hear muffled sounds from the farm. Someone was sawing wood, flails were lashing in one of the barns, the blacksmith was hammering a horseshoe in the smithy behind a clump of willows. They came to a stop at the side of the highroad, not far from where it was joined by the allee at Bohin.

"Don't ever come back," she said in a whisper. "What's done is done. Now we have to go back to our lives. You to yours, me to mine."

"Let's see each other again. Even just once."

"Don't try to talk me into it. There's no need to see each other again. It'll be easier to part now. Later on it might be too late."

"Look at me. Didn't God create me to love you?"

She smiled sadly. "No, go. It's easier this way. You'll forget, and I'll forget too."

"But I wasn't able to forget all those years. You dreamed about a strange city that doesn't exist on earth. And I dreamed of you. I dreamed of you when I was asleep and when I was on the march, and when I was at sea, when I was awake and when I was delirious with fever."

"And now it's all come true. Goodbye."

"It can't be. Everything I did in life was because of you."

"Don't think badly of me. It has to be this way."

She began backing away, looking at him with darkening eyes. "We have to say goodbye."

"We don't have to. That would be too terrible. It's better that we just part like this. You stay by the road and I'll back away looking at you."

He was about to reach for her.

"Stop!" she cried in a whisper. "I'll pray for you."

"I don't want your prayers," he said in despair. "Let's run away to the world together. I'll make boots for a living—I learned how to make beautiful boots—and you'll bring up our children."

Her smile grew sadder and sadder as she withdrew into the cool dark of the allee. Behind her, by the ponds, was the old maple that had been cleft and felled by lightning, its frighteningly white interior scorched by the flames which the rain had extinguished.

"Farewell. I won't forget you either," she said quickly, then set off almost at a run toward the manor, feeling his gaze on her trembling shoulders. He remained at the end of the allee and stood there for a long while after she had disappeared onto the porch behind reddening vine leaves.

A large carriage stood off to one side, almost in front of the farm buildings. The driver was dozing against the cushioned seat, and as she ran desperately for the porch Helena thought she knew that old carriage from somewhere.

Back in her room, still out of breath, she changed her clothes to receive their guest. While changing, she glanced out the window at the aged park lashed by gusts of a wind that had shifted and was now coming out of the north and blowing over the river, which could not be seen from there.

As she began pulling off her skirt stained by the wet green moss and flecked with golden pine needles and reddish drops of resin, the glittering little stone fell from somewhere, probably her pocket, and rolled along the floor, flashing iridescently. Before Helena was able to bend down and stop it, it had rolled under the heavy chest of drawers. She didn't know what to do—look for that opal, which had been brought to her from the other end of the world, or finish dressing and go to receive her guest. Helpless, still trembling, shaken by spasms, she stood by the table with hairpins held in her teeth. I'll find it later, I'll have plenty of time for that, it's not going anywhere, she thought. That little May bug from Australia won't be going anywhere.

In the sitting room she found Korsakov on the settee alongside a woman who was overly rouged and heavily made up. There were glasses and a small carafe of a ruby-red liqueur on the table in front of them. Michal Konwicki sat stiffly in the armchair, drawing sweetish smoke from a large pipe. Korsakov was already quite flushed in the face, drops of sweat gleamed on his forehead creased with a network of lines, and he was breathing heavily, his lungs wheezing.

"Please excuse me," said Helena, "but we have a lot of work here on the weekdays. I apologize for being late."

Korsakov tried to rise in courtly fashion from the settee but couldn't find the strength and so only made a circular gesture with his hand while wheezing all the more.

"It's we who have to apologize, Miss Helena. We made so bold as to bring you flowers." He pointed to a wooden kneading trough which had been placed on a cracked sewing box; its black water contained a few dozen black roses.

Those are our roses, she thought. Mother planted them before I was born.

But what she said was: "What a surprise. I'm grateful for my neighbors' kindness, but my birthday was a while ago."

"Still, we didn't forget it. And while I'm here I'd like to apologize for my intrusion the other night. As I recall, I came by here in the night a few days ago. I don't remember anything, I had a fever at the time. Please forgive an old man if he did anything wrong."

Michal Konwicki cleared his throat and up went a few large puffs of smoke redolent of the pink flowers Konstanty used in drying tobacco.

"We were just chatting with your father, even though he's not much for talking. Oh, I'm sorry, I've done something wrong again. I've neglected to introduce my wife, Safona Platonovna. Darling, stand up and say hello to our hostess." He tried to rise and present his wife, but only faltered, wheezed, and remained on the comfortable settee. Seized by a fit of infectious giggles, Safona Platonovna covered her face with a handkerchief and bowed politely to Helena, while blushing and giggling all the more.

"My wife is from a good Belorussian family, but unfortunately she doesn't know any Polish, so I must ask you to excuse her. What I mean is, she understands everything but she feels awkward about speaking."

Then the clock on the wall opposite began striking. Everyone looked in its direction and even Safona Platonovna fell silent, her face still hidden in her lace handkerchief. I forgot to count the hour again, thought Helena. Every tick of that clock puts distance between us and everything we still can't forget. Does that man feel how funereal the sun is here, how mournful the wind? She glanced over at her guest, who, uninvited, was pouring some of their domestic liqueur into a tall glass.

"Autumn's come," said Helena, glancing out the window. Why am I constantly looking out the window? I never even used to notice the windows, though they were always there.

"Yes, God makes the seasons change," said Korsakov with a sigh, his wife giggling briefly again. Nudging her gently with his elbow, he whispered, "What are you giggling about, you fool?"

A long silence ensued. For no reason, Michal Konwicki stared at his gun, which he had hung on the wall that day. Someone was calling out to someone else a few rooms away. Flies mated indolently on the windows.

"It's so hard to speak from the heart," said Korsakov with a sigh. "A person has the feeling he's with his own people, but it still somehow doesn't feel right."

"Should I put on the samovar?" asked Helena, not knowing what to say.

"Your father already offered us tea, but why drink tea when a person has ambrosia like this in front of him? Miss Helena, I did come here on a bit of business as well."

Korsakov raised his glass, looked into it, collecting his thoughts, and burped delicately into his sleeve.

"I'll come right out with it. I'm a forthright person and I don't know how to beat around the bush. My wife and I don't have any children, we'll leave this world without any heirs. And so, with my wife's consent, I've decided to bequeath Milowidy back to the Konwickis after we die, and may God grant us an easy death."

He broke off, his bloodshot eyes glancing back and forth from Michal to Helena. Safona Platonovna was stifling an untimely giggle again.

"That's a very noble intention, neighbor," said Helena in a weary voice. "But after all, there's an imperial ruling encumbering the property."

All of a sudden Korsakov struck the table with such force that the glasses jumped and the carafe quaked. "I shed my blood in the Caucasus and in the war against Turkey. To this day those old wounds give me trouble." He began unbuttoning his coat, but then changed his mind. "Then there was emigration, that's bitter bread too."

He seemed suddenly to realize that his wartime service and emigration did not go well together.

"Yes, it's true, I adopted Russian ways, but I never renounced my religion. Father Siemaszko will tell you that. And I got him out of trouble too. He'd started playing with nationalism, as some people call it—with Belorussian nationalism—pretending to be collecting folk songs and dances. There was a little group of people interested in folklore. But we know these folklorists. What, are you laughing at what I'm saying, Miss Helena?"

"All I'm doing is just listening," said Helena quickly.

"All right then, keep listening. Because all you people think that Korsakov is this, Korsakov is that. But I was insulted by my own people here, stripped of my dignity, my honor trampled in the mud."

"When was that, how did that happen?" asked Helena to put a stop to Korsakov's confidences. "We never heard anything about it, isn't that so, Father?"

Michal Konwicki nodded and laid aside his pipe.

"You never heard about it?" asked Korsakov in a menacing tone of voice. "You've forgotten, because that's more convenient. I had to leave here and seek my fortune elsewhere. Foreigners—how can I put it—took me to their breast. Yes, I served the Tsar of Russia, it's true, and I don't deny it. But there's nothing in that anyone can hold against me. People plotted against me in Paris, and there was a citizens' court where General Mieroslawski presided. And what was its verdict?" All of a sudden Korsakov gave the finger to heaven, the sky, or perhaps just the ceiling. "That Korsakov is pure and honest. And they all had to admit it. I used to visit Prince Adam at home, and Prince Jerzy. Or maybe you don't believe that?"

"We believe it," said Helena, forcing the words.

"We have to get going, Eduard Adolfovich," interjected Safona Platonovna, covering her mouth with her handkerchief.

"Be quiet," said Korsakov in Russian, swaying on the settee. "I'm here on business. I'll give you Milowidy, and you can enjoy it until the end of the world. It doesn't matter to me. I'm here today, gone tomorrow. Something keeps driving me through this rotten, lousy—how can I put it—sinful vale of tears. I'm a sinner though I wanted to find something sacred, oh did I. My God, how

I wanted to be noble, and loved by people, and blessed by heaven."

Suddenly he grasped his head with both hands and rapped it against the tabletop. Clearly accustomed to such situations, his wife nimbly caught the carafe that was sent flying toward the floor.

"I helped so many people. My own and foreigners, patriots of every stripe, revolutionaries. I even helped those German Communists, you may have heard of them. I gave them money to publish news bulletins, even though they won't amount to anything and people will forget all about them. And I supported our uprising for ten months."

He regained control of himself, raised his head, and looked around the room. Just then the clock began striking the hour.

"That's strictly hush-hush," stammered Korsakov. "Not a word to anyone. There was something important I wanted to say. But all this got the better of me. I've never felt good here. This land hates me. I suffered terrible humiliation here when I was young. I could have become an artist, a bard, maybe even surpassed Mickiewicz himself, but I was ground under by people's malice, their contempt for one of their own. They're ready to kiss a foreigner's ass, you'll excuse my French, but they grind their own people into the dust."

Safona Platonovna slumped against the back of the settee, her face convulsed behind her handkerchief.

"You don't believe me?" Korsakov asked menacingly.

"We believe you," said Helena desperately.

"With your leave, we'll be going now, the horses are waiting. You can have your Milowidy, I'll go off with a sack and a stick. We don't have a home anymore, Safona Platonovna. Get up and follow me."

Korsakov managed to rise to his feet, which took him first toward the stove, then he turned in the middle of the room and began looking for the door. "Yes, brothers, I'm doomed to die an ignoble death."

Reeling across the room, he struck the door with his fist. The door flew open with a thud and Korsakov disappeared into the darkness of the front hall. Hampered by her long skirt, which made her take small steps, Safona Platonovna followed her husband out of the room.

When they were gone at last, Helena glanced up at the faded sky, where unfamiliar birds were flying south. She sighed. Her father nodded.

Later, in her room, she knelt in front of the chest of drawers and used a curling iron in an attempt to retrieve the little stone from distant Australia which, who knew, might really exist or might not. Finally, she located the stone and rolled it out with the curling iron onto the floor in front of her, where it glistened with all the colors of the sky just before sunset. She picked up the stone, the size of a hazelnut, and, without quite knowing why, suddenly kissed it with her hot, dry lips.

2 1

A tightness in her breast or some sound in the night awakened Helena. Her room was completely dark except for the little heart carved in the shutter glowing with the last of the moonlight. The wind careened around the old park, at times slamming against the house, rattling the shutters. Somewhere an iron bar rang with fury, as she lay listening to the irregular beating of her heart.

Then she heard a muffled, plaintive voice. Someone was speaking to someone else, in a persistent attempt at persuasion or in humble request. Now Helena recognized her father's voice.

Shivering from the cold, she groped her way to the door, opened it quietly, then stepped into the little corridor. Her father's study, which also served as his bedroom, was on the other side of a thin partition, built during a past remodeling. She hugged herself against the cold, her arms covered with gooseflesh as she waited by that wall of unplaned wood on which a coat of whitewash had been slapped.

But the house was quiet, and it was quiet right there too. I must have imagined it, she thought. It must have been the wind moaning in the attic or gusting through chinks in the wall. She was about to go back when she heard a throat being cleared, followed by a dry, piercing cough.

"Maria, send down my death." It was her father's muffled voice. "Intercede for me and ask that I be given a sudden and unexpected death. My life is over, I'm sitting on my luggage waiting for the hearse to come, and it's late again. It didn't come the year before last, or last year, and there's no sign of it this year either."

She had already raised her fist to strike the partition and interrupt her father's blasphemous prayer, but something held her back—a wicked curiosity, some foreboding. Michal Konwicki groaned again as if trying to rise from his knees but unable to.

"Maria, if you can hear me, if you're here in this house, if you've come to us from Milowidy, watch over our child, and keep her from sickness and sorrow, and from being too horribly lonely in this world which is as empty as a cemetery."

Floorboards creaked, a door banged, someone was running about in one of the rooms in the middle of the night. We're all alone now. Emilka's in another world, sleeping in back of the kitchen stove with Antoni Sieniuc at her side. Was that really my father's voice or just my own thoughts, still at sea from my waking up so suddenly? Is Father crying or were those my tearless sobs?

She pressed herself to the rough wall, whose planks seemed to be giving back the heat of the day. She listened intently for a long while, but no more sounds reached her from her father's study.

She returned to her room and was relieved to be back in her cool bed. There's a terrible sadness here, it hangs in the air like morning mist, she thought. Disappointed hopes, dead expectations, poisoned misgivings. Yes, ghosts and specters are only deathly reflections of our fears, our guilty conscience, our despair.

Now the air seemed thick, as if the heat of a bread oven were coming from the wall by her bed. She turned over on her other side and stared blankly into the darkness of the room. Love is nothing but trouble, she thought.

Later during the day, she chanced into the sitting room and saw Korsakov's roses in the kneading trough, forgotten, even disdained. They were lying scattered, their tops leaning against the edge of the trough. Drops of water still gleamed on a few of them.

They were so fresh, so beautiful, steeped in the blackness of the night, the mysterious blackness of the night.

She counted them; yes, there were thirty. Korsakov had a good memory. Mother planted them years ago. What did she think, and who was she thinking of, as she tended those fanciful flowers?

Hearing the clatter of wheels, Helena drew the curtain and looked out the window. Mr. Plater's cabriolet was coming down the allee. In a white linen duster covered with bits of freshly threshed grain, her father was on his way to greet their guest. She whirled around and ran breathlessly back to her room, where she untied her work apron made of coarse, undecorated cloth. Checking the mirror, she found that her hair needed fixing—the glistening strand woven by a gypsy moth which had somehow landed on her head looked like her first gray hair.

Then, despite herself, she shifted her gaze to the window. Someone was standing on the far side of the old park, out by the meadows and the river, and looking at their house. It must be the black trunk of an aspen killed by lightning, she thought. Yes, it's a tree; only for a second had it seemed to be a person. But just then that tree trunk shook slightly and moved like a person shifting weight from one foot to the other. Who could it be? Her heart began racing. I'm not myself at all. Once again that uncanny sound rose from the ground, vibrating through the house from foundation to attic. It's the poles shifting, like Szyra said. The old poles are refusing to serve the old earth. I discouraged all my suitors for so many years. I wanted to be free. I had a strong need to be self-reliant. I dreamed of living my own life.

Someone was definitely standing at the far end of the old park and looking at the manor house, which was sunken in heavy, clay-rich soil where practically nothing grew, and never easily. So, let him stand there. It's a tramp, a shepherd, or a spy.

She ran down the little corridor to the front hall, from where she could see her father standing on the porch with Plater, who was propping himself up on a thick walking stick.

"What happened?" Helena called out. "Did you hurt your leg again?"

"Good day," said the count with a strange seriousness, doffing his hat imported not from Wilno but from Warsaw itself. "Nothing's happened. It's just that it's fall now and the bone's acting up. The doctors say I'll be feeling the effects of the strain for a few years more."

"Sit down, please, and we'll set the table right away. Or would you prefer the sitting room, since you know it so well?" said Helena, springing into action.

"No, no thank you. Please don't put yourself to any trouble."

Michal Konwicki cleared his throat, in a tone somewhere between threat and helplessness. How good-looking the count is, thought Helena—but completely without emotion, as if commenting on something she'd noticed through a carriage window. Dark hair graying slightly at the temples, a high forehead lightly tanned, thick eyebrows, big dark eyes, and lips that weren't large but were conspicuous because of their indecent redness. And his expression, one of pouting anger and disdain for the world, never left his face, even when Plater was speaking almost tenderly to Miss Helena.

Emilka came out from the house carrying the samovar, whose firebed was puffing with passion, expelling ash the color of autumn snow through the grate.

"We'll make some lunch," cried Helena with feigned enthusiasm. "Everything'll be fine, she thought. Why shouldn't it? Our life is like everyone else's. Like everyone else's in this great, green, lush cemetery.

"Thank you again," said Plater. "But I've just stopped by for a moment. There's a little something I need to discuss with you. Mr. Konwicki, might I speak privately with your daughter?"

Michal Konwicki cleared his throat and nodded.

"In that case, let's go inside," said Helena with a sense of trouble to come.

"Or how about a walk through the park or the orchard?" suggested the count.

"Of course, of course," she agreed with unnatural fervor, and ran down the stairs ahead of him.

Malwinka was grazing on the overgrown lawn amid clusters of sorrel. Ildefons the rifleman was standing by the head of the horse hitched to the cabriolet and holding it by the reins, while taking an obvious yet cheerless interest in Malwinka. The huge trunk of the maple felled by lightning lay on the ground on the far side of the ponds.

Limping slightly and bracing himself on his cane made of some foreign wood, Count Plater caught up with Helena and took her by the arm with his free hand.

"Would you permit me this intimacy?" he asked.

She lowered her head, not knowing what to say. Once again her heart thumped chaotically against her rib cage. For a long while they walked in silence, each immersed in thought, until they reached the neglected orchard, whose trees had been carelessly whitewashed against infestation and on whose drying, weary branches apples moldered.

"Helena, my dear, everything's going swimmingly, and soon we'll have to set the wedding day," said Plater gravely.

"That's all I think about, Alexander," whispered Helena. "But I'm racked by doubt. I'm very fond of you, and I respect you. I've just gotten used to being alone all these years. My dear Alexander, I'm not sure whether we're not doing something foolish."

Suddenly he stopped, his grip on her arm detaining her. Slowly he raised her hand to his lips. Helena felt they were being watched by that intruder who had been standing stock-still for hours out past the orchard and the old park.

"I understand your concern," said the count softly. "And I

respect your doubts. But please trust in me. It's fated, if there is any such thing as fate."

They began walking again down a little path barely visible amid grasses that had turned gray and in some places were yellow. Apples brown with rot and coated with a white deposit lay all over the ground.

"I stopped by Bohin because I wanted to take the opportunity of asking a small favor of you."

Helena's heart began racing absurdly again, but she was quite calm as she said, "Go ahead. I'll certainly be happy to do it."

On trunks long stripped of their whitewash by rain grew huge and horrifying mushrooms, blue and pink, like the tumbling entrails of a dying animal.

Plater released Helena's hand in order to lean more of his weight on his cane. "It would be better, in many respects, for you to cease giving lessons," he said, not loudly but emphatically. "And I'm specifically referring to that Jew from Bujwidze who's always drifting around the district."

"Oh, I see," whispered Helena in confusion. "So that's it. He asked me to teach him the alphabet, and the rudiments of reading and writing, because he'd been promised a job in the Niemen assessor's office."

The count was observing her intently now, with eyes that Helena thought were without a modicum of benevolence.

"Still, I would be grateful if you'd stop. I'm also concerned about nasty gossip. And you believe him when he says he's illiterate?"

Helena could feel the blood rush to her face. She began plucking a bluebottle, oddly fresh in the withering grass.

"I believe he's literate in Yiddish. But why should he lie?" she asked, her voice trailing off.

"Still, I would be immeasurably grateful if I could ask that favor of you, if I still have rights in regard to you, my dear Helena."

"Oh, he's already stopped coming himself. I think his desire to study has passed."

"All the better. In that case, there's nothing to say. So, let's go back to the house."

Everything's getting more and more tangled, she thought, with Plater limping elegantly beside her. A time of confusion has come. It comes to everyone. But why did Mother have herself buried near Bohin? Did she have a premonition this would be our last home? Last before what?

She glanced at Plater out of the corner of her eye. He was walking along calmly with that slightly offended or rather haughty expression on his handsome, alien face. In the tangle of woods behind Plater, Helena kept catching glimpses of that drifter halted by the sight of human habitation.

After her guest departed, Helena set about various tasks but found she lacked the patience for any of them. Finally, she ran from the house and took the shortcut past the farm buildings, heading for the dirt road that ran by the river, an alternate route to Woloki. At the very beginning of that sandy, winding road, near the wooden cross that supposedly memorialized the epidemic that had struck at the end of the fifties—but which was really a monument to the uprising—was the smithy, ringing like all smithies with the echoes of a hammer striking an anvil.

When Helena entered the small dark building, the blacksmith stopped working and looked questioningly at her.

"Antoni," she said casually, "I'd like a word with you."

They went out and stood by the side of the road in front of the smithy. The wind was tinged with the smell of seared steel. A horse due to be shod was hitched to a pine post. Sparrows were waiting in the bushes in hopes of manure.

Antoni Sieniuc smiled to mask his confusion. The gleam of his front tooth capped in metal somehow lent him a touch of dignity, urbanity. Helena now noticed that Sieniuc was missing two fingers on his left hand. He might have lost them during the uprising, she thought, but it's more likely he got his hand caught in the chaff cutter.

"Antoni, you used to work for Mr. Plater in Woloki, didn't you?" she asked with seeming indifference.

"Yes, in the smithy there."

"And how was it there?"

"All right. Like anywhere else. The work's always the same."

He regarded her intently out of the corner of his eye, while using his foot to dig an old, rust-eaten horseshoe out of the sand.

"Then why did you come to work for us, Antoni?"

He burst out laughing, his lordly tooth flashing again. A few strands of yellow hair were stuck to his high forehead. Christ God, she thought, his face is so red it's almost black. How can I even question him? And is it worth it anyway?

"You know the answer to that, ma'am. I want to marry Emilka if you and your father will allow it."

"And why shouldn't we?"

"I don't know about any of that, I just like to do things right," said Sieniuc, kicking the old horseshoe aside with the toe of his boot.

"You don't have to worry, we'll take good care of you. But what's this Emilka's been saying about Mr. Plater?"

"When was that?"

"The night after the storm."

Antoni Sieniuc deliberated for a long while, looking off to one side toward the wormwood tall as trees in the orchard.

Finally, he spoke: "I'm not going to say anything about it, ma'am, because it's none of my business. But word is that the count has to get married now. If he doesn't marry before he turns forty-one, his estate will go to the Order of St. John of God in Wilno."

"Oh, that's just idle talk," retorted Helena, bridling, her ear cocked for his reply.

"I don't know anything, and I'm not saying anything." Antoni Sieniuc began rolling a cigarette, sprinkling tobacco from a battered leather pouch onto a scrap of paper that was not particularly clean. "But people do say that's what the count's father put in his will. If he doesn't marry, he'll lose everything, and he'll only have Bohin left to live on."

"Oh, what do I care about all that?" said Helena nonchalantly. "I wanted to ask you something, Antoni, but now I've forgotten completely what it was. Why don't you stop by the house this evening?"

Still, she didn't walk away. The hammer in the smithy would ring out after long intervals of silence. Why am I asking all these questions, he can see well enough what I've come here about. It's all so wearisome. Oh, I'd love to fall asleep, sleep and never wake again. Christ God, what utter nonsense. She was about to cross herself, but Sieniuc was standing in front of her patiently waiting.

"The old countess has probably passed away in the madhouse by now," said Antoni. "The count wrote his will like that to fix her wagon."

"And why was that?"

"So she couldn't keep her son tied to her apron strings his whole life."

She rubbed her eyes wearily. "What do you think, Antoni— am I doing the right thing in marrying Mr. Plater?"

He began kicking the sand again. "I don't know anything, and I'm not saying anything. But someone more suitable might turn up yet."

Helena suddenly burst out laughing and for a moment had a desire to whack the blacksmith on his stooped back. "We shall see," she said merrily.

She started back to the house at a quick pace, which slowed as she passed the farm buildings; her merriment gradually deserted her at the same time.

"You have to look before you leap," she said softly to herself. "Why does everyone dislike him? That's not true. It's not everyone. It's the servants who dislike him."

Her pace kept slackening as she walked through a tall stand of grasses called Our Lady's Tears because the clusters of gray-green seeds which hung from the slender blades resembled copious and heartfelt tears.

"Animals don't seem to like him either," she said to herself. "I still have time. I can even run from the altar."

A light shudder ran up her spine again. A small spasm of the fear of the unknown. An instant of sudden dread for her future, dark and obscure.

She stopped at one side of the orchard. The same dark and slender silhouette was still visible out past the park, though it had now shifted position a little. It must be a Gypsy, she thought. I'll have to send one of the farmhands out to chase him away.

But she didn't send a farmhand out to chase the Gypsy away, she only went back to her room and sat on the bed so heavily that the dilapidated old damask canopy, stained by leaks from the ceiling, began to sway back and forth.

"It's getting hot again," she said almost aloud.

She changed into a light dress in front of the mirror. One of these days something has to be done about those trees, she thought. And, first thing, a fence has to be built. Anyone can just walk right in, even that Schicklgruber who burns people.

Then she ran back to the sitting room where the flowers were still drowsing in the trough. She selected one rose that was almost pure black and stuck it in her hair above one ear. It's an evil flower was what flashed through her mind. Christ God, I'm tempting fate. So what, let things fall as they must.

2 2

He stood by an old, half-rotted chestnut tree, playing with a gleaming brown chestnut. She immediately spotted the reddish-purple welt on his left cheek. It curved around the cheekbone and ran past his ear to his neck, like a long leech swollen with blood. He was standing by the tree rubbing the chestnut on the palm of his hand, an uncertain smile on his face.

"What are you doing here? Are you out of your mind!" she said angrily.

"Yes, I must be out of my mind," he said half aloud, a somewhat foolish smile reappearing on his face.

"I told you never to come back here again. What happened, happened. But it's the parting of the ways for us."

"God, are you beautiful," he said softly but with immense conviction.

Momentarily confused, she began walking down the faint path through the freshly mowed meadow—the last mowing of the year. He started timidly after her. Both of them walking slowly, they entered a vast lake of aroma—fall hay mingled with herbs of every kind at the peak of their ripeness, unknown grasses that had been scythed down, mysterious grasses that had hidden from human sight all summer.

"You must leave this part of the country," said Helena. "There must be somewhere you can go. The job in the assessor's office was just part of the comedy you were playing. And your parents are waiting for you in America. They could probably use their son's help. You're so uncaring."

She didn't even notice when he took her by the arm, by the wrist, as if wishing to check her pulse.

"Why aren't you answering?" she asked.

"I'm listening to your voice. At least I can get my fill of that."

"I've done a terrible thing," she said with a sigh of despair. "How could I have allowed it?"

They walked in silence a moment. The sound of the river went right through them.

"It's already the new year," said Elias, "the new year for us Jews."

"What do I care? Let go of my hand. And what happened to your face?" she asked, coming to a halt.

He stopped right beside her, so close that her breasts were just touching him. "Count Plater treated me to a thrashing."

"Christ God, I knew it right off. Why did he strike you?"

"You know why," he said softly.

"Do I? And how could he know anything?"

"The priest read the banns on Sunday."

"Oh, it's all such a tangle." Almost at a run, she headed toward the river, which flowed calmly past a low cliff. Wild-berry bushes and a branching bird-cherry tree clung desperately to the clay face of the cliff.

She sat on a black log that had been there for years, too heavy to tempt the peasants. It was the trunk of an oak tree that had fallen into the river thousands of years ago, possibly nudged by a glacier from the forest into the river, where it petrified and remained until floodwaters brought it to that sandy shore sparsely marked with razor-sharp blades of gray grass.

"Let's go to America together," he said, sitting beside her.

"You must be running a fever. I can hear your pulse." She laughed without laughter. "Now what are you going on about?"

"We're fated for each other," he said quietly. "Look how far I traveled to come back here. I even stopped in Greece on the way."

"Why are you always telling me these stories? I'm no little provincial goose, you know. And you probably don't know, how could you, that after the uprising I didn't go out of the house for a year. We were still living at Milowidy. I wanted to understand myself and the world around me. For twelve months I never left the house, never went anywhere, not even to the woods or to the river. I read every day until late at night. I read every book I could find, all the special annual editions of the local magazines, everything one could have sent here from Wilno or Kowno. You've done a lot of reading too, if you can read—travel books."

"I really was in Greece on the way back here. I located Colonel Borowy, who's now a general in Greece. I even enlisted in his corps of engineers, they were building fortresses. But he kept telling me again and again—go back home; you, at least, go home; Poland will rise out of slavery, and maybe the country's just waiting for all its far-flung sons to come back, you're young and you can be useful there around the Wilia and the Niemen, maybe I'll slip back in too when I get the signal."

He looked directly ahead at the opposite shore, dark green as the sopping moss in the marshes, and at the sky, pale violet but darkening at the zenith, where yellowish clouds moved leisurely east. And some of that violet glow would be in the water whenever the heavy autumn sun suddenly flared.

"Why are you telling me all that? Nothing can change anything now. It's too late for that."

He put his arm around her. On the verge of tearing free, she decided that this would give her away. She obeyed herself, and him. She began to tremble slightly. I've got a fever too, she thought. Again, a whiteness lashed her eyes, as if colorless lightning had flashed overhead. I might be dying, she thought quickly and with fear. Maybe it's better that way.

Reaching over her shoulder, his thin, entirely un-Jewish hand touched her breast, scalding her through calico and silk. With sudden ferocity she tried to tear free.

"Wait, I want to smell that rose. But it has no smell. Why does such a beautiful flower have no smell?"

Desperately, Helena wrenched herself back. They fell to the warm sand and the sharp grass that rustled softly.

"Let go!" she shouted, blindly pounding her fists on that head surrounded by cold fire, that forehead which bore faded traces of freckles. "Get out of here or I'll call a plowman or a mower with a scythe. Get away from me, get out of here, you Jew!"

But it was too late. She saw his forehead engorged with blood and seeming to pulse with an accelerated rhythm, his irises rimmed in gun-metal gray, and a broad stretch of sky where the clouds had come to a sudden halt. I'm falling, she thought. I'm falling into hell.

Her head was pounding and she had trouble breathing the air that smelled of river water and fresh river vegetation. He was speaking to her again, perhaps reassuring her, and himself; then suddenly she felt that it had started, he was inside her, and she was seized by a gust of joy, and for a moment she marveled at the joy; she began to be overwhelmed by pleasure, and she rose higher and higher in that cloud of pleasure; but suddenly he wrenched himself away from her, as if wanting to tear free of her arms, and she came to a stop right beneath the zenith of the violet sky, frozen there for a long time by the painful pleasure which was suspended unfulfilled somewhere above her. He was pressing his face into the warm hollow between her neck and collarbone, breathing very heavily, as if he had used the last of his strength to climb the highest mountain in the world.

They lay beside each other for a very long time, lulled by the river's dispassionate whisper. Then he began slowly arousing her again. She felt his lips on her neck, forehead, eyes, and finally her lips. Once or twice he tried to say something. Through the purple lining of her closed eyes, she could see him part his lips, then close them again with tender resignation. He made his way under her skirt and she could feel him trembling as he sought the same route he had taken before.

"No," she said without opening her eyes, herself surprised by this nonsensical resolution. "No. Just lie by me."

She was taken aback that he obeyed. She didn't open her eyes, but she could see that he was also lying on his back and looking up at the sky. Knowing he felt it too, she could feel the resilient, crunchy grass that domestic animals would not eat and which the forest animals avoid, grass that had once been a tree or which might be a tree on Judgment Day.

"You said that the South Pole was once located here," she said out of nowhere, her voice entirely natural.

Assured by her tone, he moved toward her a little. "I think that the Garden of Eden the Bible tells about was located here. When Adam and Eve were expelled from Paradise, they walked alongside this river until they reached the Niemen, which flowed south, no, then it was north. That's why the Wilia is so winding— because Adam and Eve were dodging God and themselves. They were so sad to leave, but finally they understood that they had to leave, so that they could return one day."

"How do you know all that? Is that what they teach in the talmudic schools?"

"I've read a lot too, but I read what nobody else wanted to read."

"Are there books like that?"

"No. But there are places like that in every book."

Her eyes still closed, she reached out for his head. Her fingertips found a few damp strands of hair, hair like cold fire. He's tired too, she thought. Our failed love's made him tired too. He sensed what she was thinking and brought his lips to her ear and a lock of her chestnut hair.

"The rose has no smell," he said with reproach.

"They did when my mother grew them."

"I'll take it to remember you by, and to punish myself with."

She smiled without opening her eyes. The sun must be descending toward the woods for a better look at these sinners lying by a river whose shores had been walked by the first people on earth.

"Do you have the stone I brought you from the next world?"

She said nothing for a moment. "I lost it."

"That's impossible."

Then she suddenly opened her eyes and sat up, brushing grains of sand from her cheeks. "But don't you see that anything is possible?"

And, after her long absence from it, the world seemed strangely pure, renewed.

"And now what?" he asked.

"Nothing," she said. "Let's try for a parting of the ways again."

"That's impossible now."

She stood up but at once reeled as if losing her balance at the edge of an abyss. He steadied her with a strong hand.

"Anything's possible," she repeated.

She began climbing up the bank, which was not very steep. Everything had a touch of early autumn about it. The bushes were thinning, the grass was bent to the ground, and strange flowers with strange colors could be seen through breaks in a greenness already tinged with rust red, flowers that must have bloomed for just those few hours and would be gone by evening, when the farmhands went to water their horses at the river.

"It's too bad there was never anything special about this river," said Elias, looking around him. "Or maybe it has a secret cave where new life is waiting to live."

She came to a sudden halt. "Stop. Wait."

She walked over to him, surprised by her own tone of voice. He thought she wanted him to embrace her and opened his arms, but what she did was to thrust her hand inside his coat, freezing in that position and looking him straight in the eye. "What's that?" she asked.

"Nothing," he said confusedly.

He did not interfere as she tugged out the gleaming revolver. She weighed it in her palm, then placed it back deep inside his tattered old coat.

"Who are you?" she asked softly.

"A Jew boy from Bujwidze."

She turned away without a word and began walking toward the old park, which stood motionless before them, blocking the horizon.

Then, apparently having regained her self-possession, Helena stopped. "Listen, Tadeusz. Is that the name you'd really have wanted?"

He nodded.

"Listen, you Tadeusz who strayed here from God knows where. I'll say goodbye to you here, and I'll go my way and you'll go yours."

He looked at her for a long time, his face surprisingly grave.

"Helena, we should go our ways together. We've got our own America right here. We have friends everywhere, in the woods, by the lakes, in the marshes. You'll be Helena to them and I'll be Tadeusz. And that'll be that."

"No, you came here too late."

"I couldn't any earlier."

She hesitated for a moment. Wild birds, looking like mysteriously hooded people on a secret mission, flew south across the dusky sky that itself seemed the waters of a calm sea.

"My time's passed now," she whispered. "I was different once. Now I'm old."

"What are you talking about?" He was about to walk over to her and take her hands, but she withdrew a few steps toward the dark edge of the desolate park.

"Goodbye. And thank you for this senseless adventure," she said softly.

"But that's impossible. It can't end like this."

"My darling, my darling," she said, as if both surprised and delighted to be saying those words, "maybe this is the best way it could end."

A slanting ray of sunlight made his hair blaze like a torch.

"I'll shoot myself."

She smiled with sudden tenderness. "I have to go back now. Everyone's looking at us. The sky, the earth, and the people in the fields, in the barns, and on the highroads that lead out to the world."

"Wait."

But she had already turned and was running toward the house as fast as her legs would carry her. He started after her, but without conviction, and remained in the meadow amid haystacks, the intoxicating aroma of herbs and perhaps of lovage; he remained there with despair in his heart, which had turned to stone.

Helena stopped at a safe distance and stood looking in his direction for a long time. Since the sun was behind her, he couldn't see her face, but he could feel that something terrible was happening there in the deep evening shadow. On the farm a dog began barking, as if trying to break free of its chain. Then she raised her hand, perhaps with the intention of waving a farewell or sending a last kiss, but her hand halted indecisively at her hairline, concealing her face for a long while, until she finally had removed the rose from her hair. She placed the rose on the ground, then with an air of determination ran off toward the park and the house.

Nearing the house, she slowed her pace. The single larch tree, ready for a winter's sleep, rose, like smoke from a straw fire, above the roof overgrown with garishly green moss. Love is just a brief happiness, she thought. That's not it, what am I talking about? Something terrible happened. I'm sick, I must be sick, worn out.

Her father was standing on the porch, holding his shotgun by the barrel. She couldn't tell if he was cleaning the weapon or had just brought it out of his study. He looked at Helena insistently, expectantly.

She hesitated for a moment, then, without a word, walked off into the darkness of the front hall. She thought she heard her father's hoarse voice say her name, but she did not turn around and disappeared down the little corridor.

She stood in front of her window, by her bed with its moldering canopy, and looked at the park again, but there was no one there among the old trees now. Life goes as slowly as a peasant's wagon on a sandy road, then all of a sudden it's charging along at breakneck speed. She sighed and began sleepily unbuttoning her dress.

Emilka appeared in the doorway. "Can I bring you some dinner? I kept it warm in the oven."

"No. No need to."

"But you have to eat something. You've got to take care of yourself no matter what."

Helena turned lazily toward the cook. "You know what, Emilka, bring the washtub to the little alcove and fill it with warm water. I want to wash, I want to wash everything off."

"But what about dinner?"

"You know what, you know what—I must be ill."

"Then why take a bath? You'll catch a cold, and then what?"

"Pour me a bath and call me when it's ready."

She sat at the edge of the bed, the tattered canopy fluttering like a night moth. Emilka left the room, closing the door quietly as in a hospital. A moment later she was back in the kitchen singing in Belorussian accompanied by clanging pails and splashing water. The lightning has flashed, but it hasn't struck yet. Christ God, how long do I have to wait for the lightning to strike?

She went right to bed after her bath. She fell asleep but then started awake, as if she'd been shaken by someone. It's my heart, she thought. I'm heartsick, she thought, smiling inwardly to herself, yet surprised by that inopportune smile.

Later on, probably after nightfall, she was awakened by the terrible scream of a person who has seen the devil. She sat up in bed, pressing her nightshirt to her chest, where her heart was racing violently. It was her father, her father was screaming in the night again. But it wasn't her father. That terrible scream was repeated in the depths of the woods and was answered from elsewhere by a similar cry. It's the cries of deer, she thought. They're starting early this year. Or maybe it's Schicklgruber crying out to God for death.

2 3

I too am sick. I'm exploding with dark thoughts, dark premonitions, dark fears. But that's not true. I'm not afraid, because even the worst is not the worst if it's over quickly, like a momentary lapse of memory, one that lasts for ever and all time.

My life is a mirror—I touch its cool surface and cannot fathom what it is in there. Is this me speaking, or am I mouthing the words of someone long dead?

We live alongside the dead and the as yet unborn, none of us seeing the other. My grandmother Helena Konwicka stood by the window in her nightshirt and looked out at the old park, my grandmother who's been gone such a long time now, or is yet to exist. At that second my grandmother was standing by the window and looking out at the old park.

I am bleary now and this is my last voyage in literature, a senseless trip without fixed destination. My head is bursting, and my heart too may be coming apart at the seams. And I don't know how to reach my grandmother and immerse myself in that long-forgotten commonality of life, when there were few people and many gods, or when there will be many people and no god.

My grandmother Helena stands in her nightshirt by the window, shivers from some fever, licks her parched lips. It's the punishment for my sins, she thinks, to console herself. At night she would wander through a city with terribly tall buildings where huge balloons sailed past, their cabins packed with passengers. I'm sick, she says to herself. And probably a good thing that I am. Did I really do all that? All what? Have those terrible meetings with the young Jew from Bujwidze. Nobody around here ever heard of a noblewoman meeting with a Jew. What a strange word, Jew. There's always a little moment of fear before saying that word.

There was a knock at her door. Emilka had learned to knock now that Helena was sick.

"Mr. Pushkin's here," she said with an odd smile.

"Oh, but I can't receive him. I'm ill."

"He knows, but he insists. He says he'll just say goodbye from the door."

"No, no. How do I look?" She cast a glance at the mirror covered with the dark traces of some mirror pox. "I'm so pale, my lips look like paper, and my hair's not done. Ask his pardon, Emilka."

"He wants to tell you something. Just from the door."

Helplessly, she fell back on the bed and pulled up the covers and the bedspread decorated with the faces of wild animals.

"All right then. I'm feeling so poorly, Emilka."

Grigory Alexandrovich stood timidly in the doorway, looking as his father would have, had he lived a few years more.

"I apologize for the intrusion," he said in Polish with a murderous accent. "But I wanted to see you before I left."

"You're leaving? For good? You didn't find a place here?"

"I'll be back. I'll come back and die here. Near that city Tsar Nicholas hated so much."

"But why forsake your country to live among strangers?"

"My father had a great love for the Poles. Maybe that's why he lashed out at them. He was jealous in his love, and loving in his jealousy."

Helena tried to find a cool spot for her head on the pillow. "How can anyone be jealous of us?" she said with a sigh.

"I didn't inherit my father's talent," said Grigory Alexandrovich, turning his gray traveling hat back and forth in one hand. "But I think you people will accept me."

"I'm terribly ill, you see. Just three days ago I was healthy as can be, never a sick day in my life."

"Miss Helena, I have the impression that we've met somewhere before."

"Oh, you're very nice. I feel so hot."

"I'll be going. I'm driving right to Santoka, where the Petersburg express is making a special stop for me. But I had to see you once more and tell you that the first time I saw you—oh, words fail me, my beautiful Miss Helena. I'll be back soon and then I'll tell you everything I wanted to say."

"Please do come back," whispered Helena. "But I don't know if you'll find me here."

"What are you talking about?" He took a step forward. "Why are you saying such things? It's just a fall cold. It'll pass in a day or two."

"Yes, it's just a fall cold. I'll drink tea with raspberry syrup, I'll keep my legs warm, and I'll be out of bed in a day or two. But up and around for what?"

"Everything will be fine."

"Oh, maybe it will. Sit down for a minute on the chair before you start your journey. That's the Russian custom."

"Yes, that's our custom," he said, and sat down at the edge of the chair and immediately stood back up. "Goodbye, Yelena Mikhailovna, forgive me for addressing you as if you were Russian, but it gives me pleasure."

"Goodbye, Grigory Alexandrovich."

He bowed Russian-style, almost sweeping the floor with his hat, then disappeared into the darkness of the little corridor.

"Everyone's saying goodbye to me," she whispered to herself. "No, it's not everybody, just that poor man who inherited a burden of ambiguous fame from his father."

She lay facing the wall and closed her eyes. But immediately she thought she saw small flies hovering ponderously before her eyes, which she then opened. The sight of the lichen-speckled wall brought her some relief. The clock in the next room struck the hour and this time she scrupulously counted all eleven strokes. Christ God, how many more hours until morning? Suddenly feeling suffocated, she tossed off the bedding and the spread. But she didn't have any pain, nothing was bothering her. No sore throat, no wheezing lungs. Just fever. I'm being purified and cleansed of sin and filth by this fever.

With great effort, she raised her head a couple of times to look out the window. But the park was empty, only the ragged shadows of clouds ran eastward through the trees.

"And what if I die and go to the hereafter with that shame still on me?" she suddenly whispered to herself.

She felt even hotter now, unable to catch her breath. She jumped out of bed and ran into the corridor, but came back to her senses when she heard her father's voice as he prayed or talked to himself on the other side of the partition.

"We've all sinned, Maria, you sinned too, and may God forgive you, because there's no other hope for us. Providence will not raise us out of the muck of slavery. Our nation is on the way to ruin. I sinned and you sinned, Maria, and our child is sinning too. Maria, intercede for us as you intercede for yourself."

Helena was overcome by another wave of panic. She ran back to her room and began calling Emilka.

Emilka came at once with Sieniuc, who was holding a sieve in both hands.

"Tell Konstanty to hitch the horses and go for the priest."

"What are you talking about? What do we need the priest for?"

"Do as I say. I want to make my confession."

"You're still young. It's shameful to act so crazy. It'll all pass, everything will be all right. You've got your whole life ahead of you."

"Go and tell Konstanty. Christ God, I can't breathe."

She raced to the window and tried to open it, forgetting that it didn't open. Gasping, she fell back on her bed gulping air like an asthmatic. After exchanging glances, Emilka and Antoni quietly left the room. A few minutes later Helena heard wheels clatter by the porch. It was Konstanty stopping, as he always did, to inform the squire where he was going.

She kept tossing and turning. The pillow and covers were hot all over. This isn't our home, she thought, and that's why nothing ever goes right here. The harvests are poor, the cattle die, the wind's unhealthy. And on top of everything, this calamity. Suddenly she saw him right at her bedside, bending forward slightly with a timid smile, the revolver swelling the left side of his coat. His hair was not bright in that dark room, which was crisscrossed timidly by the faint shadows of the trees in the old park. Why do you keep coming after me? Why do you torment me? But he did not ask for anything and did not even extend his hand, whose thin fingers she still remembered from their first meeting, when, with sudden, shocking audacity, he had touched her hand. She drank in his face greedily. But maybe I do remember him from the past. I must have met him a long time ago or in some other life, if there's any such thing.

"Leave. I look terrible, my hair's all snarled and I don't have the strength to comb it," she said in the darkness that had begun seeping swiftly into the room as low, heavy clouds approached outside the window. "Leave, and stay away, if you can, if I can. But you've gone now. You took a look at me and you tiptoed out of the room. I wasn't dressed at all properly." Christ God, I can feel the sweat on my forehead and I'm cold.

Then Sieniuc came into the room, grumbling loudly as he carried a great armful of resinous wood to the tile stove.

"Where'd he disappear to?" asked Helena.

"Who?"

"Him. My lover."

Antoni Sieniuc rose from the stove and took a long look at Helena, blinking his eyes. Even his metal tooth seemed to have lost its luster.

"There was no one here," he said, looking through his pockets for a match.

It cost Helena an effort to raise herself on the bed and study her room for a moment.

"You're right. Who could have been in here? But why are you lighting the stove, Antoni?"

"Emilka told me to. The air in the house is damp, that's what gave you the fever."

"It's so close in here."

"You have to sweat the fever out."

"It's disgusting to sweat on purpose." She fell back on her pillow and closed her eyes. Outside, the wind raced along the wall, rattling the window glass softly.

The resinous kindling crackled into flame. Antoni closed the little stove door and listened to the mounting roar inside. All the logs were on fire now.

"Old Mr. Plater used to sleep on that bed," he said, then squinted out the window at the park, which a north wind had brought to life.

"Why did he sleep here and not at Woloki?" asked Helena without opening her eyes.

"He used to run away from that woman, I mean his wife. He used to stay at Bohin for months at a time."

Helena said nothing, and so he said nothing for a while too.

"He was a good person." Sieniuc began speaking again. "An honest man. The son takes after the mother."

"He slept in my bed? I'm sleeping in his bed? I never knew

him. He was always either on the way to the train station at Bezdany or on the way back. You say he was a good person, Antoni?"

"I don't want to say anything, but all the young ladies in the district were wild about him."

Helena smiled, without opening her eyes. "I remember, it's like a dream. He wasn't as good-looking as his son."

"But he was a man, and what does a man care about looks?"

"You're right, what does a man care."

"I'll come back in the late afternoon and fire the stove back up."

"Where's my father?"

"He went down to the river with his gun."

"To the river?" she asked, with a sudden constriction of her heart.

"That's right. Maybe he's hunting for birds. But your father doesn't shoot much. God forbid he shoots a bison when he finally does fire his gun."

"The stove's on, but I'm cold."

"It's the fever, ma'am. You have to rest."

"Yes, I'll rest. But for what? Go, Antoni, I'll try to fall asleep."

Sieniuc wiped his hands on his pants and began tiptoeing toward the door. Helena watched him go. When his hand was on the latch, she suddenly asked, "Alexander Broel-Plater took part in the uprising, didn't he? He had his own unit in the district?"

Sieniuc turned around and said indistinctly, "I don't want to say anything, but how could he have taken part in any uprising? He'd be off hunting for days and days, but he tried to make people think he was the military commander here."

"And he found my Piotrus," whispered Helena.

"It was his pointers that found him. They were out after foxes and they found him."

"Piotrus looked terrible."

"Better not talk about it."

He went out, closing the door softly behind him. I haven't been sick for a very long time, she thought. When was the last time I was in bed with a fever? Must have been just after Piotrus died. But did he ever really exist? I might have invented him to justify being a widow in mourning all these years.

All of a sudden Father Siemaszko was leaning over her. She could see his wire-framed glasses, the slanted eyes, the bristle of hair, the low, creased forehead.

"Are you feeling bad, child?" he asked, wheezing deeply.

"Not good."

"Do you want to confess?"

"Yes, I have to be purified of sin."

He put on a short surplice and tossed a violet stole around his neck. With a terrible sigh he sat down at the foot of the bed. She was about to rise, to make her confession in a sitting position at least, but he took her by the arm.

"Just lie there. The sins weigh the same whether you're kneeling or lying in bed."

The poor man, he has to listen to so many terrible secrets. He helps people cross the abyss, though he stays on this side. But maybe it's all a hallucination. Is this my room in Bohin? Who's that coughing in the corner? No, that's just the pine logs crackling in the stove.

With the tips of his thick fingers, the last of the wax from his hives still under his nails, he made a small sign of the cross over her. She crossed herself uncertainly, finding it difficult to swallow, for she was overcome by shame and fear, and now she regretted her decision. But he had covered his homely face with the palm of his hand and was waiting for her to begin.

She began speaking slowly, falteringly, not finding the words, waiting for him to react with an angry gesture, an impatient tone of voice. But he continued to sit motionless, his hand over his face, like a pensive Christ in a folk sculpture carved out of oak from the bottom of the Wilia. He looked asleep, or far away in thought, perhaps even as far away as Molodeczno.

When she had finished, he continued to sit without moving for quite a long while; then, his hand still over his face, the priest said softly, "Your penance is ten Hail Marys in the evening. Do you understand, child?"

Without looking at Helena, he granted her absolution and gave her the end of his stole to kiss. Then he walked over to the window, where he stood a long while watching the trees slowly submerge into the darkness of the night.

"What do you think?" he said. "Which alphabet would be better for the Belorussians? Latin or Cyrillic?"

"I'm sorry, Father, I don't know. I never thought about it."

He walked slowly back to her. Removing his stole, he kissed the cross embroidered in the center, then began carefully folding it up.

"You're right. What am I asking you for? Centuries ago they used Cyrillic. So maybe Cyrillic's better. But, you see, child, later on the Belorussians took part in the Renaissance, and so they're not Asiatics, they're real Europeans. And they have great Latin poets, and they have Skoryna. Even though he got involved with the heretics, Skoryna still made contributions to Poland, and Belorussia, and even to Russia. Are you listening to me?"

"Yes, but my head's reeling. Did I make a good confession?"

"You did, you did, but what's wrong with my memory?" whispered the priest in shame. He took his viaticum from the table and walked over to the sick woman's bed to give her Communion.

"What am I doing?" she whispered to herself, using her tongue to free the wafer that had stuck to the roof of her mouth. "Am I really parting ways with life? No, I wanted to be free of the burden that I will carry forever."

She opened her eyes and looked into those of Father Siemaszko, who was leaning toward her. Those were not the kindly, slightly

Tatar eyes of the good-natured country priest who claps his breviary shut and runs off to his beehives. She was being regarded intently and without sympathy by the eyes of another person, one who had also known suffering. That beggar woman of his who came all the way here from Belorussian Holyszy hasn't turned to dust yet, thought Helena. That beggar woman can still rise up and come here to frighten us. But we're the ones who frighten ourselves.

"If I die . . ." she said all of a sudden.

"What's that? You're not dying, you'll be suffering along with the rest of us for a while yet."

"I don't know. I have no possessions to dispose of. I don't have a last will. Is that good or bad?"

"Turn to the wall and go to sleep. You'll get well again. I'll dance at your wedding yet."

Embarrassed by his dubious choice of words, the old priest briskly removed his surplice, rolled it into a ball, and stuck it under his arm.

"I feel better now," she said.

"That's good," he whispered, avoiding her eyes. "It's always a great relief to be reconciled with God."

And what about your own faith, she wanted to ask, has it returned, or are you still hopelessly waiting for it to come back while you go on baptizing children and burying the dead? But instead she said in a soft voice, "I keep blacking out and coming to. Will God be satisfied with my confession?"

He touched her cheek with the rough palm of his hand and sighed deeply. Emilka came in and lit the lamp. The light hurt Helena's eyes and she closed them. She thought she could hear a distant music, but it was probably just the wind blowing leaves through the empty park. Dying would be good, she thought. To die, to rest for a long time. But maybe it would be better to live awhile longer and see what happens in this world whose end has been predicted for so many centuries now. The world's scarcely born and already it's under threat of death.

She suddenly opened her eyes and saw the small shining stone on the floor. Elias's opal. It shimmered with rays of pale green, like the glowing embers of a fire made from a rotted willow log. Someone threw it on the floor. Maybe it was me. It'll get stepped on and ground into sand. I'll go and pick it up.

She tried to lift her head but it immediately fell back down, as if the illness weighing on her weighed a hundred pounds. It's going to be a long and terrible night. Nights are endless when you're sick.

At some point later on, she saw Korsakov standing by her bed wearing a light overcoat with a velvet collar, pressing his black hat to his chest. His gray hair was tousled, sparse patches pointing in all directions. I'm dreaming this, she thought. But the dream is as clear as if I were awake.

"You shouldn't think it's my conscience that keeps me always on the move," he said almost in a whisper. It was only then that she noticed that he was missing quite a few teeth.

"Where's Safona Platonovna?" she asked.

"Let's leave Safona Platonovna out of this. She doesn't understand any of it. She doesn't understand the country I've brought her to. Do you think I can't sleep and that's why I go from one house to the other waking people up in the middle of the night?"

"I don't think anything. I'm sick. I'm running a fever."

"And what about me?" he said in an ear-splitting tone. "I'm running a fever too. I've had it since the war with Turkey. I was lying there with the dead. A good priest found me, he heard me groaning. I caught his attention because I was groaning in Polish. You see—how can I put it—my native language saved me from death."

"Is it night yet?"

"What do you mean? It's still evening. The ghosts won't be out for quite a while. But wait." He fiddled with the watch he'd withdrawn from his vest pocket. "My watch's stopped. A bad sign."

She closed her eyes, their lids heavy now.

"I'm leaving here. You'll never see me again," said Korsakov, flaring up. "I apologize, I mustn't impose. *Aura-voir.*"

But instead of leaving he pulled over a chair and sank into it. She wanted to open her eyes but could not find the strength.

"What was it I wanted to say?" grumbled Korsakov, sounding far away. "It's all just frippery. You have to look reality in the eye. I'm through playing the buffoon."

But it was a bad and bothersome dream, she thought. Or maybe Korsakov had really come there. He'd grown very old and was becoming more eccentric all the time.

She felt a cold, wet palm on her hand.

"Wake up, don't go to sleep," he whispered. "You shouldn't sleep when you're sick. Death can only get you when you can't see it. If you're awake when it comes, it'll see your open eyes and turn right into an old woman or a dog with its tail between its legs. I've got a long way to go, it's time for me to get going."

She raised her eyelids and looked at him for a moment. Maybe my death just turned into Korsakov and now he doesn't know how to leave the room and wait in the hall till it's time. She glanced at the floor. The opal was shining like a large firefly.

"It's all nothing but—how to put it—a fantasy. Our fate is to merge with the Russian sea. To stop offering resistance and seek to survive as part of the great Russian people. I was the first to realize that. When I was on military campaigns in the Caucasus, Central Asia, and on the shores of the Black Sea, I saw it as clear as clear can be. It's resistance, opposition, revolts that are bringing us to ruin. Destroying our language, culture, our whole nation. We have to survive within Russia, there's no surviving outside it. In the belly of the whale, not under its nose. We have to join hands and take that new path. That's the only way. I've dedicated my life to that. I want to save you people. I'm redeeming your sins."

She wanted to speak, but could do no more than make her lips move. He rose from his chair and stood leaning against one of the canopy posts. His faded eyes were bulging in their sockets, there was a yellowish foam at the corners of his mouth. Holding his crumpled hat in his extended hand, he began speaking in the direction of the window, as if playing to a theater, but the dark glass contained only his reflection and a bit of the lamplight.

Then she must have fallen asleep, because when she woke again, Emilka was breaking up the glowing firebrands with a poker.

"Is that you, Emilka?" she asked.

"It's me, sure is." Emilka laughed.

"You sleep near here, right?"

Emilka said nothing for a moment.

"That's right, sleep is what I do. Antoni's not allowed to stay with me. I'm not the kind to allow it right off. After the wedding, that's a different story."

"After the wedding," repeated Helena. "What's wrong with me?"

"You caught cold. And you've been worried lately. It's everything together."

"Just before twilight I thought I was dying."

Emilka laughed merrily. "It's not that easy to die. When a person wants to, he can't, but as soon as he's got the fear of death in him, death's on the way."

"Was the priest here or did I only imagine it?"

"He was here. Sure was. Then he went off to the village to visit a sick man."

"How about Korsakov?"

"He spent a little while here. Your father ran the length of the house to get away from him. But then Korsakov left."

"We're all alone now."

"Autumn's always like that. It's a sad time of year. I can hear the wind howling in the chimney."

"No, that's people singing. They're out walking in the night and singing to give themselves courage, even though they're out of tune. But why does that Schicklgruber murder people?"

"He says people failed the test. Anyway, that was one student's idea."

"Which student?"

"Some student. Or maybe he wasn't a student."

"Then why did you say he was?"

"Did I say anything, ma'am? It's all the same to me. Just so long as things are good."

"Just so long as things are good," repeated Helena in a whisper.

2 4

Every step an effort, Helena went out to the porch. She put both arms around a cracked column and looked for a long time at the little world of Bohin, unable to recognize it. She felt she was seeing it through a piece of tinted glass from a broken bottle. At one time that was a game children liked to play—to look at the world through a lens of cracked glass. Now the roads and paths lay in an altered perspective, and the trees and bushes were bare. Only the wild hops had been flourishing in the meantime, yellow threads stitching the park, the orchard, and even the allee of lindens. Yes, while she'd been sick, the world had turned yellow, and was stained blood red in places, black in others. Even the larch had turned scarlet, as if someone had sprinkled it with berry juice.

"How many days was it," she asked herself, descending the steps carefully, her hands extended like a blind man's. "I'm so weak. And maybe it's a good thing I am. But the knot inside me didn't go away while I was sick."

She raised her head. There was a thin layer of cirrus clouds in the sky. But where's Maciej the stork, she thought. His nest was empty, black, lifeless. It's a pity Maciej's gone. Everyone's leaving here. We're the only ones who have to stay.

Then she sensed that someone was behind her. She turned around with her hands still extended and seeking support. Michal Konwicki was leaning on his shotgun and observing his daughter.

She was about to walk over to him, but then, for the first time in years, he began moving his lips and, having finally opened them, seemed on the verge of saying something of importance.

It cost Helena an effort to start toward him across the stone driveway. She thought that he would reach out to her, catch her on the move, and help her back to the porch. But all he did was open and close his lips, unable to break his silence.

"What is it, Father? What happened? What do you want to say?"

Michal Konwicki groaned like an old harmonium, then finally wheezed out, "He's never to set foot here again."

She came to a stop in front of the stairs.

"Did you ever love me, Father?"

"I'm warning you, and him."

She felt dizzy. The gilded world around her, changed beyond recognition during her illness, and the sky mildewed with cirrus clouds were reeling and swaying while blacksmith hammers pounded at her temples. Am I like my father or my mother? From whom did I get my chestnut hair and reclusive nature?

"That's all you have to say to me after all these years?" she asked.

Suddenly she noticed that his mustache was trembling desperately, as if he were trying to keep his teeth from chattering.

"He must never set foot here again."

Struggling to keep her balance, she started up the steps. "Papa, what's been going on inside you all these years?"

Her father began shrinking from her as if she were a ghost. "Remember what I said, Daughter. And tell it to him."

She caught hold of one of the porch's columns and felt a splinter prick the palm of her hand. I'm healthy again, she thought. I can feel ordinary, everyday pain again. And now she was seized by a sudden fear of the life that lay ahead of her, that life which might have its origins in heaven, or in hell.

"Why didn't you ever tell me about my mother? I don't know my own mother."

Her father had withdrawn to the doorway. He lowered the barrel of his gun, his elbow pressing the butt to his side.

"It would be very bad. Our line would die out."

Helena thought she could hear the weary earth sounding again. I must be the only one who hears it, was the thought that flashed through her mind, which felt both desolate and too vast. The fever's burned everything out of me. She felt a sudden pain in her heart, a pain that was real or imagined on the spot.

"But what if I love him?"

Her father stared at the sunken planks of the porch floor for a moment, then, looking her in the eye, said softly, "It'd be better for you, and for him, if you hated him."

Helena took a few steps toward her father, but he withdrew into the darkness of the front hall.

"Father, don't you see what my life's like? Do you ever think about me like other fathers do about their daughters?"

Her lungs wheezed badly as she filled them with air. Deep within the house the clock struck yet another hour.

"Everyone's dead. And we're not alive either. It's fate. The will of heaven."

"I'm still alive. Do you hear me, Father? I've come back to life even though I had one foot in the grave. I want to live my little moment my own way."

Her father raised the barrel of his gun. "Look." He broke the shotgun open. "I have a cartridge here that's been blessed against evil powers. Even the devil can't do anything about it."

He closed the gun, then seemed to tiptoe away into the house, as if trying not to wake anyone.

"I'll sit out here in the air," she said to herself. "I'm so tired. I'm always talking about being tired. I must think my salvation's in being tired."

She looked over at the haggard bushes by the porch, the black nettles, the last of the fall flowers. She was trying to collect her thoughts, which were diffuse, still scattered from the fever's delirium. Suddenly she saw that head of red hair and was about to scream, but it was only a gleam of the autumn sun flashing through clouds and red vine leaves.

"Is he that strong or am I that weak?" she whispered.

She went down the porch steps again and automatically began heading through the old park. She kept stopping by the trees and putting her arms around their dark trunks, as if they were old friends. Pressing her ear to the damp bark, she heard only the sound of her own heart. Garlands of dried wild hops hung everywhere. I'm dizzy, she thought. It's the fresh air. I stayed in bed too long. The world didn't wait for me. It went its own way. I'll just take a quick look at the river.

She walked through the meadow, a russet red now and almost devoid of life.

"I was sick an awfully long time," she said. "And the sickness hasn't passed yet either."

For no apparent reason she burst out laughing. Small red animals were scampering inside a large fallen tree whose roots reached, like hands, up to the sky. Those were little foxes left all alone in their nest without their mother to protect them. Instead of hiding in the deep hole under the uprooted tree, they had stopped in front of their home and, with great curiosity and childlike carelessness, were observing Helena walk by. She waved to them with sudden gaiety. Why am I laughing, she thought. I have no reason to laugh. Maybe that's why I'm laughing.

She stopped by the bank of the river. The wild hops were lush there as well. Where were they before? Why didn't I notice them earlier? Now they were even growing in the wild currant bushes. Down below, the Wilia flowed patiently west or, rather, northwest, for the river was very sinuous in those parts, forming intricate loops, as if in memory of the indecision and despair of those first human beings leaving Paradise.

Using bushes for handgrips, Helena went down almost to the edge of the water. Where was their place? It had been washed away by rain, covered over by wind. The razor-sharp grass had turned yellow and was dying, the sand was darker now. That must have been the bush where a spider had spun a silvery web glistening with drops of moisture.

She felt weak again and barely had the strength to lower herself onto the black stump of a river oak. She looked at the shimmering water that reflected the violet of the sky behind cirrus clouds fine as lace.

"Love is nothing but trouble," she said softly, and was about to repeat that short phrase, but shame prevented her.

She caught sight of something floating close to shore. It looked like just another tree stump or a gray log that had broken free from a raft. The even current turned it slowly end over end. Then one end snagged on some riverside bushes or loose clods. It struggled against this obstacle for a moment; then, suddenly free, it floated on.

But it wasn't a log. It was an empty boat, of the sort used by the local fishermen or to take people across the river in those places where no ferries ran. There were no oars in the boat and only a little water had seeped in.

Turning a full circle, the boat went past Helena, then unexpectedly began heading for shore, where it was snared by a black tree stump whose wet tentacles spread over the water riddled with eddies. If it gets free and keeps going, everything will be all right, thought Helena. If the boat floats away, it'll mean a new page has been turned in my life.

Now she began to peer with all her might at the boat, which

was planting its prow submissively into that tangle of roots. Inwardly she began urging it on to action, to boldness, until finally she was cursing it.

The boat was motionless now. Every so often its stern glanced against the shore and it seemed about to prevail and tear its prow free, but a moment later the boat would return to the position in which it had ended that journey of indeterminate length.

Later on, Helena ran into Konstanty in front of the house. His hands spread wide, the old man was carrying a piece of wire from which dazzlingly yellow tobacco leaves hung.

"There's an empty boat on the river," said Helena.

"It must have been tied up with rotted rope."

"I don't know, but it was strange. It stopped right in front of our part of the river and it's still there."

"The current'll take it." Konstanty started on his way.

"I waited a long time, but the current didn't take it."

He walked away without replying and Helena noticed that the old maple that had been felled by lightning wasn't there anymore, only large bone-white pieces of burned wood scattered among the crumpled bushes.

"I'll go to my room and lie down," she said to herself.

She entered the front hall reluctantly and looked about the dark interior with equal reluctance. Then she caught sight of the stairs in the right-hand corner. I've never been in the attic, she thought. I've lived here ten years and I've never been up there once. I was always afraid of this house, which was never really ours.

She started abruptly up the narrow, creaking stairs until she reached a huge space that was divided by white chimneys and crisscrossed with black beams from which hung long-forgotten herbs and moldering lengths of cord, the remnants of someone's clothing or of half-considered suicides.

The old dust tickled Helena's nose and she sneezed into the

sleeve of her dress. Her feet shuffled through a thick layer of maple leaves that had been spread over the attic's clay floor. She noticed a trunk under the slanting roof. Beside the trunk were demijohns encased in disintegrating wicker. Of different colors, dark blue, green, sky-blue, and silver, the demijohns were made of frosted glass. The liquids they had contained had long since evaporated and the bottles themselves were covered with dust, the dust of old attics, all the attics of the world.

She opened the lid of the trunk and saw plates of glass, open cardboard boxes containing powder, sheets of paper with a shimmering surface. It must be old Mr. Plater's, she thought. He's the only one around here who'd take up a modern invention like photography. But he didn't take any pictures of anyone or anything. He started but he didn't finish. She sneezed again, this time from the sharp smell of the chemicals, which still retained some of their potency.

She let go of the lid, which, as it fell, raised a large cloud of dust particles that rose all the way to the roof and then began slowly floating down to the leaf-covered floor.

Now she noticed a window at the far end of the attic. A small square window whose black frame had never been painted. She walked over to it carefully, and pushing the moldy festoons of cobwebs from the window, she looked out the thick glass at the world and the day. She could see the allee down below, the woods like a swirling carpet, the sky now clouding over. And she thought she could hear the distant sound of the church bell in Bujwidze. She held her breath, trying to catch amid those faint echoes of life the infrequent, protracted sound of the bell's tongue striking.

Hearing the rustle of careful footsteps behind her, she turned around with lightning speed and felt so weak that she had to lean against the rough planks of the roof. Without opening her eyes, she said softly, "Leave fast or my father will kill you."

"That's impossible. I'm immortal."

She opened her eyes. Yes, there he was, bent forward, as if in an uncompleted bow, his hair burning with a cold fire. He showed young, healthy teeth as he smiled that smile of his.

"Christ God, how did you get in here?"

"I can leap over mountains, swim the seas, and walk through walls. Were you very sick? Was it over me?"

"Why should it be over you? I was due to fall ill, I hadn't been ill for a very long time."

"I came here to heal you."

"I know how to heal myself. I know spells against toothache. And I've cured hemorrhages a few times."

He took a few steps closer. "I missed you terribly," he said.

"You musn't come here." She turned her head away. "It's over and done with. I'll forget, you forget too."

"But we can leave here and see what happens next."

"What can happen? Love dies like everything else."

Suddenly he put his arms around her. She tried to free herself but did not have the strength.

"What are you doing?"

"Nothing bad. I just wanted to hug you."

"No, no, I'm still sick," she said, aware of heat and a clamor mounting within her.

"Wait, I just wanted to see you, that's all. To kiss your eyes, ears, breasts."

"No, no, you mustn't," she whispered desperately. I'm so exhausted, so wrought up, so on edge. But the edge of what, she thought in a panic.

"You're trembling."

"I'm still sick, this is my first day out of bed."

But he wasn't listening. She could feel the terrible heat of his lips on her eyebrows and her lips. He was already unbuttoning the top of her dress, his red-hot hands slipping under the cool material. She wanted to burst into tears and go running away—if only in thought, to tear free and fly as high as she could, lose herself in the icy sky—to avoid what was now making its inevitable approach, frightening and frighteningly delightful, what had been within her for so long waiting to be set free, desiring to explode and slowly expire in thrilling crimson, and which now had suddenly arrived and so stunned her that she forgot everything, even he who, startled, held her rigid body bent back in his arms, frozen in a soundless cry, a cry ending in a long and almost painful sigh.

Then she grew limp in his arms and he pressed her to him with all his strength, shaken by her muteness, her unconsciousness. She lay like that for a long time in his arms, then very slowly opened her eyes, glancing through half-shut lids at his face, finally bringing her lips to his cheek, where very lightly but very tenderly she kissed the traces of freckles by his ear.

"What happened to you?" he asked, still shaken.

"It was nothing. I felt faint," she whispered, not in the least distressed.

"You're so beautiful."

"Are you out of your mind?"

"No. Look, the last ray of sunlight's on you, the sun won't come out again this fall."

"I can't see myself."

"Look in my eyes."

"Yes, I can see myself in the pupils of your eyes."

"We have to escape from here before winter."

"I have to stay here."

"Stay here for what?"

"I don't know. But I must stay."

"You have to break those old restraints. Enough is enough."

"You can say that because you've got no ties."

"Then I'll take you by force. Where were you a minute ago?"

"Where was I? I can't tell you. But I do thank you."

"Thank me for what?"

"This has to be goodbye. All this can't end well."

"Why don't you ever call me by name?"

"Farewell, Tadeusz. Farewell once again. And, for the last time, farewell."

"I'll stay here and haunt you like a ghost."

"It's all such a tangle, I don't know myself what the future holds."

"I can't leave here alone."

She kissed him lightly on the lips. "Go out the same way you came in."

"And then what?"

"Nothing. The end. The final period. The story's over."

"I'll never give up."

"I'm not listening, I'm not listening," she called quietly as she ran shuffling across the leaves to the stairs.

It came to her on the porch.

"Christ God, he's still up there. Maybe for good."

She felt like crying and laughing at the same time. Looking anxiously about, she straightened her hair and buttoned her dress. Then she caught sight of Konstanty over by the ponds with a grappling hook in his hands. She was worried that he had spotted her confusion and disarray, but he was occupied with thoughts of his own.

"The boat belongs to that Roosky, Korsakov," he said. "He was crossing the river in a hurry during the night. People think he drowned."

"Oh, he'll turn up," said Helena distractedly. "He always turns up."

"Everyone's time comes sooner or later."

But she had already run into the house. Taking refuge in her room, she sat between two canopy posts and listened to the sounds of the house. Emilka was singing in the kitchen; a ventilation window had been left open in one room and was rattling; from time to time the floor or walls creaked, as they will in old wooden houses.

"He disappeared," she whispered with relief and regret. "He appeared like a spirit, a redheaded spirit, and he disappeared like one too."

2 5

A huge bank of black clouds had closed off the sky for the winter.
Actually, it had closed off the earth, protecting it against evil forces
for the half year when blizzards blow in from the north and ice
approaches with a crunching tread from the east. The bank of black
clouds closed from the northwest like a cast-iron lid and clicked
shut on the bare top of the solitary larch. An icy wind raced ahead
of those clouds, pressing the tall grass and bushes to the ground,
bending the trees low. There was a roaring and a rumbling in the
woods. An enemy army is rolling past Bohin, thought Helena. A
foreign army going west or returning to the east. An army of ghosts.
An army of the recent and the not so recent dead.

She looked out the window behind her father, who was eating
pancakes for breakfast. He'd roll them up and dip them in sauce.
The time for the hard work of threshing and winnowing had come.
The plowing was done. Michal Konwicki had shifted from summer
to winter fare. Every so often he would raise his eyes and contem-
plate his daughter for a moment, and at those times, she would
shift her gaze to him. He could not bear her gaze and would deliberately lower his lids. I'll tell him now, she thought. One more
minute and I'll tell him everything. Through the window she could
see wild hops, wild sorrel, and a wild pear tree growing by the
barn. Life's returned to the wild. A paradise that's gone back to
the wild, gone to seed, never to return here again.

"Father," she said, breaking the silence.

He raised his head, his hair gray, his face lean, his nose aquiline, and regarded her with clear eyes.

"Father, I'm pregnant," said Helena.

Michal Konwicki tried to swallow the mouthful that was in his throat but without success.

"I want to have the child."

The clock began chiming, as usual striking the hour at the worst possible moment. It was always silent when you wanted to know the time, and when you didn't, it would strike insistently, endlessly.

"I don't have anyone to give me advice. I'm alone and you're alone. Mama certainly wouldn't have allowed any interference with my pregnancy. I must have the child."

Michal Konwicki lowered his head and spent a long while chewing a piece of pancake. Then he raised his head, gave his daughter a fleeting glimpse as if wishing to conceal his feelings, then lowered his head again and sat without moving. Helena couldn't wait for it all to be over. He must be crying, it flashed through her mind. But that's impossible. He's never cried. Except for Mama. Probably only for Mama.

Michal Konwicki finished eating, wiped his mustache, crossed himself, and stood. He hesitated for a moment as if wishing to say something, but went off to his study without a word.

"Thank God that's over," whispered Helena. "Now I'll finally be able to sleep. Maybe the child will bring us together."

She was about to clear the dishes when she heard a clamor of hoofbeats. She ran to the window. Yes, it was her father on horseback, galloping down the empty allee where the wind swirled clouds of yellow leaves. Askew on his gray horse, his shotgun bouncing on his back, Michal Konwicki turned to the right, where the allee met the highroad. Christ God, thought Helena, he's going to Bujwidze. But that probably doesn't mean anything. He's galloped to town on his charger a thousand times.

But her hands had begun to tremble. She pressed her forehead to the cold window glass. Malwinka was running as fast as her thin legs could carry her after the master's horse. Konstanty emerged with an unlit pipe in his hand. His mouth opened as he looked to where Michal Konwicki had just disappeared.

"It doesn't concern me anymore," said Helena to herself. "It was fated. Who used to say that? He was always saying that. He was here, then he was gone. No, he's waiting up in the attic. He's up there with the webs that'd been woven between the chimneys when they were cool in summer."

Starting to clear the table again, she suddenly set the dishes down and ran to the stairway in the front hall. Panting for breath, she clambered up the creaking steps and with an anxious heart leaned into that dark opening.

But there was no one in the attic. A wind was butting the gable wall, and angry drafts were lashing the inside of the roof. There was no life in the attic except for the penitent souls of the old house's former inhabitants, who hid in that ice-cold darkness. Maybe he vanished back into the mist he came out of in late summer, she thought. Maybe he's disappeared back into the obscurity from which he first emerged at the beginning of the harvest.

She had a desire to walk over to the trunk full of chemicals but decided against it.

"It's not important. Nothing's important now," she said to herself. If only I knew why Father went flying off to Bujwidze. He probably won't do anything crazy. Dear Mother, who looks down on us from heaven, don't let anything bad happen to us.

Suddenly she crossed herself, but only because she had forgotten to do so when rising from the table. All the folly's been burned out of Father, if he ever had any in him. Why did Mama die so young and why does Father pray to her every day? Maybe I'll die young too. No, I won't die young, because I'm not young anymore.

She went back downstairs to look for the wool shawl which must have been her mother's at one time. Passing the open door of the kitchen, she encountered Emilka's watchful gaze. She has her own life too. She's older than I. And no one knows anything about her life before she came here. Maybe I'll go into the kitchen and sit by the stove; the logs are crackling. I'll tell her everything, make a clean breast of it.

But she didn't go into the kitchen. Wrapped in the wool shawl, she ran through the park toward the river. But it was sad and empty there too. The Uzla's white water blurred the dark, swollen river, where eddies kept forming and fading. On the other shore, the tall woods took a blow from the wind on their reddish chest, bending, but with dignity, sighing piercingly.

Then she thought she heard distant gunfire. But she could not identify its location because of the icy wind blowing from all sides and the great, ubiquitous roar that always accompanies every change of season in that land.

"What's on the other side of the river?" she said, using her shoulder to shield herself from the wind. I've never been there. Probably just more woods, marshes, enchanted groves, and sparse settlements. Where was Korsakov going in such a hurry? Maybe he was running away, maybe he was seeking salvation. But nobody was chasing him, no one wanted to take his life. What do I care.

With an abrupt drop in her spirits, Helena headed back for the house. Was he that strong or was I that weak? And what was he like? I never really took a good look at him. Christ God, why did it turn out like this? Why do I think about him day and night? It's the disease of solitude. Crippling isolation. People always looked at me as if I were touched. I wanted to be free where there was no freedom. I wanted to be myself, though I never knew who I was.

Back in her room, she began looking for the opal, which she had not picked up from the floor when she was sick. The opal had gleamed anemically from the floor like a fading star. But now she couldn't find it. It had faded and died. But when she was on her bed resting her head on the pillow, she glanced at the dark floor and the opal suddenly gleamed again, seeming larger and more powerful than before.

She picked it up and walked toward the table, her fingers toying with the stone. The opal was real, even if the rest was made up. But mightn't it also have lodged in the sand here, forgotten by the first people in Paradise?

Just then she noticed his tablet and slate pencil. He forgot his writing implements, she thought with a sudden smile. Beside the traces of half-erased letters, she began drawing a man's face with a great head of hair. If he's my invention, it was a good one. But he left me with this burden to bear. Which I have only just begun to bear. How will it all end? She raised her head and listened intently, but it was only the sound of the wind feigning life.

She went to the sitting room, whose windows looked out on the front drive and the allee of lindens. A farmhand walked by with a sack on his back. Children were chasing a dog by the ponds, then the dog started chasing the children. I've got to collect myself now, right now, she thought. I've tried to so many times. But it's already too late. Something terrible happened. Or maybe it's only just starting.

The door creaked behind her and she turned around quickly. But it was only Emilka poking her head into the sitting room, and she closed the door at once. She's probably looking after me, thought Helena, suddenly shivering. I'm still sick. And probably always will be. Sickness is my ivory tower, my tower of ivory. There was a flare of light outside. No, it was only in my eyes.

The clock started striking in the next room. No, it was in there, in the sitting room with the furniture in its coarse cloth slipcasing. That clock had always told the hour in that room. It had been left by old Mr. Plater and was still counting the hours as they passed lazily at Bohin. She looked at the ceiling. Someone was up there shuffling through the dry leaves. No, the wind had just gotten into the attic and was dashing by the chimneys, tearing the useless webs away.

Just then she heard the sound of hoofbeats—sensed them more than heard them. Michal Konwicki was returning from his expedition at a hard gallop. His gray horse slowed at the sight of the house and began snorting, his heavy head bobbing to the ground. Helena could not hear any of this, because the wind was wailing strangely, drowning out the few other sounds there were.

The rider turned toward the farm buildings. Helena noticed that she had clenched the edge of the curtain in one hand. She deliberately took a deep breath, but it afforded her no relief. Finally, she caught sight of her father walking with a weary step toward the house. The butt of his shotgun was under his arm, the barrel pointing toward the ground. Her heart began striking her rib cage with such force that she thought everyone in the house could hear it, everyone in the whole district, everyone in hell.

Her father crossed the porch, which rumbled like a bridge. He lingered for a moment in the front hall, then finally locked himself up in his room. Emilka was whispering to someone in the front hall, probably Antoni Sieniuc.

Helena began walking stealthily toward the door of her father's study. She groped her away along the old, cracked planks with her fingertips. She remembered that there was a chink in the wall that at night allowed a thin shaft of light into the dark corridor. She found the chink. Looking through it, she saw a slice of the window, a part of the desk, and the dark shape of a cross on the floor. But that wasn't a cross, it was her father lying face down, with his arms spread wide in penance.

She pressed the latch and the door opened with a soft groan.

Helena knelt beside her father and began tugging him by the back and sleeves of his jacket.

"Father, what happened?"

Michal Konwicki lay motionless. It was only then that she noticed the shotgun on the desk.

"Papa, why don't you answer?"

He looked as if he were sleeping after an exhausting day. A few drops of sweat gleamed on the skin at the back of his neck, which had turned blue.

"Where did you go? Why are you lying there like that?"

Her father still hadn't moved. No pulse could be seen at the side of his neck and his shoulders did not rise and fall.

"Papa, are you sick, or did something terrible happen?"

Suddenly she jumped up from the floor and ran to the kitchen. Emilka and Antoni were kneeling in front of a holy picture in one corner of the room. The cook was plaintively reciting a prayer over and over, accompanied by the blacksmith's husky voice.

"Emilka, get up and help me. Father's sick."

Emilka and Antoni turned from their prayers, Emilka saying softly, "The master's killed a man."

Helena rushed to the door, flinging it open with a blow from her body, and dashed through the front hall to the porch, then to the farm buildings. Konstanty was grooming the road-weary horse with a wisp of straw.

"Konstanty, hitch up the carriage!"

Saying nothing, his hands trembling, Konstanty began dragging the carriage out of the coach house. Helena herself led out the horse that was nearest the stable door. She helped the old man harness the horse, putting the collar on crooked and not tightening the girth. Then she hopped up on the box.

"Wait, I'm coming!" cried Konstanty, running after the carriage, which was already in motion.

"I'll go alone. I don't need you. You stay home."

Now she was racing down the allee, clouds of red and yellow leaves rising behind the carriage, as if the wheels were striking fire from the flintstone of the road. Malwinka didn't come back either, she thought. If she didn't, she didn't.

Then she flew across heather which had fused into a ruddy stream that flowed into the woods, flooding pine, birch, and a solitary aspen.

It was only at the edge of town that she stopped the horse, which was shaking from emotion or exhaustion. She hitched it to a rowan tree and with an uncertain step walked to the sloping square in front of the church. An early dusk had fallen. How can I find him, she thought with despair. Maybe the priest knows.

Just then she caught sight of a stout figure pacing anxiously in front of the church. It might be Father Siemaszko driven from his house by his own sins and those of others. He was pacing in a circle in the gathering dark, as if waiting for someone or lacking the courage to be with people.

"What will I say to him?" whispered Helena.

Instinctively she hid by the fence of the nearest building, which was The Golden Apple, Goldapfel's grocery store. Suddenly her heart stopped, halted in mid-motion like a spinning wheel. She'd seen a flickering light in the window and heard a man's muffled voice speaking in Yiddish.

"Maybe his body's in there and they're praying over him."

But candlelight was also flickering in the next house; and in the one past that, the cold window glass also shimmered with light. Shaken, she stayed by the dark bushes. Why are there candles in all the houses, and why are they all moaning and lamenting, in that language that none of us had ever learned in all those centuries.

"Should I go from house to house and ask?"

Just then she realized those were Sabbath candles in all those houses, the Jews of Bujwidze were celebrating the Sabbath. But where is he? Maybe we passed each other and he's already warming himself up by the chimney in the attic at Bohin.

"Oh, my husband's dead," she said to herself with great amazement.

She lifted up her eyes. "God, is it true?"

But all she saw above her was the darkness, dense and lifeless. Suddenly she felt something cool and damp touch her face. I must be crying, she thought. But it was only the first, fleeting snow of late fall or early winter.

"It's started snowing," she said to herself on the way back to the carriage, her lips dry and numb. "Look, it's snowing already."

Without untying the reins, she got into the back of the carriage and stretched out her legs.

"Let's go. We have to get back," she said, and it was only then that she noticed she was all by herself and that the old, terribly old Konstanty, who could still recall the Saxon kings, was not on the coach box.

And it was only then that she began to cry. Concealed by the autumn night and by the snow, thicker now and treacherously quiet, she wept without constraint. Wishing to see her, the horse jerked its head back twice, tearing the reins free of the rowan's slender trunk. Looking at the road ahead with worried eyes, the horse began pulling the carriage home, to Bohin.

Chief of Police Dzhugashvili arrived the next morning. But there had been a terrible night before that cloudy, cold morning. Helena's father had not showed his face all evening and Helena had shut herself up in her room. She lay down on her bed without undressing, but then she kept getting up, walking around the room, and pausing by the window, whose shutters were closed. Finally, she tried to undress, but then suddenly gave up on it. My mind's a terrible blank, she thought. May everything be set right. Any minute now I'm going to start to understand.

Her eyes kept going to the ceiling, and it was only now, after so many years, that she noticed the cracked white beams that supported the ceiling. Maybe he's still up there, the immortal Elias Szyra. Or maybe it's better that he isn't. Christ God, I'd like to slam my head against the wall and forget the whole world.

Suddenly she sensed that someone was walking around the house. Doors squeaked, steps creaked, a muffled voice called out to someone from the corridor. Finally, there was a knock at her own door and her heart was in her throat again.

"Come to the kitchen for something to eat, ma'am. You can't go around all day on an empty stomach."

"Thank you, Emilka. Go to sleep. I have a headache. I have to rest."

"It's better to be with people on a night like this. We'll wait for you there."

"God bless you good people. I don't know myself if I'll live through the night."

"We'll be waiting. It's always more frightening when you're alone."

But I don't know if I am afraid, thought Helena with despair. I don't feel anything. I'm like a log, a block of ice, a fieldstone. I should be howling and threatening heaven. But all I do is walk around without being able to stop. I'll walk and I'll walk to the ends of the earth.

She knelt by her bed and began praying. But she kept making mistakes and losing the thread. The priest had assigned her a penance. What penance did he assign me? I don't remember anymore.

She wanted to wash, but there was no water in the pitcher. It had been forgotten in all the turmoil. But I'm not normal, she thought with sudden relief. I was always different and people could always see that, and they were all afraid of me for that.

Then she fell asleep standing up, just dozing off by the window, her eyes constantly closing as she looked through the little heart carved in the shutter at the dark-blue night raked by an obstinate, mournful wind. When she woke up, a gray light was glimmering through the carved heart. She felt cold and began shivering, her teeth suddenly aching and chattering slightly.

It was then that she heard the clatter of hooves on the first frost of the year. The whole world was white. Actually, the whole world was gray, even though it was covered by a thin layer of snow, the first snow of the winter to come. The children of the villagers or farmhands were running around by the ponds, eating the tasty new snow by the handful.

Its hood raised, Dzhugashvili's runabout approached at a walking pace down the allee. Sitting beside him was a gendarme in a light-blue overcoat with its hood up too. Malwinka didn't come back, thought Helena. She ran after Father and never came back. The clouds parted over the horizon and the woods, revealing patches of sky, the pale-green sky of late autumn or early winter.

Konstanty was coming toward the house from the farm. For some reason he'd removed his Astrakhan cap and the light wind tousled what was left of his hair, not gray but green-blue with old age. Shadows moved among the trees dusted with snow. Everyone can see our disgrace and tragedy, she thought.

The runabout pulled up to the porch. The chief of police was the first to jump heavily down from the runabout. Landing awkwardly on his feet, he grabbed on to the coach box, his legs stiff from the cold, even though he had worn a wolf-skin overcoat for the trip. Next, saber clanking, spurs jingling, the middle-aged gendarme clambered down from the carriage. Turning discreetly to one side, Dzhugashvili blew his nose, holding it with numbed fingers.

A flock of rooks, black and nasty birds, rose over the ponds.

The chief of police looked at the porch for a moment and

Helena had the impression that he was observing her with new interest, but his eyes were fixed above her head.

"Mr. Michal Konwicki," he began in a hoarse voice, "you are under arrest as a suspect in the murder of the Jew Elias Szyra, who had temporarily been residing in the town of Bujwidze."

Helena turned around. Her father was behind her, wearing only an unbuttoned shirt that revealed his painfully prominent ribs and the same riding pants he'd worn when he went to Bujwidze. He was listening to the chief of police and nodding his head slightly.

"Do you understand what I'm saying?" asked Dzhugashvili.

"Yes," replied Michal Konwicki unexpectedly. "I understand. I'm of sound mind."

"Well then, get dressed, and take some of your things with you, you'll need them in prison. The gendarme will make a search of your room. But that's only a formality."

The gendarme went obediently to the porch, his saber's black sheath and brass chafings slapping his leg as he went, his spurs clanking heavily. He followed Michal Konwicki into the house.

Then Emilka came out from the front hall. As always, she was neat and tidy, her hair smoothly combed, but there were dark circles under her eyes now. She was carrying a tray with a decanter of vodka, two glasses, and a sliced pickle.

She approached the chief of police and curtseyed in courtly style. "Would you care for a little something to drink, Your Honor?" she said softly.

Dzhugashvili gazed greedily at the carafe, not put off in the least by this liberty on the part of a servant.

"A drink'd be good. It's terribly cold and everybody knows the first cold spell's always bad for your health, but how can a man take a drink when he's here on official business."

"We beg your indulgence, Your Honor." Emilka curtseyed again.

Oh, the poor thing, she thinks she can help her master, thought Helena dejectedly. When will this all end, and how will it all end? Can it be that for the first time in his life my father will leave the house and never come back?

Antoni Sieniuc appeared at the door with his pipe. He opened his mouth as if about to say something, but his metal tooth only glinted like the head of a nail.

Unable to resist the temptation, the chief of police removed his glove and poured himself a full glass. He nodded. "He killed a subversive. But subversives are human too. This means Siberia."

"And what about him?" asked Helena suddenly, frightened by the sound of her own voice.

"Who do you mean?" asked the chief of police.

"Him."

"Oh, him. His body was taken to Wilno. An autopsy will be performed. It's all the same to him now." He shifted his glass to his other hand so he could cross himself.

He's awfully Russian for a Georgian, she thought. And Korsakov's terribly Russian too. We're all probably Russian now. Far away a shot rang out, but the chief of police paid it no attention. He puffed out a cloud of steam, then poured himself another drink. Could he be Schicklgruber, Helena asked herself. Let him burn us all up, our houses, our woods, our cemeteries.

Someone was riding up at a trot from the highroad. It was the rifleman Ildefons, and she knew immediately why he was there. When he had drawn up to the porch, he jumped down from his horse, brought his hand to his forester's cap in a silent salute, and handed Helena an envelope with the count's seal on it. Then he stood in front of the porch, gazing with sullen curiosity at the little group assembled there.

"Are you supposed to wait for a reply?" asked Helena with sudden anger.

"No. I wasn't told to."

He made a show of leaping up into the saddle, then trotted away. Helena weighed the letter in her hand, aware that Emilka and Antoni were peering at it avidly. He's breaking the engagement, thought Helena. And thank God he's breaking it. My life is over.

Then Michal Konwicki came out to the porch wearing a black fur jacket and carrying a good-sized bundle. He was followed by the gendarme holding the squire's shotgun.

It was only then that Michal Konwicki lost his self-possession. His mustache began to tremble, he cleared his throat violently while adjusting the fur cap on his head. Suddenly he turned toward his daughter, only moving his lips for a moment, then saying in a voice not his own, "Forgive me."

Then he bowed to the people gathered on the porch, or to that manor made of larch wood that had never really been home. With a sigh he went down the steps and got into the carriage. Dzhugashvili followed him in, and last came the gendarme, who climbed up on the box, casting a glance at Emilka, who was still standing tray in hand.

"Move!" growled Dzhugashvili.

Michal Konwicki was no longer looking at those who had been near and dear to him; very clear, his eyes were fixed on that gray world whitened a touch by the snow. With a groan of its springs, the runabout rolled off down the linden allee as empty and eerie as a tree-lined road in a cemetery.

But now I have to leave my grandmother Helena Konwicka, happy to have accompanied her to that moment, happy that my heart did not collapse or my head explode, and that I spent the whole winter and spring flying north across the sky like a crane to the place where I was born and which has been nourishing my soul now for many years; or was I in fact bound in another direction, past the very zenith of the sky and into the mystery of the future?

It's night, my time, almost the witching hour—for ghosts of

my own invention or real ghosts patiently looking for me in a haystack of stars and planets.

I wanted to say something of importance—for so many days and nights I have kept an idea in store in my soul, a warning or words of farewell, for the time of farewells is close at hand; I wanted to scratch something onto the wall of common memory, and now I've forgotten what it was, and I'm still in mid-flight, because I am no longer back there, nor have I returned here yet either, and I am suspended somewhere in the sky, waiting without knowing for what, ashamed to be using the literary device of flight and the view from above, since floating in the air beside me I can see ordinary ducks, mangy hounds, and even cows fat with calf.

Still, it all ended well, because, despite everything, I do exist and am among the living. But how can *I* be the upbeat ending to any story?